JANET MILLER

TASTING Nightwalker WINE

Cerridwen Press

What the critics are saying...

Five Angels! "Stella, oh wow, I loved her. She was courageous, even when an amazing world is exposed to her and her life view is turned upside-down. With a traitor after Sebastian they are forced to run and the twists and turns that the plot took were suspenseful and well written." ~*Paranormal Romance Reviews*

"Vampire lovers alert! Janet Millers TASTING NIGHTWALKER WINE is a thrilling and sometimes chilling read." ~*Romance Reviews Today*

A Cerridwen Press Publication

www.cerridwenpress.com

Tasting Nightwalker Wine

ISBN 9781419951299
ALL RIGHTS RESERVED.
Tasting Nightwalker Wine Copyright © 2006 Janet Miller
Edited by Ann Leveille.
Cover art by Syneca.

Electronic book Publication November 2006
Trade paperback Publication May 2007

Excerpt from *Night Visions* Copyright © 2007 Ariana Dupre
Excerpt from *All Night Inn* Copyright © 2005 Janet Miller

With the exception of quotes used in reviews, this book may not be reproduced or used in whole or in part by any means existing without written permission from the publisher, Ellora's Cave Publishing Inc., 1056 Home Avenue, Akron, OH 44310-3502.

This book is a work of fiction and any resemblance to persons, living or dead, or places, events or locales is purely coincidental. The characters are productions of the authors' imagination and used fictitiously.

Cerridwen Press is an imprint of Ellora's Cave Publishing, Inc.®

Also by Janet Miller

☙

Hollywood After Dark: All Night Inn

If you are interested in a spicier read (and are over 18), check out the author's erotic romances at Ellora's Cave Publishing (www.ellorascave.com).

Divine Interventions 1: Violet Among the Roses

Divine Interventions 2: Echo In the Hall

Divine Interventions 3: Nemesis of the Garden

Ellora's Cavemen: Dreams of the Oasis III (*anthology*)

Ellora's Cavemen: Legendary Tails I (*anthology*)

Ghosts of Christmas Past

Holiday Reflections (*anthology*)

Hollywood After Dark: Fangs for the Memories

Memories To Come

The Doll

Two Men and a Lady (*anthology*)

About the Author

During the weekday Janet is a mild-mannered software engineer who writes code and design documents. At night and on weekends she turns to the creation of offbeat stories about imaginary pasts, presents, and futures. But no matter when or where the story happens, there will always be some adventure, some humor, and meaning to the tale. For Cerridwen she's writing a new line of parafolk tales about modern day vampires, called nightwalkers, along with psychics and shapeshifters of all kinds.

Janet welcomes comments from readers. You can find her website and email address on her author bio page at www.cerridwenpress.com.

Tell Us What You Think

We appreciate hearing reader opinions about our books. You can email us at Comments@EllorasCave.com.

Tasting Nightwalker Wine

Dedication

To my mom, who is one of my biggest fans even with all the naughty stuff.

And to my editor Ann, who knows just how to encourage me into finishing a book – by telling me she's as excited to see it come out as I am.

Trademarks Acknowledgement

The author acknowledges the trademarked status and trademark owners of the following wordmarks mentioned in this work of fiction:

Better Homes and Gardens: Merideth Corporation
Diet Coke: The Coca-Cola Company
Dodgers: Los Angeles Dodgers
Ghirardelli: D. Ghirardelli Company
Giants: San Francisco Baseball Associates
Gulfstream: Gulfstream Aerospace Corporation
Mercedes: Daimler Chrysler AG Corporation
Transamerica: Transamerica Corporation
Uzi: Israel Military Industries Ltd.

Chapter One

When she got back home she was definitely going to fire her agent! Stella Robertson leaned back in her chair and examined the empty bookstore around her, the reason for her decision. She was Estelle Roberts, author of Vampa-Regency, the most successful historical paranormal romance series in publishing history. She wasn't used to this kind of situation.

Instead of dealing with her usual long line of rabid fans, she sat behind a still-high stack of books on the narrow display table, with not a customer in sight.

What a *marvelous* idea Helen had had, she thought sarcastically. What a publicity stunt—to have a book signing for Stella's latest novel in the late evening on Halloween. Helen had been sure that the San Francisco book-loving crowd would be dying—*ha, ha!*--to buy signed copies of Stella's new book...so much so that they'd be sure to come to the bookstore that night.

Persuasive, that was Helen. She'd convinced the bookstore owner to keep the shop open, she'd convinced Stella to add this one last stop to her already overlong book tour.

It had been a wonderful idea. Too bad no one had shown up.

Stella sighed. Of course no one had shown up. It was Halloween night in a city that took the holiday seriously. Everyone was in costume, running around the Castro district and other parts of the city and having a wonderful time.

San Francisco was a party town, particularly tonight. No one was going to come to a book signing, not even to see her.

Glancing at the clock, Stella noted she still had thirty minutes to go until the pre-announced eleven o'clock store closing. Even if there weren't any customers she couldn't really leave. She sighed and grabbed the book on the top of the stack, opened it to the title page and scribbled her name. At least she could leave a few signed copies for the store manager. Those would sell better in the next couple of weeks, when her fans were more interested in reading about vampires than running around pretending to be one.

Finished with the last book, she turned to page one and began reading. If nothing else, she'd keep her mind occupied. It had been nearly a year since she'd seen this manuscript. Was it as good as she remembered?

Soon she was completely engrossed in the tale, the poor but plucky English governess heroine having just met the suave and sophisticated hero, a mysterious man of dark habits who appeared only at night in his gloomy European castle. He'd hired her to take care of his adopted daughter, but would soon have his fangs—as well as other body parts—sunk deep into the heroine's no-longer-virginal body.

But that wasn't until chapter eight. Impatient, Stella skipped forward to the couple's first sexual encounter and a tingly warmth spread through her as she imagined herself in her heroine's place as the hero's hand made its way between her thighs...

Stella grinned appreciatively. It really was as good as she remembered.

"Well, that answers my first question, if you read your own books."

A deep and exceptionally masculine voice dragged Stella from her eighteenth-century fantasy world and back into the bookstore. Startled, and feeling guilty at having been caught reading her own erotic prose, she glanced up at her customer. And up.

And up.

And up, until her gaze met gray eyes framed by golden-brown lashes. Gray eyes set in a pale, thin and aristocratic face surrounded by a wealth of wavy gold hair that fell to his shoulders. Silvery-gray eyes with a molten gleam in them that stared at her from under sardonically arched brows.

Stella's jaw dropped. *He was absolutely beautiful!* Forget tall, dark and handsome, this guy looked like Apollo, god of the sun. Or, she thought, noting the wicked twinkle in his eyes, perhaps like an angel who'd fallen to earth for sinful thoughts. Most excellent sinful thoughts.

The sensual tingle she'd started by reading her book fired into overdrive under his heated gaze. Suddenly it was no longer her dark-haired hero she was envisioning with his hand between her thighs, but a blond Adonis.

Stella flushed clear to her toes at her naughty thoughts, then more when she realized what he'd said about her reading her own books.

Closing the book, Stella grappled for some semblance of self-possession. "Of course I read my own books."

One eyebrow arched higher. "And do you *enjoy* them?"

His deceptively polite tone suggested that he knew just what pages she'd been reading when he'd interrupted—and their effect on her.

Stella gaped, a niggling thought wriggling about in her mind. *Could he know what she was thinking?*

No, of course not. How could he know her thoughts?

A smile curled the edges of his closed lips. Pulling a book off the stack, he opened it to about where she'd been reading. The edges of his mouth curled higher, but it was the dancing lights in his eyes that told her how deeply amused he was.

"Very nice..." His voice trailed off as he continued to read, turning the pages as he finished the scene. She watched his mobile features, noting when he was amused and when he was intrigued. Toward the end he was far more intrigued than amused.

When he closed the book, his silvery gaze looked hot enough to melt lead. Certainly it was hot enough to melt her. For a moment she was lost in the furnace of his stare, her own senses aflame.

He put the book on the table in front of her. "Add 'to Sebastian with love', please."

"Huh?" Stella stared at him, open-mouthed, still caught in his erotic spell. Tearing her eyes away from his face, she glanced at the book in front of her and realized he wanted her to add a dedication to the signature.

Reassembling her scattered professionalism, Stella snatched her pen off the desk. "Oh right," she told him with a rueful grin.

She scribbled the desired message onto the title page but as she handed the book to him, their hands met for a moment and a jolt jumped between them, rocketing up Stella's arm.

She jerked back. *This guy was lethal. What kind of man was he?*

But when she looked at him, she saw that he'd felt that spark too. And she saw something else…he hadn't liked it. His smile vanished, he stepped back from her, and for the first time since encountering him she was able to focus on something besides his beautiful face.

The sight of his outfit took her by surprise. Dressed in a black tuxedo and wearing a crimson-lined cape, her customer might have stepped out of an old horror movie.

Released from her spell, Stella burst into laughter. "Are you supposed to be a vampire?"

His eyes narrowed and his upper lip drew back, and she could see he'd even had fangs added to his teeth. They looked impressively realistic, not cheap plastic…must have cost a pretty penny.

But then the entire outfit was pricy. Of course, it could be a rental, but even so he'd clearly spent money on it. Now he looked at her in annoyance that she'd made fun of him.

Trying to make peace, Stella waved her hand apologetically. "Sorry I laughed. I keep forgetting it's Halloween night. You going to a party?"

Some of his irritation fled. "The whole city is a party tonight." He glanced at her own empire-waisted gown in buttercup-yellow, a duplicate of the one gracing the buxom heroine on her cover, although Stella's gown didn't display her cleavage in quite the same fashion. Even so, she felt his silvery gaze linger there as if he could see through the fabric.

Some of the heat returned to his eyes and he held out a hand to her, his voice like rich velvet. "I was on my way to walk the streets and enjoy the merriment. Perhaps you'd care to join me? You are certainly dressed for the part."

Sudden panic hit fast and hard. *Oh that would be a very bad idea.* The way she was reacting to this man, she could be in big trouble real fast.

"I couldn't," she stammered. "I don't even know your name."

He pulled back the hand and nodded as if he'd been reminded of his manners. "Forgive me. Of course we haven't been properly introduced. My name is Sebastian, as I told you. Sebastian Moret." He performed a courtly bow so natural that he might have done it centuries ago in front of royalty.

His sardonic brows arched higher and he smiled with a bit of fang showing. "As you've noticed, I'm in costume for the celebration. Tonight you may call me 'Prince Sebastian'."

Another fit of merriment assailed her. "Prince Sebastian?" She tried for a royal nod. "Well, of course, your royal majesty."

"Your highness is more appropriate. I'm not a king, Ms. Roberts."

No, more like a loon. Still, he was a devastatingly handsome loon. And he had a great voice, deep and rich, vibrant, with an odd accent. He sounded like he might have actually come from Europe.

Perhaps not a loon. He was probably just pulling her leg, she decided. After all, she wrote books where the hero was often some sort of royalty turned vampire. Sebastian was a fan and he'd no doubt thought that pretending to be one of her heroes would be a good way to garner her approval.

Not that he needed a costume to do that. She couldn't help but approve.

Still, there was no way she was going anywhere with this guy, handsome or not, loon or not, approval or not.

"I'm afraid I couldn't possibly join you tonight, Mr. Moret. I've an early flight tomorrow and once I'm done here I've got to get back to my hotel."

Tonight was the last night of her book tour, and Stella was glad for it. Much as she loved getting out and meeting her fans—at least when they weren't dressed up like vampires— she was looking forward to a couple of weeks of leisure at her home in Los Angeles before jumping into her next project.

"Perhaps you could take a later flight. Or I could fly you myself…I have my own small jet."

A princely vampire with a pilot's license and a plane? A giggle escaped her. "I'm afraid not," she told him, attempting to temper her rejection with a smile.

It didn't work. A look of annoyance crossed his handsome features, and Stella realized that "Prince Sebastian" must have rarely had to cope with rejection. He didn't like it much either.

He leaned over the table, his voice a liquid purr. "I'd make it worth your while."

Did he think he could pay her and she'd go with him? Face flaming, Stella resisted the urge to slap him. "I'm not that kind of a woman," she told him angrily.

Now he looked affronted. "I didn't mean what you clearly think I meant. If you'd accompany me tonight, I'd promise to be a perfect gentleman. I just want to talk about your books. I could help you with them."

She wasn't buying the "gentleman" line for an instant. Those silver-gray eyes still held enough heat to melt the resolve of a vestal virgin—and she was no virgin. Besides that, after seven books, two on the bestseller list, she certainly didn't need assistance with her writing.

"I don't need help with my books. I'm doing just fine with them."

"You need a great deal of help, Ms. Roberts. Your books are well-written, and your stories intriguing, but when it comes to vampires you don't have the slightest idea what you're talking about."

Stella jumped to her feet and stretched to the limit of her five-foot five-inch height. Unfortunately her adversary still held a one-foot advantage over her, so she let her fury make up the difference.

"I have written seven books, won dozens of awards and pleased thousands of people, none of whom have ever commented that my vampires were anything but true to their natures. Who are you to tell me that I don't know what I'm talking about?"

For a moment he glared down at her, his molten stare boring into her. Only her own anger kept that stare from melting her into an incoherent puddle.

Prince Sebastian's jaw tightened and he turned, striding rapidly to the door.

"You forgot your book!" Stella snatched it off the table and held it up.

Without glancing back, he addressed the wide-eyed clerk near the cash register. "Put it on my bill and send it with my usual order. Add to it the rest of the signed books on that table."

Opening the bookshop door, he paused in the opening and turned for a final frown back at her. Stella felt the weight of his anger as if it were her own but met it with a determined glare.

Then she heard his voice again, rich and vibrant—but he hadn't opened his mouth to speak. Instead of in her ears, his voice sounded in her head, and that shook her to the core.

What I am, Stella Robertson, is someone who does *know what he's talking about!*

Jaw dropped, she stared as the door closed behind him.

* * * * *

Sebastian pulled the covering blackness of his cloak closer around him and stepped farther back into the shadows as Stella darted out the front door of the bookstore. He held his position as she searched up and down the street, obviously looking for him. Only after she went back inside, shoulders slumped in defeat, did he move.

Well, she'd followed him. That was good. He'd tried to get Stella's attention, and he had. Not quite the way he'd wanted—instant messaging her mind had been an act of desperation, but after the way she'd dismissed him what else could he do?

Getting her attention, that's what tonight had been about. He'd wanted to meet the woman behind the books he so enjoyed and see if she really was a latent parafolk. She got a lot in her stories wrong, but there was sometimes just the littlest ring of truth to them. Somewhere, she'd obtained information she shouldn't have.

Either that was because she was lucky, or because she'd accidentally read the mind of someone who was one of his kind. He was betting the latter given the fact she lived in Los Angeles and that was a hotbed of parafolk activity, even more than the Bay Area.

Now he'd met her and he knew one thing for certain. She was a latent psi and a strong one—someone who needed to be watched at the very least, particularly with her penchant for gaining attention through her writing.

He wouldn't admit that he'd become a little infatuated with her through her writing. She showed such a strong sensual spirit and the way she described her heroes almost made him wish he could be one of them. Or at least find a heroine similar to the ones in her books.

Weeks ago he'd begun an email correspondence with her agent, convincing the woman that San Francisco would be a wonderful place for a book signing and Halloween evening an excellent time to do it.

Most of the time Stella's signings were in the late morning or early afternoon, best for her usual customers of adult women, but also when he was forced to be indoors and asleep. Arranging this signing at his favorite bookstore had been the one way he'd found to finally indulge his curiosity about his favorite author.

And for her to meet him, even if that hadn't worked out as well as he'd hoped. In retrospect, the costume might not have been the best choice, even if it did allow him to smile and laugh normally in public without his fangs inviting comment.

The act of a desperate man—or nightwalker. How had he become so intrigued by a woman whose books, when they didn't tell too much of the truth, continued the lies and old prejudices about his kind? It was inexplicable, particularly since the last thing he wanted was to be involved with anyone.

Too long ago he'd learned his lesson in wanting a woman's love and he'd sworn never to lose control of his heart again. But somehow that hadn't stopped him from arranging to meet Stella.

Who could explain the workings of the human, or in his case, the not-so-human, heart? Certainly not him. Many who knew him would argue that he had no heart and would be amused by his current predicament. He could almost hear the peals of laughter from his old friend Jonathan, whom he'd twitted from time to time about his domestic problems.

Sebastian Moret, four hundred and eighty years on this earth, and Prince of the California Nightwalker's Association, was enamored of a woman who wrote vampire romances. It really was funny if you thought about it.

Or if you weren't him. After all, he wasn't laughing.

Yes, Jonathan would laugh. Just six months ago Jonathan had had one companion in near revolt and another he was too much in love with to feed off of, but his friend had managed to fix his domestic problems for all time. He'd taken his companion, Sharon, bartender and singer-songwriter, to be his bloodmate—his lover and the sole source of the life-sustaining blood their kind needed.

Now Chief Jonathan, leader of the Los Angeles parafolk, wallowed in domestic bliss. It was enough to make a dedicatedly unattached nightwalker such as Sebastian nearly sick...with an envy he hadn't thought he could feel.

After all, he had no interest in finding a bloodmate, or even a long-term companion of his own. He liked his life the way it was, hunting his supper when he wanted, using bagged blood when he didn't. He didn't need someone the way Jonathan needed Sharon.

But thinking of Sharon and Jonathan led his thoughts back to Stella. Heavens above she was pretty. Sebastian hadn't really expected that. Her glamorous picture in the back of her books didn't do justice to her natural beauty. In the store she'd been wearing limited makeup, just a little bit of mascara around her velvet-brown eyes, and her hair had been tumbled into a loose pile of auburn curls, in keeping with her period dress.

She was younger than he'd thought too. Probably not even forty years old yet.

Not that it mattered to him...she was still a younger woman.

A much younger woman.

Sebastian sighed. Stella had looked every bit as scrumptious as the heroine in her book with her slight décolleté and long, slender neck. Especially that long, slender neck. Thank heavens his thoughts had been hidden as he'd admired that part of her!

Yes, she looked delicious and probably was too. As unaware as she was of her mental powers, she had them, strong ones, and that, he knew, would give a luscious flavor to her blood.

Strong mental powers in a beautiful body and an intelligent mind to match. He'd been able peek into her thoughts as soon as he'd walked into the store—and entertaining thoughts they had been.

Such a sensual woman. That was the one thing that had rung true in her books, her love of sexual adventure.

This evening, the thoughts she'd had when she'd seen him... Unexpectedly, Sebastian felt a coil of tension thinking about just what Stella had imagined about him.

A woman like that could coax a monk out of his robes. And he was no monk.

Too bad she'd been too timid to act on her delightful ideas, or to even to spend further time with him this evening. For a moment Sebastian considered reentering the store and inviting her once more to attend the celebrations in the city or, failing that, perhaps a private celebration with him in his townhouse could be arranged. Later he'd see to it she went home. He'd meant his offer of a private jet down to the home he knew she had in Los Angeles. He knew a lot about Stella, including her real name.

A little quality time spent with Stella could be most entertaining. Between his hunger and desire for sex, he'd keep her busy.

But no. Sebastian reined in his imaginings of what he could do with the lovely Ms. Robertson. He'd be better off letting the woman go. Tonight he'd go out on the town to hunt his dinner and sample as many necks as he wanted. It was Halloween, party time, and the city was a buffet of intoxicated humans waiting to serve him.

Sebastian tried to work up a healthy enthusiasm for that, but it was harder than he expected. Tasting Stella would've been delightful, an appetizer beyond compare. Trouble was, she didn't seem like a one-bite stand. If he weren't careful he'd develop a taste for her.

Stella was the kind of woman that was habit-forming, and better not to sample her creamy sweet blood if that were the case.

No, far better it would be to head downtown. He'd feed off the revelers in the streets, clouding their minds to make it easy. The alcohol they'd consumed would only enhance the experience for him and he'd be happily making merry within the hour.

He'd probably even be too intoxicated to care that none of those he took from had auburn hair and velvety-brown eyes. Maybe he'd hang outside one of the Mexican restaurants and catch someone who'd indulged in margaritas. He felt like eating ethnic tonight.

Yes, he'd head downtown soon, but not right now. Hungry as he was, Sebastian waited until the store was closed and Stella exited into the taxi that arrived shortly thereafter. With his sharpened hearing, he heard her give the driver the name of her hotel, and an odd melancholy took hold of him.

Stella was following the plan she'd given him, returning to her hotel and preparing for her flight in the morning. For a moment he'd hoped she'd ask the storeowner about him. He'd even given the woman a mental push to give Stella his address, on the off chance she decided to look for him there, or even maybe seek him out tomorrow.

But rather than enjoy her last night in San Francisco, she was going to her hotel. She'd probably go to straight to bed and tomorrow catch the plane that would take her home…and out of his life.

Fighting the unusual desolation that thought gave him, Sebastian watched the cab drive off. When it was gone, he drove his motorcycle out of the alley and rode off toward the heart of the city, where laughter, frivolity and sweet hot blood waited.

It might not be quite what he wanted, but it would have to do.

Chapter Two

Stella stared the front of the North Beach row house and wondered for the tenth time that morning just what she was doing here. The house, with its unassuming façade, kept close company with the buildings around it, and with its shuttered windows and carefully trimmed bushes in pots on the narrow porch, it looked just like its neighbors on either side, right down to the door painted a deep forest green.

It didn't look like a house that a man who read vampire romances and wore a Dracula costume would live in. Or maybe it did. What did she know about men with vampire fetishes? She hadn't met more than a couple of dozen or so in her lifetime so far, and she'd never hunted one of them back to his lair before.

Besides, what had she expected? A dark and gloomy house on a haunted hill, or a ruined castle? Maybe something like an old abbey? That seemed more in keeping with the character of "Prince Sebastian".

On the other hand, this was San Francisco. Real estate options were limited when it came to the dark and spooky, and he probably had to compromise at least a little. Also, real estate prices were extremely high. Maybe he was a vampire on a budget and this unassuming row house was all he could afford in the city.

Maybe he had an old castle someplace else.

This was the address the bookstore owner had given her, the place her mysterious customer of last night gave as a mailing address for his monthly book deliveries, so this was where the mysterious Sebastian Moret lived, even if it did look like every other house on the block.

Last night Stella had learned that in addition to buying her romances, Mr. Moret had a standing order with the bookstore to send him a copy of every book that they came across that featured the supernatural, in particular werewolves and vampires. She wasn't his only fetish when it came to reading material...although she apparently had been the only author he'd seen fit to visit at the bookstore.

Of her books, he always purchased several copies. The clerk had mentioned he bought them for friends of his as gifts. Stella hoped Moret's buddies were grateful they were going to get her signed book for Christmas—or whatever holiday he celebrated during the year. If not, they might come looking for her. And friends of Sebastian's might not be the type of people she'd want to find on her doorstep. Even if she was nearly on his.

Why she was here was another question. She really had planned on leaving this morning but had trouble falling asleep last night. Some of it was the noise from the amorous couple in the room next door and the returning partygoers who had been tramping up and down the corridor until nearly dawn. By early morning she'd been inclined to stay an extra day to relax and catch up on her sleep.

But much of it was the mysterious Sebastian and the voice she'd heard in her mind last night. She wasn't sure she believed in mental telepathy, but what he'd done to her mind sure had felt like the real thing. If that was the case, she wanted to see if he could do it again.

Stella used mental telepathy in her books but didn't believe in it any more than she believed in vampires or werewolves. Here was her first proof that something beyond the norm actually existed in the world.

She spent hours of research to make her Regency world as realistic as possible and thought what she did with the paranormal parts of her story were equally well done. But he'd said she didn't know what she was talking about. Sebastian had implied that he could help bring verisimilitude to her stories. If so, she needed to talk to him.

Of course the fact that he was a golden-haired fallen angel of a man didn't have anything to do with her decision to cancel her plane reservation this morning and have the hotel extend her stay another night. This was research, not lust.

She was after information…not his body. And she'd keep telling herself that until she believed it.

Stella climbed the narrow steps to the green front door, stepping between the ceramic planters that graced the porch. The ornate doorknocker featured a wolf's head in full snarl. Studying the fearsome metal beast, Stella wondered if it was meant to warn against knocking on the door.

It would certainly deter the usual solicitors, including the local children selling candy and cookies. She could almost imagine a dear little girl in a green uniform running in terror to the next house instead of grasping that fearsome doorknocker.

But she wasn't a little girl. Summoning her courage, Stella seized the beast by the jaw and rapped it firmly on the metal plate. The sound was louder than she'd expected, echoing in the quiet neighborhood.

The next door neighbor's dog barked, the yappy sound of a small animal. Once more Stella questioned why she was here.

Sebastian Moret was probably perfectly normal. It was very likely only an act last night, the costume and the fangs giving him that appearance of being otherworldly. She'd probably imagined his voice in her mind.

He could be married, with kids. Heck, this was San Francisco, he could even be gay…although she dismissed that thought right away. No way a man who made her blood boil that fast could be same-sex oriented, at least not exclusively.

Even so, he still might not be happy to see her at his door.

She'd turned to leave when there was a flash at the window near the door, the appearance of a face near the edge of the curtain, then it was gone.

A moment later the lock twisted and the door slowly opened. Clenching her teeth to keep them from chattering, Stella stood her ground.

The man in the doorway could have answered the door of an English upper-class manor house. Dressed like a butler in formal black, his black shoes were as shiny as his bald head. He seemed as surprised to see her as she was to see him.

One gray eyebrow arched inquisitively. "How may I be of service?"

He even talked like an English butler. "I was looking for Sebastian Moret."

The second eyebrow joined its mate. "Indeed. And you would be looking for him here because…"

"This was the address I was given."

"Mr. Moret gave you this address?" Patently, he didn't believe her.

"No. The bookstore owner gave me it. She said he was a fan and he wouldn't mind. I met him last night…" Stella's voice trailed off, feeling more foolish all the time. Some mistake had been made and she was certain it was hers.

The butler looked like he agreed. "Might I have your name?"

"Stella, that is, Estelle Roberts." This was stupid. She turned to leave. "I'm sorry I bothered you."

"Estelle Roberts? The writer?"

The sudden enthusiasm in his voice pulled Stella back to see a surprised look on his face. At her assenting nod, he stepped out onto the porch, the surprise morphing into pleasure. "This is an honor, Ms. Roberts. I've read all your books."

The dog next door went into a yapping frenzy and the man called something to it, using words Stella didn't recognize. Immediately the dog quit barking with a sharp yip. With a pained look, the man opened the door farther. "Perhaps you should come in."

Feeling like Alice stepping into Wonderland, Stella followed him into a dark and elegantly decorated front hall. On a narrow, obviously antique table stood a massive vase filled with fresh mixed flowers, which perfumed the air. Taking a deep whiff, Stella recognized lilacs, as well as some fragrant roses in the bouquet.

Maybe her would-be vampire wasn't on that much of a budget after all. Expensive furniture, a vase she could swear was Ming dynasty, and what looked like a butler in this day and age. Apparently Sebastian Moret wasn't a poor man.

"As you have surmised, Ms. Roberts, this is, indeed, Mr. Moret's home. I'm Harold, his manservant."

Harold. The author in her turned the name over, matching it to the man and his occupation. Yes, she supposed that was a good name for a butler. "Is Mr. Moret at home?"

There was a moment of hesitation. "He is but isn't receiving visitors at this time."

Stella glanced at her watch and nearly groaned aloud. It was all of eleven-thirty in the morning. How stupid could she be? Sebastian had been on his way out to party last night and even in her hotel she'd heard revelers in the streets until just before dawn. The man had no doubt been up all night.

"Oh of course. He's probably still asleep."

A faint smile crossed the man's ever-so-proper face. "I quite imagine that he is. But he seemed to anticipate your coming. He left a message for you."

A message? From the table Harold produced a faintly scented envelope with her pen name scrawled across the front in elegantly done letters. Inside was a note in the same handwriting.

Ms. Roberts,

If you are reading this, then you will have no doubt reconsidered my invitation. If so, I'd be delighted to have you accompany me out tonight. If this is acceptable, please leave word with my manservant and I will collect you at your hotel at seven o'clock.

Until then,

Sebastian Moret

How had he known that she'd hunt him down? Unsure but intrigued, Stella pulled out one of her business cards and wrote her hotel name and room number on it. "Please tell Mr. Moret I accept his offer."

With a slight inclination of his head, he took it from her. "I'd be delighted. And I hope you'll return to visit us, Ms. Roberts."

Once back on the street, Stella started the hike down the hill to the bus stop. At least in San Francisco you didn't really need a car to get around, although sensible shoes were a must.

With the rest of the day stretching before her, Stella decided to visit the little shops near Union Square. Outside of the period costume she was using for the signing, she didn't have a nice dress with her, and from the looks of Sebastian's English butler, she'd need something more formal than her black jeans and a turtleneck sweater for her date tonight.

* * * * *

He was late. Stella glanced at the clock, which read ten minutes past seven, and frowned. Just because he was wealthy, had a "manservant" and expensive tastes in household furnishings didn't give Sebastian Moret permission to leave her sitting around waiting for him.

Standing and pacing, Stella stopped in front of the mirrored closet door, pulling at the tight skirt of her new dress. The darn thing looked great on the hanger and even better in the dressing room, but now just seemed too short, too skimpy and far too expensive for her to have bought.

Not to mention too red. She'd thought the color complimented her red-brown hair, but now she had misgivings about even that.

Stella sighed and examined her reflection again. At least her new boots were nice. They'd not only been the most comfortable pair of boots in the store, but a bargain at half price. The sleek black leather ended just inches short of her knees and made her legs look long and sexy. She smiled, anticipating Sebastian's silver eyes going molten when he got a glimpse of them.

Assuming the man ever showed up. Stella checked the clock again. Seven-fifteen. Maybe she should have said she'd meet him in the bar. Her room had seemed a good choice this morning but now that she'd thought about it, a more public place might have been better.

She wasn't sure she wanted to see Sebastian in a room that contained a bed, even though when they'd met last night, a bed had been pretty high on her list of proper meeting places for the pair of them.

A knock on the door broke her aberrant thoughts. After a last panicked glance in the mirror, Stella moved to open it.

Six feet plus of gorgeous, golden-haired male waited on the opposite side, his gray eyes alive with pleasure. Even his sensuous lips curled up in a closed-lipped smile. "Ms. Robertson. I was pleased you accepted my invitation." He moved past her into the room, which immediately seemed smaller with him in it.

Stella started to reply then glanced down and noticed what he was wearing and again silently cursed her purchase of the red dress.

Blue jeans, tight, the kind with a button fly, topped by a black T-shirt that hugged his upper chest, displaying some impressive muscles. Well-worn western boots completed the outfit. Over his shoulder he carried a black leather jacket.

From prince of darkness to king of the road. In this getup Sebastian might have stepped from the pages of a biker magazine. So much for dinner at a fancy, intimate restaurant.

Sebastian was doing his own checking out of her outfit, the increased sensuality of his smile telling her just what he was thinking. "Nice," he said, indicating the dress. "Is it new?"

"This old thing?" Stella told him, lying through her teeth. No way she was going to admit that she'd gone shopping for him.

She pointed to his jeans. "Are we going to a biker bar?"

He looked down and laughed. "Not really. I thought you might enjoy visiting one of the better Chinese restaurants in town. The food is quite good, I'm told, but the dress code minimal."

"You haven't eaten there?"

A look of chagrin crossed his face. "Alas no. I'm on a rather limited diet and it's hard to keep to it with restaurant dining."

Skepticism colored Stella's voice. "Limited diet? Are you kidding me?"

"Not at all. It's a physical problem I've had for more years than I care to count. My body just doesn't digest most food appropriately." Sebastian shrugged. "I can drink, though, in moderation, of course. I've already had my evening meal so I'll keep you company with a cocktail."

Stella swallowed her disbelief. Maybe he really did have some digestive issues, although he looked healthy enough…

"There is just one thing though," he said, giving her dress a long steady look. "You might want to change…"

"Change?"

He pointed to her new dress. "Much as I like it, and believe me, I do, you would be more comfortable in pants. I thought we'd take my motorcycle."

"You want me to ride on the back of your bike?"

"I have an extra helmet for you and I'm a very good rider. Quite safe. It makes it so much easier to get around this town and its parking restrictions."

This evening was getting weirder all the time. Well, she'd wanted an adventure. Riding a motorcycle through San Francisco with a golden god who had digestive problems sounded like an adventure. At least there was likely a good scene for a book in it.

"Why don't you wait downstairs while I change? You can get a beer in the bar."

He leaned against the wall, his silvery gaze sliding along her legs. Stella could feel the heat across the room.

"I don't mind waiting here..."

Seizing his shoulders, Stella turned him toward the door. "Out. I'll see you downstairs."

He quirked one eyebrow in amusement but he let her push him from the room.

* * * * *

The hotel bar was pretty quiet, only a few people about. Sebastian sat at the bar and ordered a martini, assuming he'd have a wait for Stella to dress for their evening.

Even though the bar wasn't busy, there were still a few single women there who glanced over at him, then their eyes returned for a longer, more appreciative look. They eyed him and smiled—smiled and licked their lips.

Sebastian lifted his drink and sipped it, ignoring the olive he couldn't eat. Usually he'd be happy with the attention. He liked women.

Pretty women, young women or even women who were neither pretty or young. He wasn't that particular. Sometimes the older ones or the less attractive tasted sweeter than their more beautiful sisters.

Like a good wine, age and adversity was sometimes needed for blood with a hearty taste, for vintage flavor. The best-tasting blood he'd known had been from a grandmother in her late sixties, her laughing eyes wreathed in wrinkles.

Sebastian smiled at the memory. Hot and sweet she'd been, that long-ago night in far-off France. Sometimes he wondered if she'd ever told her husband about the mysterious young man who'd shown her such a good time after he'd abandoned her for the evening, leaving her to dine alone. Her laugh had caught his ear, her smile his eye. From across the room her aromatic blood had called to him.

He'd offered to show her Paris at night. They'd gone to the river to view Notre Dame, and he'd sipped lightly from her neck beside the Seine, clouding her mind to the experience.

If she'd been younger he might have offered far more than a single bite, bound her by giving her his mark and taken her to live with him for a time. It was one of the few times he'd been tempted to take a companion.

She could have lived a long time with him, the mark giving her the ability to create enough blood to feed him regularly, the mark slowing her aging to a crawl.

But under it all he'd sensed her love for her family, so instead he'd sent her back to her undeserving husband with a smile and a memory of a kiss that surpassed all others.

Sebastian smiled, careful to keep his fangs covered. He was fond of women and they of him, and it was sometimes hard to resist their lure.

He was glad the women here kept their distance and didn't approach to flirt with him. He might have flirted back. He might have been tempted to disappear upstairs for a nibble and he might have forgotten what he was there for.

But then again, probably not. None of the ladies here appealed to him more than Stella and it was no hardship to wait for her. Stella, whose sweet blood had also called to him from the moment he'd walked into the bookstore last night. It had taken effort on his part to not seduce her away for a quick nip, as hungry as he'd been.

Tonight he'd taken steps to assuage his appetites, for blood at least. If he became hungry later for other delights…he mentally shrugged. The night was young and Stella had sought him out. Clearly she was a woman with unmet needs, and he was just the nightwalker to satisfy them.

That would mean losing a little control, but that could be just what he needed right now. He wanted a night spent not being Prince Sebastian, but just a man showing a woman a good time.

Stella walked into the small, intimate bar and his own needs took center stage. In black jeans and a black blazer over a dark red turtleneck, she caught his breath. Literally. Dazed, Sebastian struggled for air as she sauntered to him.

She eyed the partially consumed martini glass. "Are you sober enough to drive?"

Instantly he pulled himself together, shoving the remains of his drink to the side. "I'm fine. Only had a little of it. You can have some if you like." Glancing down, he realized she'd retained the black boots he'd admired upstairs.

The image came to mind of Stella wearing those tall black boots and little else, and he felt his sex go on full alert. No, he wasn't at all interested in any other woman tonight.

Stella reached over him and grabbed his drink, taking a sip. Her smile widened. "Not bad… I like a good martini."

He liked a woman who liked a good martini. "Finish it."

She lifted the olive and held it out to him. "Don't you at least want this?"

"No."

"Ah. Your diet?" She put the olive into her mouth, rolling it around on her tongue.

He wordlessly nodded as she sucked the olive off the toothpick and then finished his drink. Throwing money on the counter, he led her out of the bar.

By the time they got to his motorcycle, stowed at the side of the hotel garage, Sebastian had decided that he might, for once, enjoy leaving control by the wayside.

* * * * *

Riding a motorcycle down a San Francisco hill on a balmy fall evening wasn't an adventure—it was one hell of an adventure! Stella held tightly to Sebastian's waist as they headed downhill, the wind of their passage whipping past her. When she peeked around his back, she could see the bay, the bridges a tracery of lights in the distance, breathtakingly beautiful.

Not that she had much breath to waste on the view, what with the way her chest heaved with excitement, her heart keeping up the tempo, only some of which she could blame on the wild ride.

Some guilt had to be borne by the arresting man she had her arms around.

They bore right, and she could see Chinatown ahead, the colorful upper stories and quaint shops below. The place was bustling with tourists and locals, and Stella understood why Sebastian had wanted to take his motorcycle. It was a lot easier to find a parking spot for it than a car would have been.

He parked in the alley next to a restaurant, the fragrant smells from inside contrasting with the sour smells of garbage. Breathing as shallowly as she could, Stella allowed him to help her off the bike and hurry her inside.

Breathing in deeply the aroma of deep fat frying, seafood and soy sauce, Stella watched, bemused, as a small Chinese woman with gleaming black hair and laughing eyes greeted

Sebastian. He gave her a tight-lipped smile and spoke to her in what sounded like perfect Cantonese and instantly they were led to a table at the back, past several groups already waiting.

VIP treatment at a popular restaurant. There was something to be said for going out with a prince.

Thirty minutes later she collected the last of her rice with her chopsticks and watched as Sebastian poured more tea for both of them. Turned out jasmine tea was one of the items he could tolerate on his diet, and he relished each sip of the fragrant brew.

She laid her chopsticks across her plate and picked up her own cup. "That was every bit as delicious as you told me it would be."

He smiled at her over his cup, and once more she saw his vampire teeth in his upper jaw.

"Hey, you still have fangs in. Did you forget to take them out?"

Immediately his lip descended, hiding them from view. "They aren't as easy to remove as you might expect."

Fangs in his head, sleeps though the day, liquid diet. "If I didn't know better, I'd think you were trying to make me believe you really are a vampire."

For a moment his silvery gaze seemed intent on the swirling steam above his cup. "Suppose I were. What would you think?"

"That you were crazy—there are no such things as vampires."

"So sure are you—we'll have to see about that." He finished his tea and signaled for the check. "Let me show you around town."

The view from the Golden Gate Bridge amazed her. They parked at one end, walked out to the middle and stared back at the city. On the water were sparsely lit small boats bobbing between the bridge and the rest of the bay. Brighter lights defined the edge of the shore and illuminated the piers. Behind the waterfront rose the tall buildings of downtown, surmounted by the pyramid-shaped Transamerica building. Nearer them stood the Ghirardelli chocolate sign.

They stood side by side against the railing. A cold breeze blew around them and Stella shivered in spite of her jacket. She pointed to the sign on the shore. "I don't suppose you'd like to go out for hot chocolate."

Sebastian gazed at it and she saw real regret in his face. "I'm afraid I can't indulge, but if you'd like some…"

"You can't have hot chocolate. Or mushi pork. Or plain white rice. How about a hamburger?"

He shook his head. Stella crossed her arms. "And you have fangs."

Laughing, he turned toward her and she could see them plainly. They were the most realistic-looking caps she'd ever seen.

Her face seemed to mesmerize him for a moment, then the heat of his stare warmed her faster than any cup of hot chocolate would. He took her into his arms.

"Yes, I have fangs, my lovely. All the better to eat you with." Then he kissed her.

How could she have ever imagined it was cold out? Just because it was November, and she was on a high bridge, and there was a stiff breeze. Locked in Sebastian's arms, Stella met his fiery lips with her own, and warmth spread through her like fire through tall, dry grass, relentless, consuming. His tongue explored the entry to her mouth and she opened to him, bade him enter and he did. When he retreated, she followed him and felt for herself the needle-sharp points of his caps.

One pricked her, and Stella pulled her tongue away, tasted the coppery blood from the pinprick hole. She pulled back to see his eyes, glowing, molten silver gray, the irises huge black holes in the middles. Her face was reflected in them, pale…with fear or passion she couldn't say, but she saw her own eyes widen and the heightened color of her cheeks.

Sebastian ran his tongue along his lips, catching a droplet of crimson blood from where he'd bitten her. The molten silver in his eyes seemed to catch fire. His arms tightened and she felt the tension in him, a passion so consuming that it took her with him. Against her belly, his arousal was rock-hard and immense.

Apprehension and common sense warred with her need. "I don't do this," she whispered.

He shifted himself closer, letting the tip of his tongue drift along her neck. "Funny, you do it so well."

Stella sought balance, space, and tried to gain both by pushing against him. He let her go and she felt the reluctance in him when he did. She felt her own reluctance as well.

"I don't go to bed with strange men, Sebastian."

"I'm not that strange…"

She couldn't help but laugh, and he stared at her before the humor in his reply must have become obvious. His mouth twitched with amusement.

"Perhaps I am a little strange."

"I meant I don't go to bed with men I just met. With strangers."

"Ah." Sebastian stared into her eyes and stroked her cheek.

"But you see, little star, I'm not a stranger to you. I've read your books and you know me—I'm in every one of them. I'm the man you want above all others, a strong man of passion who sweeps you away."

She felt his hand along the back of her neck, caressing without possession, and within her rose a hunger for more of that touch.

Sebastian leaned closer to whisper in her ear. "I'm the dark soul you seek, the man you yearn for in the middle of the night. If you'd let me, I'd fulfill every one of your dreams, the ones you've written of in your books."

He licked the pulse point of her neck and a shiver that had nothing to do with the chill air of the bay swept through her. "I'm not a stranger, Stella. I'm your fantasy."

Chapter Three

What did he think he was doing? Sebastian shifted gears, heading up the hill that would take them to Stella's hotel. Stella rode behind him, her arms tight around his waist, her breasts soft against his back. He could almost feel the hard pebbles of their tips as she shifted against him.

Urgency told him to speed up their trip, to arrive as soon as possible, but caution made him stay to the speed limit. Last thing he wanted was to be pulled over by the police. Any delay would give Stella the opportunity to reconsider their actions.

He didn't want Stella reconsidering anything. She was primed for him now as much as she'd ever be, just as he was for her. It had been years since he'd wanted a woman this badly. Perhaps he should have taken her to his place. It was closer, but she'd feel more at ease in her hotel, particularly since he'd need to leave her tomorrow before the sunrise.

She said she didn't sleep with strangers and she didn't need to know just how strange he was. Later would be soon enough to tell her more—if it became necessary.

The parking garage yawned in front of him and he took advantage of the smaller spaces near the front to park his bike. Heightening his senses, he could hear Stella's heartbeat, staccato with excitement—from the bike ride and from him. He pulled her off and into his arms, and then they were hand in hand, running for the front door.

At the lobby elevator they stood close, waiting for the doors to open, anticipation in every breath. The bell rang, the doors slid open, they slipped inside and Stella pushed the button. Then she was in his arms, his lips locked with hers, a kiss even more passion-driven than the one on the bridge.

Sebastian drew back, keeping her close. The mirrored interior of the elevator car showed him multiple views of her face, her eyes bright with excitement, cheeks flushed, lips swollen from his kisses. Auburn hair tumbled down around her ears and across his hands, the color of fire, but soft and silky.

His own face he avoided looking at. It had been years since he'd taken a good look at himself. Hundreds of years, the truth be told. Each nightwalker saw something different in the visage after they crossed over, an unnaturalness that haunted their souls.

Even as prince of his kind, strongest of his people, Sebastian could not easily look at his face and see the stranger there. Instead he looked at Stella's eyes and the recognition in them. Recognition of the stranger he'd said didn't exist and who'd soon be her lover, at least for this one short night.

The bell rang again and they were in the hallway. Stella struggled with the card key, the light on the door stubbornly staying red, and for an instant Sebastian thought it a warning. Red meant stop, don't, and he almost drew back, but then she tried again, pushed and pulled and the light blinked green.

In the room now, and Stella's jacket was off, then his. She was in his arms again and nothing was more important than her warm body in his arms, her mouth on his.

He tried to keep some control. He wouldn't let her risk her tongue in his mouth again, where his fangs had nicked her. That had nearly undone him back on the bridge, forced him into bloodlust when he'd tasted her sweet essence.

Blood unlike any other he could remember. Her flavor was rich like honey but not as sweet. There was tartness in it that added spice to the sweet. A shame he didn't dare nibble her, taste her more. He wanted her blood as part of their coupling but in his current state he couldn't be careful enough.

Control was important and he must maintain his to avoid revealing too much.

It would have to be enough to possess her body and bring her to ecstasy.

He had her shirt untucked from her jeans now, the red turtleneck lifted to reveal her breasts, swollen, the tips jutting outward through the silk of her bra as he cupped them. He pulled the top off, then the bra and she was naked from the waist up, her skin golden in the light of the bedside lamp. Soft cries erupted from her as he fondled her softness, then he pulled one rosy tip into his mouth and suckled it.

Boots came off, then the rest of their clothing. Now he'd pulled the covers off the bed to reveal the plain cotton sheet, and for the first time Sebastian regretted not taking her to his home instead.

Stella would've looked glorious spread out on his red satin sheets. That there might be another time for them seemed too much to ask for. If he possessed her again, he might never want to let her go. He would have to be satisfied with just this once.

Then she stretched out, her hair a red flame on the bed behind her, and satisfaction was never a doubt. Her body wasn't as slender as some women's, but filled out in the hips and with heavy breasts that seem to beckon to him. Then she gave him a wicked smile and crooked her finger in teasing invitation.

Breathing heavily, he crawled over her, widening the gap between her legs to make room for him. Eyes wide, she seemed to examine his rod, the half smile on her face telegraphing her anticipation. He stopped when his body covered her, the tip of him resting between her thighs, keeping his weight on his arms.

He spent a little more time worshipping her body, tasting the skin of her neck with his tongue, keeping his fangs away. She moaned, her hands on his back stroking him, her mouth dipping to catch his forehead, the shells of his ears. Stella's breathing sounded like the ocean, deep and rhythmic, her soft cries as he tugged on her nipples could have been the cries of a bird.

Sebastian dipped lower, finding soft folds already slick with need, waiting for him. He tasted that liquid desire, its flavor reminding him of her forbidden blood, honey-tart.

The urge to dip lower, find the vein in her thigh, pulled at him. He breathed through it, knowing he'd never be satisfied with sipping there. Instead he applied his tongue and drank her nectar. When he applied his mouth to her sensitive bud hiding in the folds, she arched beneath him.

As she climaxed, he let his mind touch hers, felt the red-purple of her essence flare out at the edges, mixing with his own silver. Some of her ecstasy bled into him, tripling the passion already driving him. Control was becoming hard, harder than anything to maintain.

He *needed* her and the realization was shocking. Sebastian, prince of nightwalkers, hadn't needed anyone, not for years. Hundreds of years.

But he didn't feel the weight of those years tonight, not here, not with Stella in his arms. He felt young, as young as he'd been the night he'd taken the gift from the Countess, his maker, and become a nightwalker. He felt as young as Stella.

Stella, his starshine.

She was coming down from her heights, her hands tangled in his hair. Sebastian allowed her to pull him to her lips and their lips mingled, tongues mingled, hers seemingly more cautious, avoiding the tips of his fangs. In the midst of this he positioned himself, then drove home within her, swallowing her gasp at his entry.

She shuddered under him and the red-purple deepened as her passion rose again. When he moved, she joined him, and it became an intricate dance between them, two people made one. Her legs slid over his, widening, deepening for him, and he took advantage of that.

Her head turned away, baring her neck, the pulse frantic. It fascinated him, that jump, the honey-tart flow through her vein, just beneath his teeth. Just within reach.

She moaned as he drove into her. Without thinking he bent to kiss her neck, just a kiss, just a touch of his tongue to taste the skin.

"That feels so good," she muttered, her voice was sultry whisper.

He licked her again and she smiled. Sebastian ran his tongue along the vein and she tilted her head, giving him better access.

It felt like permission. The silver of his mind covered hers, touched her passion, drove it further. With the next slide of his tongue Sebastian heard her thoughts.

More, more.

With the next pass his fangs glided along with his tongue, her mental cry frantic in his mind. She whimpered, her neck rippling against his mouth.

Bloodlust, hot, red, the color of her hair, the color of blood, seeped into his mind and without further thought his fangs found her pulse, sinking into the soft skin above it. A happy whimper fled her throat as he pulled the first sip into his mouth.

Flavor, honey-tart, flooded his tongue, and like flint to steel it sparked, like fire to tinder it flamed. Bloodlust flooded him and each mouthful was just enough to encourage the next, none was enough. He drank from her as he would from a deep well, an ever-replenishing spring.

Caught up in their passion, Stella's untried mind reached out to his, the red-purple swirling around his impassioned silver. She trembled then climaxed in ever-increasing waves, her sex tightening around him. Pulling his mouth away, he shuddered, pulsating deep within her, orgasm dragging him from his bloodlust haze.

Still breathing heavily, Sebastian stared into Stella's face, her eyes and lips dark in her face.

He blinked, horror seeping into him. *Her features weren't that dark — her skin was pale!* On her neck twin puncture wounds seeped, the blood trickling onto the sheet beneath her, her complexion nearly as white.

Stella's eyes were full of astonishment. She smiled and laughed, her breathing labored. She probably thought it was simply due to their having sex. "That was really something."

But then her astonishment faded, touched by concern. Reaching for his face, she ran a finger along his lips and stared at the blood coating the tip, her eyes narrowing in confusion.

"I don't understand…what did you do?" She stared at him. "Did you bite me?" she asked, her voice barely a whisper. Then she fainted.

* * * * *

For a while there was only darkness, then there was darkness and voices, several of them, soft, urgent, concerned. She wanted to open her eyes to see them but somehow couldn't.

Something wouldn't let her. Something was keeping her eyes closed, she could feel it. It was like a big silver bowl had been put over her mind, enclosing her, locking her within and keeping her from seeing. But she could hear.

She stopped fighting the bowl, focused on listening instead and eventually she could make out independent voices.

"I need you to hold her still." That sounded like a woman, her voice crisp, businesslike, with a soft accent she couldn't quite place.

Her arm was seized and immobilized against the bed, strong hands holding it firm. She felt a sharp sting, like that of a needle. Coolness flooded into the area as if something cold was being injected into her vein. There was a sound like tearing tape and her arm skin grew taut.

"She jerked when I put the needle in. Try to deaden the area." A tendril of silver licked at her mind and she didn't feel her arm anymore.

Fear encompassed her. Who were these people? What did they want?

Soothing silvery thoughts flickered through her mind, dampening her panic. *It's all right, starshine. We aren't going to hurt you. This is to make you better.*

But she had been hurt—she'd been bitten. It had been Sebastian with his false fangs that perhaps weren't as false as she'd thought they were. Now it was his voice she heard in her head, just as she had in the bookstore.

She fled deeper within her mind to where the silver thoughts couldn't find her. Safe, disconnected from her body, she could still hear.

"Will she be all right?" Sebastian's voice, anxious and guilty.

The woman answered him in her soft lilt. "Given time, yes. She didn't lose all that much and you stopped before it was too late. Finish the transfusion and let her sleep. She'll be fine in the morning."

"I'll take that. It will leave your hands free." The new voice spoke with a rich, familiar British accent. *Harold, the ever-so-proper butler?* The desire to cover her naked self rose before she realized she had no control over her body. Hopefully Sebastian had thrown a sheet over her. If not, she was going to kill him for letting other people see her naked and if she died instead, she'd haunt him forever.

"My lord, while I'm holding this little bag of blood over our favorite author, would you mind telling me just how this came about?"

Stella heard a heavy sigh and thought she felt someone pass phantom fingers through her hair.

"I lost control. First time...since I can remember."

"Certainly the first time I remember. Interesting. Have you considered the possibilities?"

Sebastian's voice held a new note, angry, and inside her hiding place, Stella felt a twinge of alarm. "This was an accident, that's all. She distracted me."

"You were distracted? Another first. It's been what, two hundred years since your last distraction?"

"It doesn't mean anything. Accidents happen. As long as I've been around, I was due for one. No harm done, I'll see to it she's taken care of and that will be the end of it."

The end of it? But they'd loved each other. It had been more than sex. Far more. A different kind of hurt took hold in her.

"You can end it just like that?" Stella thought Harold sounded skeptical. "A woman who distracts you and makes you lose control isn't just rare, my lord, she's unique. A true prize, one might say."

"One might say many things but I'm not interested in a relationship with a normal woman."

"Normal? I thought she was a psi."

"She's untrained. Not even aware of what she is and in all likelihood she'll stay that way the rest of her life. We won't speak of it anymore."

"Very well, my lord." Stella heard him shift. "I say—you did put her completely under, didn't you?"

"Of course I did."

"I was just wondering... There seem to be tears coming from her eyes."

"What the devil!" Silver mist flooded her, and she blanked out again. When she came back the mist was faint, like a fog around her brain. She tried to open her eyes, only to fail again, but this time it felt more like a dream.

She heard the door open and hushed voices, Sebastian saying thanks, the others acknowledging. The silver mist grew deeper and she knew he was just above her. Again it was like phantom fingers touching her face, her hair.

I'm sorry to leave you this way, starshine. If I were other than I am, it would be very different. But I've met you far too late, you see.

Phantom lips touched hers, a kiss that went nowhere without her response. She heard his sigh, mental and physical, then his rich voice.

"Goodbye, Stella Robertson. It was wonderful knowing you. Dream of me, now and then, for I shall never forget you."

Silver mist pushed her into sleep and when she woke it was gone. Through the heavy drapes the sun shone. Sitting up too fast, the world whirled around her and she held her head until the dizziness stopped. Stella examined her arm and saw a tiny bruise near her elbow, but no sign of a needle mark.

Had it been just a dream? Gingerly she crawled from the covers, noting that she was still naked, stood and found the mirror over the desk. No pinprick holes on her neck.

What had happened last night? She'd gone out with Sebastian, he'd watched her eat dinner, then they'd toured San Francisco on his bike. They'd kissed on the bridge, then come back here.

They'd made love… She examined her bare body, noted the small bruises, scratches, marks of a passionate lover. Stella sighed. More than passionate. Sebastian had been a magnificent lover. Best she'd ever had. On a scale of one to ten, with all her other lovers ranking between two and six, Sebastian had been a twelve. No, make that a twenty.

Make it a hundred and twenty.

She thought of what she'd overheard last night, Sebastian and Harold discussing how many years he'd seen. Several hundred years, his age as a vampire.

Stella collapsed onto the bed. A vampire. She'd made love with a real vampire and he'd taken blood from her. Too much blood, because he'd lost control. He'd said she'd been dreaming of someone like him, and he was right. This could have been a scene right out of one of her books…except she'd never had her hero call in the paramedics before.

But proof of what had happened? There was none. She was a little faint, but not that bad. Of course she'd dreamed that Sebastian, his faithful butler and some unknown woman had given her a transfusion, but only the little bruise on her arm was evidence of that.

Sebastian wasn't here and it was daylight, but it wasn't the first time a man had sneaked out on a woman in the middle of the night. It hurt, but it wasn't that unusual.

Stella shook her head, determined to put things into perspective. She'd made love to a man, that much was obvious. Perhaps the rest was just some sort of whacked-out dream.

She took a deep breath and let it out slowly, forcing calm into her shattered nerves. It *had* been a dream—that was the most likely explanation.

There were no such things as vampires. They were the stuff of myth and legend and she wrote about them in her books. A guy had tapped into that and shown her a great time but now didn't want anything more.

It hurt, but she could live with that.

She rose and went past the end of the bed, heading for the bathroom. As she passed something caught her eye and she stared at the bare sheet where her head had been last night while making love.

Two brownish-red spots decorated the sheets, blood spots that had been hidden under her pillow. Stella raised her hand to her seemingly uninjured neck.

As she fainted Stella decided it was fortunate that she had just enough time to aim for the bed before she finished blacking out.

Chapter Four

In rueful satisfaction, Stella stared up at the rough-cut stone exterior of the Napa County Nightflyer Winery, a building that looked as if it could have been airdropped from a French countryside.

Well, this is a little more like it!

The solid rock walls, gilded by the late afternoon sun, looked strong and impenetrable, and large metal studs reinforced the heavy wooden doors at the front. The structure looked able to withstand any kind of a siege, including that of an unruly mob of peasants carrying pitchforks and torches.

It looked like the home of a mad scientist—or a sorcerer.

It may have been a little of both. From what she'd found out, the mysterious, unnamed owner of the winery had a reputation for being exceptionally good at the creation of new wines, a mix of sorcery and science if ever there was. He was also reclusive and never seen during the day. Stella eyed the walls. Dark, narrow slits decorated them along the upper edges but otherwise there were no windows to invite the entry of undesirable visitors.

Or to permit the light of the sun. Perhaps it was the home of a mad scientist-sorcerer who was also a vampire.

Stella climbed out of her car and gazed at the uninviting edifice. Since waking in her hotel room, she'd spent every day of the past two weeks in her hunt for the elusive Sebastian Moret, both in San Francisco and from her home in Woodland Hills. In her studies she'd uncovered a remarkable amount of information, not only about him but also about other people who were reported to be of paranormal origin.

She'd started with the address she had, but apparently the man had abandoned his San Francisco house that same morning. A curt note left at the front desk of the hotel had pled urgent business elsewhere and briefly apologized for what had turned into the strangest one-night stand in Stella's experience.

She still didn't quite believe what she remembered happening, his mouth sucking at her neck, the telltale bloodstains on the bed. But something way out of the ordinary had happened, and she wasn't about to let it go unexplained. Besides, the comment made about her being a psi continued to haunt her. If there was something different about her that she didn't know about, she needed to pursue that.

For ten years Stella had honed her skills as an investigator in the pursuit of better and more complex storylines. She knew how to use the Internet as well as public records to find out what she wanted. Tracing through the tax records of the townhouse had revealed a commonality in ownership to the winery, and investigating the winery had revealed the oddities of its proprietor. More records had unearthed other properties scattered throughout California, customized land vehicles, as well as a small fleet of Gulfstream jets, leading to another fact about the mysterious Prince Sebastian.

Her vampire really did know how to fly a jet plane.

Assuming he really was a vampire.

Stella had considered the possibility that her mysterious man hadn't been anything more than an overanxious fan with a flair for the dramatic. It could be. It was even most likely to be. Up to now she'd never believed in the existence of vampires, werewolves and the like. At least that's what she'd thought before researching the matter and finding so many unanswered questions. Now she wasn't at all sure.

But she was sure of one thing. Whatever had happened had been out of her control and that was something she didn't care for at all.

She stared at the building before her. This might not even be the right location. The fact that the same company owned both this winery and the San Francisco townhouse might be a complete coincidence.

Stella whipped her courage into shape, climbed the tall steps to the heavily armored front door of the winery and reached for the doorknocker. Immediately she felt a chill, gazing on the metal fixture.

It was a wolf's head, forged from golden metal, eyes set with red stones—a doorknocker exactly the same as the one on the door in San Francisco.

She wasn't wrong. *Sebastian lived here.* It was the only explanation. Heart pounding, Stella raised the metal hammer to bang on the door. Inside she heard the sound echo around, as if the interior was large and empty.

On her back she felt the last warm rays of the sun as it dipped toward the horizon, and abruptly realized that sunset was merely minutes away. What was she thinking, investigating a vampire after dark? She should have waited for morning.

Courage failing, she considered making a mad dash for the car and heading back for the little hotel she'd spotted by the main road. She could come back in the morning...

"Miss Roberts!" Stella turned when the door opened. In the open doorway stood Harold, dressed as before in perfect butler regalia, a look of genuine delight on his lean features. "What a pleasant surprise to see you again. Come in, come in!" Seizing her hand, he pulled her inside.

It was open and echoy inside, the room cavernous, its stone walls covered in tapestries, and thick oriental rugs cushioned the wooden floor. On one side stood a fireplace, flanked by heavy chairs of dark wood with soft, colorful cushions. Over the mantle were arrayed an impressive display of weapons, some medieval, some modern. A heavy broadsword stood side by side with an ancient blunderbuss, a brace of dueling pistols and what she could swear was an Uzi sub-machine gun as well as a pair of American M-16 rifles.

None of the weapons appeared to be new. They looked well used, in perfect order, ready to be snatched off the wall and put into action.

A glance at Harold told her he'd noticed her stare. He seemed to be suppressing a chuckle. "Yes, my lord does enjoy collecting things."

Bitterness over her abandonment in San Francisco rose within her. "Like authors of books? Or is it just women in general he enjoys 'collecting'?"

Some of Harold's formality slipped. "I've been with him for many years, miss, and in my experience what happened with you was unique. Please don't judge him quite yet."

Harold glanced through the narrow window at the setting sun and once again was the perfect butler. "Perhaps you would like some tea? Or perhaps something stronger? We have some very fine wine you could sample."

She had to laugh. "So I hear. Perhaps I'll try some later. For now, tea would be fine."

The tea was better than fine. It was made perfectly, in the proper British fashion, and accompanied by a selection of small sandwiches and biscuits. Served in an intimate drawing room that could have been lifted from one of her Regency-era vampire books, Stella was happily pouring herself a second cup when a tall blond shadow suddenly appeared in the doorway.

Sebastian startled, and for a moment she thought he looked delighted to see her. That moment passed quickly.

A dark scowl crossed his face. "Ms. Roberts. How... What the devil are you doing here?"

Stella held tight to her equanimity. After all, she had expected something like this response to her uninvited presence. "What I'm doing here is having tea and it's lovely. Would you like some?"

He hesitated, then apparently remembering his manners, nodded and took the seat at the tea table opposite her. Stella poured him a cup and served it, omitting the biscuits she knew he probably couldn't eat.

He sipped deeply and sighed appreciatively. "Ah, that hits the spot. One of the advantages of a British butler is just how well he does tea. I'm sorry for my outburst. You must forgive me, I didn't expect to see you here."

She smiled at him. "I'm not surprised. You did a very good job of giving me the slip. I don't think you've been back to your San Francisco home in the past two weeks. Given the kind of time we spent together, I could take considerable offense."

"I often spend time away from there. It wasn't to avoid you. And what happened between us... I do apologize for leaving the way I did. It was rude."

"I'm glad we agree on one thing. As for your slipping out of town, it was effective."

"Then might I ask how you found me?"

Stella laughed. "Oh I have my ways. The Internet, you know."

He blanched, and Stella saw his already pale complexion grow paler. "You found me how?"

"Search engines. I did a lot of research and found several websites that talked about real vampires...and other people. There were a lot of references to parafolk. You know what those are?"

She thought a whisper of a smile touched his lips, but he sipped his tea to cover it up. "No, can't say that I'm familiar with the term."

"Well, parafolk are people like vampires and werewolves and people with psychic abilities, called psis." Stella had thought a lot about the latter since finding that reference. When she'd been unconscious in her hotel room, Harold had called her a psi although Sebastian had said she was untrained.

That had been one of the many reasons she'd hunted him to his lair, to find out just what he'd meant by that.

One of the reasons, although not the most important, and she'd wait until later to bring it up. She didn't want her reluctant host to know that she'd heard and remembered what had been said that night.

"And so you believe me to be a vampire?" He cast an amused glance at her. "What would that make Harold I wonder? A werewolf?"

A bald werewolf? Stella almost snickered.

"I thought you didn't believe in vampires," he said. "They were just legends and stories, like the ones you write."

"That's what I thought too. But I'm not so sure now. You see, I think you really are a vampire. All the evidence I found on you, on the winery here, all of it points to exactly that."

Sebastian put his teacup down. "If this is true, aren't you taking quite a chance coming here? If I'm what you think I am, I could do you harm."

"I don't think you are going to hurt me. You could have done that in San Francisco and you didn't."

He nodded. "Then what is your purpose in coming here? To get your hypothesis confirmed?"

"Partly. I also wanted to take you up on your offer."

"What offer?"

"The one you made in the bookstore the night we met. To teach me what you know about the supernatural."

Sebastian frowned. "You are that curious?"

"I'm curious. But more important, I've been writing books for years. I do tons of research into the historical aspects of my books, trying to get things right. If I've been wrong about the paranormal parts all these years I want to know what the truth is."

"The truth…" That seemed to amuse him. "To what purpose? Would you change the way you write your books?"

"Maybe... It would depend on what I learn," she said. "That might be tricky as my readers expect a certain kind of book from me and wouldn't be happy to have me change too much right away. But more important is that I just want to know the truth."

He gave a great sigh. "You are asking a great deal, Ms. Roberts."

Stella took a sip of tea. "Given how intimate we've been, don't you think you should use my real first name?"

Again he looked uncomfortable at being reminded of the time they'd spent together. "You have a point...Stella. Even so, your curiosity isn't important enough for me to risk giving you information that could be used against the parafolk...assuming such even existed. I'm going to have to refuse you."

She stiffened her back. "You don't want to do that, Sebastian."

"I can do anything I want. After all, suppose I am what you think I am. Why shouldn't I just wipe your memory of all this and send you on your way?"

"You tried before and it didn't work," Stella pointed out. "Besides I'm not relying on just my memory now."

Some of his confidence seeped away. "What are you talking about?"

"I took precautions before coming here. I took all my research on you, and the parafolk, and put it someplace safe. There are people who need to hear from me, and if they don't they are going to take that information and send it to a number of places. Have you heard of the Paranormal Watchers Society?"

It was Sebastian's turn to stiffen. "I've heard of them. They are a group of fanatics who hate whatever isn't the same as they are. They tried to kill with sunlight what they thought was a vampire just a few months ago. What business have you had with them?"

Stella had heard about the attempted destruction of a female vampire, and the method they'd employed had sickened her. Death by exposure to sunlight in front of a live audience? Horrible! Fortunately it had turned out that the woman hadn't been a vampire at all, just an actress with false fangs, and the Watchers had been discredited.

But she couldn't show weakness now. She knew what she wanted and was willing to let Sebastian think she'd deal with the PWS if he didn't give her what she wanted.

She met his stony stare with one of her own. "I've done no business with them…as yet. But they are one of the groups I targeted to receive my information."

"I don't like being blackmailed." His silver-gray eyes narrowed, and if he were capable of killing her with a glare, she was sure she'd be dead already. For a brief moment she felt fear.

Still she forced herself to keep her voice even and answered him in the same even tone. "And I don't like it when a man uses me then runs away like a thief in the night."

He flushed and for a moment he actually looked guilty. Finally he sat back and steepled his fingers together, considering her for a moment. "What is it exactly you want from me, Stella?"

"Only what you offered before. You were going to teach me about your kind. To improve my books, remember?"

"How would you expect me to do that?"

She hadn't actually worked that out. "I suppose you could let me stay with you for a while and see how you live. That's the best way to study a culture."

"You'd be willing to live with me? Perhaps as a nightwalker companion?" He made the suggestion casually.

Stella wasn't sure she liked the sudden gleam in his eyes. He was up to something. "I'm not sure. I know what a nightwalker is…that's another name for a vampire. But what is a companion?"

He didn't answer her right away but reached for his teacup and refilled it from the pot. After taking a deep sip, he put both cup and saucer back on the table. Stella watched him clearly delaying answering her and wondered why. Perhaps he was just trying to make her nervous.

She had to avoid a shiver. It was working.

"A companion is a human who lives with a nightwalker. They are normal people other than carrying the mark." He reached over to her and gently laid his fingers on her throat and she felt her heart sputter at his touch. "A companion carries the scars from their nightwalker's fangs here, to show to whom they belong. The mark also helps them create more blood."

"More blood?" she heard herself squeak, pulling away from him.

A shadow of a smile crossed Sebastian's face. "Yes. Blood. A companion is a blood source for a nightwalker. Someone to feed from."

Stella squirmed in her seat. Was Sebastian honestly expecting her to feed him her blood? He'd done it that once, but she'd been pretty overwhelmed by the sex at the time. To do it now…in cold blood, as it were? Stella shivered.

Sebastian continued to nod as if thinking it over. "Yes, that would be the best way to do the research you want. To become my companion for a while. That way we'd both get something out of it. You'd get your information and I'd have a convenient source of blood."

He almost sounded cheerful, and in spite of her dismay it caught Stella's attention. Why was the man suddenly so enthusiastic about this when he'd clearly not wanted her around at all?

Then it came to her. He was expecting her refusal! He'd deliberately picked something that she'd be uncomfortable with so that she'd change her mind and leave him alone. It was all Stella could do to not jump to her feet and scream at him.

Stella settled back into her chair and watched as Sebastian picked up his teacup and refilled it from the pot. She could almost see waves of self-satisfaction coming off him. The smug bastard was sure he was going to scare her off.

Well, if he thought that, he had another think coming, as her grandmother always said. Once Stella had a plan, she never gave up on it. So he'd take a little blood from her, how bad could it be?

She waited until the cup was nearly at his lips. "Okay, I'll do it."

Sebastian jerked and hot tea sloshed over the edge of his cup and onto his fingers. "Damnation!" he said, and quickly put both cup and saucer down, grabbing a tea towel to wipe his hand.

He glared at her warily. "What do you mean, you'll do it?"

"I'll become your companion," she told him with a cheeriness she didn't really feel, although seeing him scald his hand had made her feel better. He really hadn't expected that answer.

"Just for a little while, so I can really get the feel of it." She smiled at him. "It really is the best solution. Thank you for offering, Sebastian."

Astonishment mingled with sheer horror in his face as she stood up and rang the bell Harold had put on the tea table. When the butler arrived she greeted him heartily.

"Harold, it looks like I'm going to be staying after all."

A pleased look graced the man's face. "I'm so happy to hear that. How many days do you think you'll be with us?"

"Oh for quite a while, Sebastian has asked me to become his companion."

The butler's eyes widened and he shot a sharp glance at his master, still nursing his hand with the towel. "He did? Well...that is happy news."

Happy and rather surprising news, if Stella read the man correctly. Harold hadn't expected this either.

Sebastian returned Harold's stare and arched one eyebrow that seemed to forbid any further comment. "Yes, happy news," he said, although he didn't sound terribly happy. "Please have Rebecca ready a room. I assume you have luggage somewhere?"

"In my car," Stella said, handing the keys over to the butler.

He took them with a far more welcoming expression than his master had. "I'll fetch them immediately."

Well, at least one person was pleased she was going to be here. Not her, necessarily, or Sebastian, but Sebastian's servant was delighted.

Chapter Five

Turned out that both of Sebastian's servants were thrilled by the news she was going to become his companion. Rebecca turned out to be a small woman of Asian ancestry who was married to Harold and served as housekeeper. She smiled delightedly at Stella when they were introduced and promised her a superb meal for dinner if they could give her an hour's time to prepare it.

Once Stella heard the woman's voice, she identified her as the third party who'd been with Harold and Sebastian in the hotel room that night. So, at least she now knew whom she was dealing with...it had been Sebastian and his servants who'd taken care of her after his "accidental" feeding too deeply.

As she'd told Sebastian, she'd uncovered a lot of information about parafolk and wouldn't have been surprised if he'd called in help from others when he'd taken too much blood from her, but apparently his household staff had been able to deal with the situation themselves. Convenient, that.

As she sat down to dinner that night in Sebastian's dining room, she realized that handling medical emergencies wasn't the only thing his staff was good at. The table was set magnificently with spotless white linens and candles providing a rich light that glinted off fine china and gleaming silver candlesticks and utensils.

Wine was poured and she finally got her chance to taste some of the winery's products, a delicate white wine to start and a rich full-bodied red with the main course. They were excellent wines and she complimented Sebastian on them.

He nodded and for once seemed pleased. "This was a good year for both my Chardonnays and Pinots. I've been very happy with the results."

He only took a small amount of each in his glass, sipping them carefully, spending most of his time quenching his thirst with a clear straw-colored liquid in a crystal goblet. She wanted to ask him what it was, but she had a suspicion she wouldn't like the answer. At least it didn't look like blood.

Otherwise he ate nothing, while she attacked her steak, baked potato and mixed vegetables with a healthy appetite. It was superb, despite the fact that she was the only one dining.

She noticed that Harold and Rebecca didn't join them for dinner. "Don't you let your servants eat with you?"

Sebastian toyed with his glass. "They wouldn't feel comfortable sharing the table with you at this time. You might have trouble with what they eat."

She paused in the middle of putting a juicy bit of steak in her mouth. "What do you mean? Don't tell me they are vampires too. I've seen Harold in daylight."

He winced. "Stella, first thing you should know is that vampire isn't a welcome term for my kind. We prefer to use the word nightwalker. Other terms you should know are 'spellcaster' for a psi trained in magic and 'shape shifter' for those who shift into the forms of animals. And to answer your question, no, they are not like me, but they are parafolk."

"Are they psis, like me?"

Sebastian shot her a sharp look. "Whoever said you were a psi?"

She shrugged. "It was something I overheard." She didn't want to tell him she'd overheard his and Harold's conversation when she was supposed to have been unconscious.

He eyed her with suspicion and she decided the best defense would be a fast attack. "I am a psi, aren't I? I have mental powers."

Caution filled his face. "Some. I bespoke you once, in the bookstore, and I couldn't have done that if you weren't able to receive me. It is also the reason I can make you a companion. Mental powers are needed so I can readily link to you and know when I've taken too much. But yours are untrained."

"So I have some powers, but they aren't trained. Could you train me?"

His smile turned seductive. "You wish this, in addition to being made my companion? I am a busy man. What would be in it for me?"

There was a suggestion in his voice that she found particularly irritating. If he thought he was going to get back into her bed, he needed to think again. She forced down the sharp retort that came to mind.

Instead she shrugged. "Well, if you're too busy to do it, perhaps someone else could. There must be lots of people who could help me. Perhaps another nightwalker, someone young, with time on his hands." She smiled brightly.

He scowled and his hand gripped the stem of his goblet so tightly she thought it might break. Leaning over, he gave her a look of sheer possessiveness. "Nightwalkers do not share their companions, Stella. That's the next lesson you should learn. If you require any kind of training, I will do it."

So he was jealous of her, was he? She settled back to eating her dinner, keeping her self-satisfied smile to herself.

* * * * *

Well, this was a fine mess. Sebastian sipped his evening glass of serum and fumed at his new would-be companion. She wasn't even marked yet and already she was manipulating him.

He'd had no intention of offering to make her a companion. He'd only made the suggestion because it had seemed an easy way to discourage her and force her away.

He'd been sure she'd be too afraid of his bite to accept. Instead the little minx had taken him up on it.

She'd even brought up his deplorable behavior in San Francisco. Not that he was happy that he'd snuck off "like a thief in the night" as she'd put it. He'd always regretted not doing more for her.

But after losing control while feeding, it had seemed the prudent thing to do. No way he'd allow a similar incident to occur with her. She seemed to have no idea how close she'd come to death at his hands.

And now she was inviting his bite, to the point of becoming his companion. The next thing he'd know he'd be like his friend Jonathan, unable to control his hunger when feeding. In nearly five hundred years of life he'd never lost control that way and he hadn't liked it.

How this one female could push him so far, he didn't understand. Certainly he found her attractive, but he'd encountered thousands of women more lovely than she was. Even so, he still remembered the exquisite taste of her blood. In the past few weeks no other woman had moved him the way she had.

He'd even taken to drinking serum on a regular basis rather than hunting so much. His heart hadn't been in the chase since that night with her. He'd even lost some weight, which his faithful servants had taken to commenting on. That was probably one of the reasons they'd been so pleased to see Stella show up. They probably thought it a wonderful thing that she was going to be his companion.

They probably didn't even think he meant it when he said it was only temporary.

But he didn't think any of this was that great an idea. It wasn't like he needed anyone, particularly a woman in his life. He was prince of his people and had been for more years than Stella had seen. He wasn't going to let a woman less than one-tenth his age lead him around.

He valued his self-control too much to let a woman who made him as off-balanced as Stella did come into his life, even if she did taste really good. He glanced over at her, enjoying her dinner. In a few moments he'd take her blood and give her the companion oath. Part of him almost looked forward to that.

Almost, but not quite. In all his years he'd never taken a companion and he didn't see why he had to have one now. He was being forced into this to keep her curiosity satisfied, so she wouldn't tell what she knew to people who could use the information to harm his kind.

She should remember that curiosity sometimes killed the cat. She was using the threat of exposing his people for her own ends and he didn't like that at all.

Of course it was possible she might back down if he could put enough of a scare into her. She might still be persuaded to leave without his mark if she gave into the fear he knew she had to have over being bitten.

Perhaps she could be persuaded to seek what she wanted to know from another source and would leave him and his people alone.

In the meantime, he decided that he no longer wanted to watch her eat and drink a delicious meal he could have no part of. Sebastian rose to his feet. "If you'll excuse me, I have several bits of work to deal with prior to the ceremony."

Stella froze and her face turned apprehensive. "The ceremony?"

He hid his smile—she *was* still uncertain about becoming his companion. "The marking ceremony. Where I take your blood and leave my mark on your neck." He leaned over and stroked the soft skin over her vein and her eyelashes fluttered wildly.

"I think we'll do it later tonight. Around midnight." He gave her a frosty smile. "I presume that will work for you."

Stella seemed to lose some of her enthusiasm for her dinner. "I suppose so. At midnight then. Where?"

He thought for a moment. Where would a good room to do a marking ceremony be? To be truthful, since it was the first time he'd taken a companion, he had no idea of what proper protocol would be. Still, he couldn't let her know that.

"I suppose we should keep it simple. My study will do."

She nodded slowly. "Very well—midnight in your study. I'll be there and in the meantime I'll get settled," she said, but her expression was anything but settled. Stella looked distinctly nervous.

Sebastian turned and moved from the room, hiding his smile. He'd be willing to bet that she'd be thinking very hard for the next several hours, and might not even be around by midnight tonight. If so, he'd head out for town and find sustenance the way he preferred to do it, quietly and anonymously, and forget all about her.

In the meantime he'd simply ignore Stella's presence and get some work done. There were invoices to go over and other aspects of running a multimillion-dollar empire that never slept...even if he must during the daylight hours much of the local businesses worked. He often had to spend the first several hours of the evening playing catch-up with his buyers and suppliers, and the time after midnight working with his clients back in Europe during their early morning.

Everyone thought that somehow vampires simply had wealth without working for it. At least in his case that could hardly have been less true. His maker the Countess had enjoyed unlimited inherited wealth, but he'd been born poor, and without being able to show clear title to her lands, he and his brother nightwalker Jonathan had been forced to leave her palatial surroundings and live by their wits for a long time after her death.

Another thing he'd held against his maker. Not the main thing, a small matter in comparison to everything else, but her not making financial arrangements for those she'd sired before she'd taken her own life had hurt him badly. After a hundred years in her service, he'd expected better than to be cast back into a dangerous world without resources.

Fortunately he and Jonathan had had some kind of useful trade. His friend had returned to making music while he'd known much about wine making, and after a short time risking his life in culverts and deserted barns he'd been able to find a small French winery willing to give him a safe home in exchange for his skills.

For several hundred years he'd helped make them rich, until he'd finally found a way to follow Jonathan over the ocean and to this place where the land was as rich as his homeland had been. Here he'd used his savings to buy his own winery and populate it with people who respected him…although no one called him by his title but his shape shifter servants.

No, he'd hardly been living a life of leisure. In fact, Sebastian had been working all his life—all four-hundred-eighty-plus years of it—and he had barely slowed down during the past fifty. He didn't have time to "take life easy" as others did.

Nor did he have time to teach a romance author about his kind, or even hers. All he wanted was to see Stella leave, preferably as soon as possible.

With that he opened his computer and began his work for the evening.

He was deep into it several hours later when a knock on the door disturbed his concentration. The first had been so quiet that Sebastian, deeply engrossed in comparing data from two spreadsheets, almost didn't hear it. The second knock was louder, and assuming his visitor was Harold with his midnight tea, he said, "Come in."

The door opened and shut, and his visitor now stood inside the room. Without looking up, Sebastian waved his hand at a bare spot next to him on the corner of his desk. "Just put it there."

He felt the figure move closer. "I'll never understand how they've managed to complicate something as simple as buying a barrel," Sebastian said, attention still focused on the screen in front of him. "In the old days we used a log book, not a computer, and somehow accounts still managed to balance."

"They also used quill pens and animal skins at one point." Stella's voice broke his concentration and he jerked away from the screen to stare up at her. Her lips twitched up in a smile and her eyes twinkled with amusement. "But most of us prefer to write on a computer. Saves a lot of feathers and hides and is a lot easier to edit."

She eyed the edge of the desk, shrugged and sat on the corner where he'd expected his tea to rest.

"What are you doing?" Sebastian asked.

Stella shrugged again. "What you told me to do. 'Put it there', you said."

Her position put her far too close to him, particularly when she crossed her legs. Much as Sebastian wanted to be indifferent to her presence, he couldn't be. He might tell himself he didn't want her around, but his body felt differently about it. One sniff and her richness, the potency of her blood, called to him.

He saved his files and pushed himself away from the keyboard, and even further away from her. "What are you doing here?"

"It's midnight. You said you wanted to mark me now."

Sebastian opened his mouth to say he hadn't really expected her to still be here, but stopped when she shook her head.

"You really thought I'd chicken out, didn't you?" A look of triumph was on her face. "That is so funny. I'm not sure if I should be insulted or not."

Sudden horror sped through him. "You're not reading my thoughts?"

"I don't have to. I can see it in your face." She leaned over and stared into his eyes, which put her far closer than he wanted. Her mouth couldn't be more than inches from his. Kissing distance.

He actually had to lean away from her to keep himself from crossing that short distance and catching her lips with his. That would never do, to kiss her now. He wanted her out of his house and out of his life.

Didn't he?

It didn't matter if he did or didn't, she was still here and he was honor bound to make good on his offer. He had to make her his companion now, regardless of whether or not he really wanted to. Harold and Rebecca were expecting it and even if Stella decided not to make trouble later, he couldn't afford to renege on the deal now.

Even so, marking her here, alone with her in this room, didn't seem like such a great idea. He needed space, distance…and witnesses, or else he was likely to do more than take blood from her.

Much more.

Carefully Sebastian cleared his throat. "I would like to make a change, I think. Perhaps it would be better if we used the great room instead. I'd like to invite my servants to attend."

Stella brightened. "Sounds great, I'll tell them."

He watched her go and wondered just what had happened to his plan to send her heading for the hills. She even seemed eager to become his companion, certainly more than he wished. After all, he didn't really want to have her here…did he?

One thing was clear. As soon as she'd sat on the desk next to him, he'd desired her more than any woman he could remember, both her body and her blood. That made her dangerous…and more than a little intriguing.

His life had gotten fairly routine in the past many years and perhaps he needed someone like Stella in his life to shake things up. One thing about it, he had her now, whether or not he liked it.

Time would tell if he liked it.

Chapter Six

Rebecca and Harold arranged themselves next to the fireplace. While neither had cracked a smile at being summoned so hastily to this impromptu ceremony, Sebastian could feel their amusement. Harold's eyebrows had arrowed up at the invitation and Rebecca had to carefully compose her face, but both now stood somberly near the door to the kitchen. Apparently they'd decided on that position, thinking they'd be able to quickly duck away if things got too sensual while he was administering the mark.

He had no intention of any such thing. It just wasn't going to happen. He'd control his urge to bed the enticing Ms. Robertson, no matter what it took. How hard could it be? He'd been resisting even more irresistible women for centuries.

In fact, only one woman had ever been able to hold his passion for long enough to be measured — the woman who'd made him a nightwalker, the Countess. But she was long dead and held no dominion over his heart any longer.

That was an empty spot in him that did not need to be filled by anyone. Not anymore…or ever.

Sebastian did not smile but held out his hand to Stella, who took it and allowed herself to be led to a divan in the center of the room. For the ceremony she at least needed to be seated. He knew that she would need the support once he'd taken enough of her blood to create the mark. He could sit or stand, but sitting next to her would make it more comfortable to feed from her neck. They needed support and comfort — but not too much comfort.

He did not need a repeat of the episode in her hotel room, where he'd fed without limit and very nearly taken his first life in so many decades that he couldn't count them. He would not lose Stella to his hunger, anymore than he would compromise her. Again.

This was a somber event, to take a companion. In all his days he'd never done it before, but she'd left him no choice. He let the gravity of the bond he intended to forge between them show in his face and demeanor. Stella picked up on it and her lighthearted mood wavered, her smile disappearing.

Joining her on the couch, he touched her neck at just the place he intended to mark her. "I will bite you and leave my mark here. Is this satisfactory?"

She hesitated and he saw concern in her eyes. "It will show."

"Marking you as mine. That is true. You'd need to wear something over them." Sebastian read her reaction. She still wanted this but didn't want the scars obvious given that she often had a public role to play.

That was a problem. Probably by the time she had to make her next appearance at a convention or booksigning she wouldn't be his companion, but in the meantime he didn't want to expose her unnecessarily. Perhaps they could come up with a compromise.

He moved his fingers lower, onto her shoulder, where her clothes would normally hide the scars. "Here would be less obvious."

Her relief made him smile. "That will be fine. It's not that I don't want your mark…"

"But a vampire's fang marks would be hard to explain to your fans. I understand. Here will do nicely."

He unbuttoned her blouse to bare the skin he wanted. It was a beautiful spot on her body, unblemished and perfect. Her fresh, sweet blood called to him and his fangs ached, wanting that skin, to pierce it and claim the blood that lay beneath.

Stella tensed under his gaze and he felt her second thoughts. "You can still say no," he told her. "There is no need for this if you don't want to do it."

"I do want it." She said the words, but he wasn't convinced she believed them. But then she looked at him, stared him in the face, and he saw she really was certain.

"All my life I've wondered about who I was," she murmured. "What I was. You say that I have mental powers I know nothing about. This is one way for me to learn."

"Not the only way," he told her, but he was no longer certain he wanted to discourage her the way he had before. He'd told himself he wanted her out of here and that he had no need for a companion. Perhaps that was still true. But right now, with her so close to him, he no longer doubted that he at least wanted her blood, this time, this night.

Later, as his companion he'd be able to draw on her again and again. She'd be part of his life and he hadn't wanted that before. But now he wasn't so sure. Inside him something reached out for her.

Even so, he felt compelled to discourage her. "You could find a spellcaster to teach you about being a psi. Many like you do that and it is far more…comfortable than being a companion."

"I don't know any spellcasters. I do know you."

"And you trust me?"

Again he read her as well as heard her words. "Yes. I trust you."

"Very well." Suddenly eager, Sebastian leaned over and pressed her to the couch, his mouth caressing the skin over her shoulder. He sensed the vein buried deep within, deep, but not too far for his fangs to reach. He licked her, once, twice, catching her taste on his tongue.

His. That was her taste, rich and spicy, and it belonged to him.

Stella's mind was the most alarming shade of lilac, purple with reddish tones that contrasted with the coldness of his silver. He let his thoughts slide over hers to ease her skittishness, calm her for the coming bite. If they were to be lovers he'd give her passion, but that wasn't for tonight...

No. It wasn't for any night! Sebastian told himself. *He'd made that mistake once already and wouldn't do it again.* He wasn't going to make love to Stella when it was so likely that if he did, he'd go too far again and take too much.

He'd only take enough to mark her. If necessary he'd feed elsewhere tonight once this ceremony was done. There was more blood in the kitchen...

Sebastian controlled his revulsion at that thought. To feed on pre-packaged blood when a warm, willing woman was in his arms? What kind of nightwalker had he become?

No, he'd feed well from Stella, but be careful not to take too much.

She was calm now, her mind engaged with his. It felt right, having her here. Felt right to be able to take her blood. Her body in his arms was warm and accepting. All he had to do was let his fangs dig into her shoulder and open the vein. She'd feel some pressure, but little pain.

No pain. He let his mind tell her that and she relaxed further.

One more lick of the silky skin and then he bit down. Blood flooded his mouth, coated his tongue. Honey-tart and rich, like nothing he could remember tasting before except for that one time in San Francisco when he'd taken her blood in her hotel room.

He sucked deeply and awareness fled. All that existed was her warm body in his arms, her blood on his tongue. Her breath rasped near to his ear, heating the side of his face. She was here for him and nothing else mattered, not the formalness of the room around them nor their silent watchers.

It was as if they were the only two people existing in the world. Her pulse, her blood, his hunger easing as he sipped deep. Warmth filled him and satisfaction with it.

His hands stroked her upper arms, the solid muscle and soft skin above it. One hand drifted her back to draw her closer. Not sexual, but sensual. It felt so good to hold her.

In his mind, the purple intensified. *Haven't you had enough?*

Startled, Sebastian paused in mid-draw. Had Stella bespoke him? But he didn't think she knew how.

I'm dizzy...

It *was* her mental voice he heard and even with his best intentions he had taken more than he'd planned. Pulling away, Sebastian cursed himself silently, particularly when she fell back faint to the couch.

With a swipe of his tongue he closed the wounds but left them as pinpoint scars. Unless she wore a low-necked top they wouldn't show, just as she'd wanted. For a moment Sebastian glared at the small wounds that bound her to him, a whirl of emotions and thoughts. Concern that he'd harmed her, anger over wanting her, dismay she wanted to hide what she was to him. He conquered all of those emotions and kept only the thought she belonged to him now.

Putting two fingers over the tiny holes, he spoke the companion oath. "I take you to be my companion, to serve me as long as you wear my mark. In exchange you have my support and protection."

"Support and protection?" She smiled at him, her eyes heavy-lidded. "I like that. Almost sounds like marriage." A yawn escaped her and he realized that for her it was very late. She was still on normal human time and even without the blood loss she'd be tired now.

He lifted her in his arms. "I'll take you to your room."

"I can walk..." she protested, but she snuggled happily in his arms. "Hmm, I think I like this 'support' business," she said as he headed for the stairs.

She felt so right in his arms, so familiar. Just as she had before... The memory of "before", of when he'd made love to her in her hotel room returned, and Sebastian's arms tightened around her. He'd taken too much blood then too, and he'd blamed it on their having sex that time.

But there had been no such distraction tonight. He'd taken more than he intended and hadn't been close to stopping when she'd interfered by speaking into his mind.

Even worse, she had interfered, without knowing how to do so. An untrained psi, Stella should not have known how to send that message into his mind...and yet she had. There was more going on between them than he was comfortable with.

Carrying her to her bedroom suddenly seemed like a bad idea. No telling what would happen if he got her alone like that. Instead he let her slip to her feet while continuing to support her.

He turned to the still-waiting servants. "Harold? Would you help Ms. Robertson to her room?"

Surprise and what might have been disappointment crossed the man's face before he resumed his usual expression of polite affability. "Of course. Rebecca, if you'll assist me?"

They took her from him and guided Stella away. She was still unsteady on her feet but she paused at the foot of the stairs. Some of the haze he'd induced to ease the experience of his bite had faded from her mind and her eyes stared more clearly at him.

"So I'm your companion now?"

At his nod, she hesitated. He waved away the questions he knew she wanted to ask. "Tomorrow I'll tell you whatever you wish to know. But you need sleep tonight."

She wobbled and Harold's arm slid around her shoulders to steady her. Sebastian felt an instant desire to walk over and remove the other man's hand from her and take back Stella for his own. But no, he'd given her up for the evening.

"I suppose you're right," she said. "I'll say good night."

Sebastian watched her leave, knowing he'd made the right decision…but not feeling nearly as good about it as he'd expected. He needed time to adjust to this new addition into his life, no matter how temporary that addition was likely to be.

How long did an author stay around when she was in pursuit of information for a story? Longer than it took to acquire it?

Somehow he doubted that.

* * * * *

Stella woke in a bed she barely remembered falling into the night before. For a moment she stared at the unfamiliar ceiling and wondered at what had happened to her. Then she remembered her impetuous decision to become Sebastian's companion in exchange for knowledge of the parafolk.

Pulling down the neckline of her nightgown, she exposed the small scars just below her collarbone. They barely looked like anything at all if you didn't know what they were. But she knew. They would tell other parafolk she was one of them now.

Sitting up was a challenge—she was dizzy immediately—but when the room stopped spinning she examined the bedside table clock. It was dark in the room…very dark, with lightproof shutters covering the windows, but the time was early afternoon.

From her research she knew that Sebastian wouldn't rise until after the sun left the sky, so at least she wouldn't have to deal with a tall, blond and sexy nightwalker for several hours.

Turning on the light, she discovered that while she'd been asleep someone had unpacked and arranged her belongings.

Her robe lay across the end of the bed, with her slippers on the floor nearby, and the last time she'd seen either of them they had been in her luggage. While she'd moved her bags to the elegant room Harold had shown her to last night, she hadn't intended to unpack until she'd determined just how long she would be staying.

Apparently someone had decided that was going to be for a while and put her stuff away.

At least she remembered having Rebecca's help in changing into her nightgown last night. After the ceremony she'd been so tired, and even more mellow, that she'd have happily let Sebastian help her out of her clothes in spite of how ambivalent she felt about sex with him.

Of course, if that had happened she doubted she'd have ended up wearing a gown to bed or waking up in that bed alone. Ambivalent or not, anxious to get rid of her or not, she had no illusions of how interested he'd been in having her last night. She'd felt every instance of his desire during the marking ceremony and knew what had been on his mind as he'd lifted her to carry her upstairs.

That she'd been in a similar mood wasn't lost on her. Fortunately he'd had more presence of mind than she had and so she'd ended up in the bedroom with his housekeeper undressing her and not him.

Her clothes weren't on the chair she'd left them on, so they must have gotten hung up. Rebecca must have done that, as well as unpack her bags. She remembered some hushed movement in the room as she'd lingered on the verge of sleep. Stella sat on the edge of the bed and contemplated the situation.

It was strange having servants move your things around. Nice in a way, but unsettling. She was used to doing for herself, including preparing her own meals.

Which reminded her stomach how long it had been since she last ate. Pulling on her robe and slippers, Stella was prepared to slip down to the kitchen when she noticed a small table set up just outside the door to her room that bore a large tray. After removing it to a small breakfast table positioned next to the window, she lifted one of the metal covers and discovered, to her surprise, a bowl of her favorite cereal. Next to that were small pitchers of orange juice and milk which had been left on ice, and an insulated carafe held piping-hot coffee.

Just what she normally ate for breakfast as she'd said in at least one of the many interviews she'd given in the past couple of years. Someone had done their homework on her.

Stella sat in the delicate chair next to the breakfast table. Obviously she didn't even need to rustle up her own breakfast...it was already here. A note on the tray rested against a folded newspaper. She opened it and read, "Dear Ms. Robertson. I hope you rest well and that this offering will tide you over until a more substantial meal can be prepared after sunset."

Was it from Sebastian or from one of his servants? At this point she didn't know, although it looked more like Harold's handwriting than what she remembered Sebastian's looking like.

Sipping a cup of what turned out to be excellent coffee, Stella turned to examine her room. It was nice. Elegant, just like the rest of the house—just like the nightwalker she was companion to. Part of her didn't feel like she belonged here at all.

Except... Stella turned her gaze to the opposite corner from where the breakfast table sat. Something had been added to that part of the room, something that had not been there the night before. Last night there had been a decorative set of shelves that had been stocked with glass birds, but now a substantial writing desk with a good-sized lamp stood in the corner. On it sat her laptop case, and pushed up to one side next to it was a comfortable-looking office chair. A small printer sat on a table next to a short bookcase.

When she investigated the desk, she found that the top drawer was filled with binder clips, colored pens, empty notebooks and a variety of items useful for a writer, while on the bookcase was a large dictionary rubbing edges with a thesaurus, as well as a book of Bartlett's Quotations.

In short, someone had prepared a space for her to continue to write while she was living as Sebastian's companion. In this very elegant room, she could do her work.

Stella smiled and tried out the desk chair, which was as comfy as it looked. One thing about it, being companion to a wealthy nightwalker was certainly going to have its good points.

After finishing breakfast and taking advantage of the lovely attached bath, Stella dressed in her usual working togs, a slightly worn-out sweatsuit. She settled herself at the desk and set up her computer, opening up her latest work in progress.

This was new...a contemporary story rather than one set in the distant past. Originally she'd envisioned her hero as one of her usual—tall, dark and befanged—but since meeting Sebastian, only blond-haired heroes had come to mind.

It was still mostly in outline form, but the project excited her more than anything she'd tackled in the recent past. Not only was it a time period she hadn't done before, but she hoped to show how someone who'd been alive in the Regency period would adapt to living in modern times. Parts of the story would be set back in her hero's youth. Again, her inspiration was Sebastian, although she didn't plan for the story to be about him...exactly.

It would be fictionalized, but with more details as to how real vampires lived. She might even throw in some other paranormal folks if she met enough of them to get a good feel for them.

After pouring herself a full fresh cup of coffee, Stella started to work on fleshing out her outline.

It was several hours later when she leaned back and stretched, working out the kinks that had settled in. She checked the time, which showed late afternoon, and wondered when the sun set around here.

Just as she was thinking about it, the blinds across the windows began to slide open, revealing a sunset-tinted sky. They must be on a timer, or were light-sensitive. Either way, the now-uncovered window revealed a glorious view of vineyards and rolling hills that she wished she could have seen during the day.

Annoyed, Stella decided to see if she couldn't get that changed. She understood why the room Sebastian slept in would need its windows covered during the day, but that was no reason her windows needed the same treatment.

It would be different if they were sleeping together…not that she wanted to sleep with him, at least not very much.

Sebastian was the sexiest man she'd ever been in bed with, that was true. At one time he'd told her he was her "fantasy" and that was most certainly true. For years she'd imagined a man like Sebastian, handsome, self-assured and unafraid of taking the lead when making love.

"Prince" Sebastian was all that and more. The one evening she'd spent with him had been the greatest romantic experience she'd ever known, and later he'd given her the best sex of her life.

But that one night had turned out to be all he was willing to give, and that wasn't enough for her. Once he'd gotten what he'd wanted, Sebastian had taken off without a backward glance… She had no reason to believe it wouldn't happen again.

A woman couldn't live in a fantasy world for very long and Sebastian had already proven to be a love-'em-and-leave-'em kind of guy.

She wasn't going to make that mistake again. She'd stay with him as his companion, learn as much about the parafolk as she could, but she'd avoid his bed at all cost.

Yes, maybe last night she would have allowed things to go further than they had. The result of his bite had turned her on more than she'd bargained for and she'd been more than happy to be in his arms. If he'd taken her up to bed, she would have been pleased to be there.

But he'd turned her over to his servants instead, even though she knew he wanted her. Possibly he too had had second thoughts. He didn't want to bed down with her anymore than she wanted him, although she knew both their bodies were still interested. Just as well he wasn't willing to act on it because she shouldn't be thinking of him that way either.

No way was she going to be fooled twice by his fantasy lover act. When she went to bed with a man, she wanted him there when she woke up, and if she was going to have a relationship with someone, it had better last for longer than what he could get out of it for himself.

All Sebastian had wanted from her was quick and easy sex and a fast bite, and Stella Robertson was not a fast-food kind of woman.

She saved her work and closed up the laptop. Given the formality around here, Stella bet her sweatsuit wouldn't be appropriate attire for dinner, so she'd better change.

Getting up, she examined the closet where her clothes had landed and planned what to wear. Dressed in her best black slacks and a silk top, she'd be ready to face whatever Prince Sebastian intended to dish out this evening.

Chapter Seven

So of course he's wearing jeans. Stella couldn't help a mental groan as she noted that once again she'd misjudged what to wear around the nightwalker she was companion to. He stood at the top of the stairs, dressed casually, while she was wearing her second-nicest outfit.

First the hotel, when she'd had to change before riding the motorcycle, now tonight? Was this going to be a common theme with them that she would forever have to change her clothes before going out with him?

Not necessarily. It could be that you'll simply get into the habit of asking me what plans exist so that you know what to wear.

Stella startled as she heard Sebastian's mental voice in her head again. He hadn't done that recently, not even last night. Sebastian leaned against the banister of the stairway of the great room. She was sitting with a cup of Harold's excellent tea, waiting for her nightwalker, as she'd taken to thinking of him, to appear.

And here he was, a golden god slumming in blue jeans and a blue-green plaid flannel shirt worn open over a black T-shirt tight enough to show off his abs. Very nice abs they were too.

Stella blushed and groaned aloud as she caught his smile and realized he'd heard that part of what she'd been thinking.

It is easier to speak to you this way now that we have the companion link. However I will not peek at your thoughts if you'd rather I didn't.

She'd rather, all right. Particularly when he was picking up on thoughts that she didn't necessarily want him knowing about. Like what she thought of his abs. He didn't need that kind of encouragement.

He seemed to read that thought too, a smirk forming on his perfect lips. But just as quickly it slipped away, almost like he didn't want to know that she was attracted to him.

"When you have finished dinner, I'll take you on a tour of the winery. That should give you some of the information you are looking for."

"I wanted to know more about parafolk..."

He folded his arms across his broad chest and Stella tried not to stare at the bulge of his biceps, visible even through the flannel shirt. "You need to learn about being a companion. I have work to do so it would be better if you simply follow me around." He peered closer at her. "You don't mind, do you?"

No, she didn't. Truth was, she hadn't been at a winery before and was curious about how it worked anyway.

After the excellent dinner Harold and Rebecca served her, Sebastian collected her from the dining room. He took her through the house to the open yard at the back and then to a long barn-like building constructed from the same old stone and wood that made up the house's exterior. This, he explained, was the winery proper, the heart of Nightflyer Winery.

The place felt timeless, like it had existed for centuries, but wasn't at all decrepit. The building felt old but strong and was still in excellent repair.

Not unlike her nightwalker host. Also old, but strong and anything but decrepit.

Beyond the house and the winery was the vineyard that she'd been told produced at least a third of the grapes used in Nightflyer wines. Along the slight slope of the hillside were lines of waist-high stakes supporting the vines, now growing dormant for the approaching winter.

As if he knew her thoughts, Sebastian pointed to the quiet hillside. "We completed harvest several weeks ago. All the grapes have been processed into must and are fermenting now."

"Must?"

"Crushed grapes, juice and the skins...at least for the red wines. For whites we remove the skins before fermenting, using a wine press. Here, I'll show you." They entered the back of the building, where several large metal tanks resided. He pointed to them. "In those are the result of our harvest, and the future wine we will produce. That is where the must sits and ferments into wine."

Sebastian's voice was oddly reverential, and Stella wondered at that. It was the most respect she'd seen him pay anything. Winemaking really was his life.

He opened a small door on one of the tanks and took a sample of the contents. "I'm checking the acidity to make sure it doesn't change too fast. That would interfere with proper fermentation." He dipped a small piece of paper into the liquid and nodded. "This is fine."

Sebastian indicated the many large metal vats around him, at least fifty that she could see. "There is not much to do here for now. All we can do is wait until the wine is ready for the next step. Still, I have other things to show you."

He led her into a room populated by large wooden barrels. It was dark and had a musky smell...old wood and old wine. Like a cellar filled with bottles of wine, which is pretty much what it was.

Stella stood on the dirt floor and tried not to think about crypts and coffins. There was a remarkable similarity between an old wine cellar and a place where bodies might be buried. No wonder Sebastian seemed so much at home here. The place had a history as old as he must be. However long that was.

He must have read her mind again. "You want to know how old I am? Very old, well over four centuries." He shrugged his shoulders at her gasp of surprise.

"To answer your first question about my kind," Sebastian said. "A nightwalker is not an animated dead person. We aren't dead but we are quite different from normal people though. We can't eat most foods and must consume blood as nourishment, plus we have a strong allergic reaction to the presence of the sun. Ultraviolet light that would only give you a slight burn is lethal to me. What's worse is that when the sun is above the horizon I must find a safe place to lie down as I can't stay awake."

Some of this she'd already heard, but she was glad to have him confirm even those parts she already knew.

He shrugged. "Such is the life of a nightwalker. But it does have its advantages. We don't get ill very often or age. We have a tremendously longer life span as a result."

He cast a sidelong glance at her. "Since our companions carry a part of our DNA, they also get some of the same benefits. Slower aging and healthier life spans, in exchange for giving us the blood we need to survive. A fair trade, don't you agree?"

Stella stared at him. "I'll live a longer, healthier life? How much longer?"

"Five to ten times as long."

"Oh." He was right, that did seem a fair trade.

Sebastian stood before a small table loaded with several bottles, a large basin and a set of glasses. He picked one glass up and examined it carefully, using a cloth to clean a smudge off the edge. Then he carefully poured about an inch of deep red wine into the glass. He swirled the liquid carefully around the inside.

"But now to get back to winemaking. This is another critical stage in the process. What I need to do now is taste the wine that's been fermenting to verify that it is ready for bottling. This has been aging about two years in oak flasks."

Sebastian sniffed and took a tentative sip. He rolled the liquid around on his tongue for a moment, closed his eyes as if in appreciation—then to her surprise spat it back into his glass.

"You don't like it? It's not ready?" Stella asked.

Regret colored his expression. "No, actually it is quite good. I just can't drink much wine, any more than I can eat regular food. Too much fruit juice, I'm afraid." He sighed. "Some nightwalkers can drink small quantities of wine, but if I have very much it makes me ill. So I'm one winemaker who must taste only."

That explained why he'd only poured a small quantity of wine when he'd stayed at dinner with her last night.

Grabbing a fresh glass, he poured an equal amount from the bottle and handed it to her. "Now you try it."

"I don't know what to taste for," Stella said.

"I will show you then."

And then she felt him again in her mind, like a silver haze. *This is nothing that will hurt you, starshine. I promise.* She felt his reassurance as if it were a hand caressing her face.

Unsure how to proceed, Stella carefully raised the glass to her lips.

Don't drink yet. Just let the smell tease your nose.

She took a deep whiff and the heavy odor made her jerk her head back and choke. She glanced over to see Sebastian trying unsuccessfully to hide a smile.

"Perhaps it would be better to not try to inhale the wine, Stella. Put your nose just inside the glass and breathe in a little."

She tried that and this time the smell did simply "tease" her nose. Her mouth watered a little at the scent.

Again she felt Sebastian's mind covering hers. *This is what you should smell. A hint of berries, as well as the tang of the oak barrel this wine has been resting in.* As his mind said the words, she sensed the intangible scents he wanted her to recognize. It was strange being taught to smell something this way, but it worked.

Yes, it does work. Now you should taste the wine. Just a little bit, and let it roll on your tongue.

At his direction she let a small amount of wine into her mouth. It had a heavy texture and was much stronger in flavor that what she was used to.

You haven't been drinking the best kinds of wine then. A good wine should have a good body.

Her mouth full, she decided to try answering him back using his method. *Body is what you call this fullness?*

That pleased him. *Yes. You learn quickly. Now let me show you what to look for in the taste.* In her mind the silver haze slid in like a mist. The simple "taste" of the wine was teased apart and she could see layers to the flavors. *This is a rich cabernet, with a lot of cherries in its make-up. There is also a smoke component.* As he named the layers, she could "see" them in her mind and noted how each one could be distinguished from the other.

When the wine warms, it changes from the heat of your mouth. He paused over that for a moment. *As a human, you are warmer than I am. That makes a difference in the flavor — I hadn't realized it before.*

Stella's mouth was still full so she swallowed her mouthful of wine, feeling it warm the back of her throat, then flow down to her stomach. An accompanying shudder came from Sebastian.

I've not felt that. Not for a long time, since I've been unable to drink the wine I taste. He looked at her hopefully. *Could you do it again?*

Hiding her smile, Stella took another sip and let it flow across her tongue and down her throat. Even without Sebastian's prompting she detected the mixed flavors of the wine and was able to distinguish them better this time.

"You're a quick study," he nodded approvingly, and she thought she saw something else in his face that was more than approval. He was pleased. Pleased with her.

She'd forced him to take her as his companion, using what she knew about him and threatening to tell it to the world. He'd started out resenting that, but now things were different. He actually seemed to want her there.

He moved closer, his hand brushing her hair off her shoulder. The fingers lingered over the place where his fangs had left their mark. Just a small press of two fingers over the spot. She looked up into his face and saw impending desire in his gray eyes. A soft glow in the irises.

Last night she'd wondered if he would ever look at her that way again. Funny how sharing a man's interests sometimes got their attention. He loved wine but couldn't drink it. All of a sudden she realized how infinitely sad that was.

On a whim she took another sip but opened her mind as much as possible, trying to send the sensation to him. He startled but leaned closer into her, his fingers gripping her shoulder. Not too tight though. A possessive grip, not painful.

Yes. Like that. She heard the pleasure in his thoughts as she sent what she sensed and tasted to him, as well as the warm glow from swallowing, the one thing he couldn't do. Standing behind her, Sebastian put his arm around her shoulders and pulled her close. His breath was hot in her ear. "You can share taste with me. That's a rare skill for a companion."

Stella giggled. She wasn't used to drinking so much and she'd nearly finished her glass. "Well, at least there is some benefit for you from having me around."

His fingers slid up her neck to her cheek, exploring the softness. His voice deepened and grew husky. "There are many benefits of having a woman around, with or without the mark. Perhaps we could explore them later this evening."

Turning in his arms, Stella found herself inches from his face, his mouth just outside of the reach of hers. It took less time than a thought to cross that distance and lightly kiss him. Maybe it was the wine making her lightheaded, making her bolder than usual, or maybe it was the connection between them.

Maybe it was both, but all Stella knew was that she wanted to kiss him. For an instant she wasn't sure what he'd do, but he pulled her closer and then they were kissing in earnest.

Sebastian tasted of wine and an odd flavor that she realized must be his own. She loved the way he tasted.

You taste good too, little star. She heard his voice in her mind and realized they were still linked. Kind of handy, being able to speak when your mouth was busy kissing. Her tongue slid into his mouth and was pricked by his fangs. Now she tasted blood, hers, and the taste seemed to drive Sebastian wild. He lifted her as if she weighed nothing and pressed her against the wall of the cellar, the coolness of the wall seeping through her shirt.

Stella shivered, only partially from the cold against her back.

Sebastian broke off their kiss and when she looked into his eyes, they glowed fiercely. "You tempt me to do more than I've bargained for. I promised myself not to touch you tonight."

That news was like a slap in the face. "Why not?"

"To have sex I must feed and it is too soon for that with you now. I find…" His voice broke off for a moment. "Around you I find it harder to keep focused and I tend to drink more than I should. You must become stronger and control the link before we can indulge ourselves that way."

He stepped back and let her slide onto to her feet. Still aroused and now more than a little annoyed, Stella glared at him. After all, he'd initiated that kiss and the up-against-the-wall action that had followed it. Fine thing for him to get her started then leave her hanging, and all because he couldn't control his thirst.

"Well, this would be a fine addition to my book. A vampire with a drinking problem."

Sebastian swung around and she stepped back at the look of shock on his face. "What book would that be?" His eyes narrowed threateningly. "You wouldn't be thinking about writing a book about me or the other parafolk."

"Isn't that what you had in mind when you talked to me that first time? You said you wanted to help me with my books."

"I didn't mean I wanted to *be* in one of your books."

"It wouldn't really be about you. Just someone like you."

He shook his head. "No, it's too dangerous. You can't write a book someone might use as evidence against me or my people. It might be better if you didn't write at all while we're together."

Stella crossed her arms. "Just what do you expect me to do then?"

"You wrote books to make a living. There's no reason for you to do that while living with me. I'll take care of your needs."

Like that was going to happen! It was all Stella could do not to spit in his face. There was no way she was going to let some overbearing male vampire "take care of her". She'd been independent for far too long for that.

He seemed to read her mood if not her mind and his eyes narrowed as well. He crowded her up against the wall again, but this time she read anger rather than passion in his attitude. "You wear my mark, woman, and it was done at your request. You agreed to be my companion and part of that will be to obey me in certain things.

"I did not ask for you to come into my life and complicate it. I do not need you any more than you seem to think you need me. You are here at my tolerance—while you are you will not write anything that could possibly hurt my people...who may well be yours by the end of your stay."

He leaned closer. "Assuming you learn what I can teach you."

If ever there was a challenge, this was it. Stella matched his stare with her own. "I can learn whatever you want to show me, nightwalker, and then some. Just try me."

Sebastian gave her the wickedest smile she'd ever seen. Had she ever thought of him as angelic or god-like? Hell, he was more demon than angel.

"Very well, little star. I will, as you say, *try you*. But be ready for anything."

* * * * *

The next several days passed quickly. Every day Stella woke and wrote for a few hours before sunset, when Sebastian would rise and join her for dinner. For him that seemed mostly to consist of a glass of thick red liquid, which she decided to think of as wine, even though she knew he couldn't actually drink that much wine. Munching on one of the excellent meals Rebecca had prepared while sitting with a man sipping blood from a crystal wine-goblet was a little too strange.

After dinner he would take her either around the winery, introducing to her the intricacies of running a winemaking operation, or into his office, where he'd demonstrate ways for her to control her psychic abilities. She grew more confident in holding the link and was even able to initiate it from time to time, but actual control continued to elude her.

She did better on the winemaking front. For example, Stella learned that skin color had nothing to do with the color of the wine. Red wines were fermented with the skins then pressed, while whites were sent to a wine press to remove the skins first. Both kinds of wine were fermented, the process started with careful measurements of added sugar and yeast.

Sebastian let her watch as he checked the vats with his more-than-professional zeal. He seemed dedicated to his work, the way she was dedicated to hers, and just as practiced at it. Occasionally she met others who worked at the winery. None had fangs or showed any obvious signs of being parafolk but Sebastian didn't hide his fangs from them so Stella assumed they must know what he was.

It was also clear that they didn't care. The nightwalker seemed well-liked and his people happy to be working for him. As far as she could see, he didn't misuse them or feed from them. She tried asking just whom it was he did dine on since the glass of canned blood he had for dinner couldn't possibly be enough to sustain him. But when she asked, Sebastian gave her an arched glance and told her that it wasn't really her concern, an answer that left her fuming.

When she wrote her books, she had ultimate control over the world, and not having anything resembling control over this one drove her crazy. But Sebastian didn't care how irritating this was for her. He answered many of her questions that way, as if she had no reason to know the answer, particularly if her question was about himself rather than parafolk in general.

There were other things he wouldn't tell her either. She was also unable to get an exact idea of how many such people were actually around. There must be far more than she realized but Sebastian didn't trust her to know just how many there were.

Sometimes she watched Harold and Rebecca for any signs of what they were, but outside of not eating with her, she wasn't given enough information to make a guess. They didn't seem to have any psychic abilities and she knew they weren't nightwalkers, if only because they were about in the daytime like she was.

She didn't press the point. Stella was confident that eventually she'd figure it out, or that they or Sebastian would tell her.

Even so, the series of half-truths and incomplete information grated on her patience until by the time Stella had been there a week she was more frustrated than she'd ever been before.

It did not help that while Sebastian continued to profess to not wanting to go to bed with her, when they were together he often would touch her or move closer than needed for the task at hand. She'd end up in bed with his smell on her skin and hair and it drove her crazy not to have the man himself. She could only hope this relationship of theirs was driving him as crazy as it was her.

* * * * *

Ten days after taking Stella as his companion, Sebastian woke in the quiet darkness of his empty bed. He stretched out on the cool smooth sheets below him. Very cool, cooler than they'd be if he had someone warmer than him sharing them.

Someone like Stella. Warm and tasty, and oh, so sexy, the perfect woman to wake with, make love to and sip at her sweet neck.

For the tenth evening running, Sebastian groaned at the thought of his companion, so near and yet not in his bed. Even now his body reacted to the thought of her with him, his cock hardening for an action that was simply not going to take place. Stella might be everything he wanted, but he was wary of what that meant. What were the implications of having Stella in his life?

He'd gone many centuries without someone like her around and he was just getting used to her as a companion. As a bed partner? His body was willing but his mind wasn't completely sure she was what he should be wanting.

Fortunately, until his lovely little companion was ready to feed him again, he wasn't going to have her in his bed anyway. He sometimes regretted the decision to keep away from her no matter what temptation she offered—and lately she'd been more than tempting, but he knew if she came to harm through him, he'd never forgive himself.

As he'd told her, they would just have to wait until she was ready to be fed from and in the meantime there'd be no sex, no matter how much his cock ached—as it did right now from just thinking about her.

Ignoring his body's response, Sebastian rose and dressed for the evening. He started to ring for Harold, but then he remembered it was the night of the full moon and his faithful servants' night off.

He sighed. The shape shifters' night of running wild didn't normally bother him that much. There would be no fresh tea tonight and he'd have to pour his own serum, but it didn't affect him otherwise. Dinner would, as usual, be in town, dining on one of the many tourists who fell victim to overindulgence at one of Napa's fine restaurants and in particular the restaurant's wine cellar. Half-intoxicated vacationer had become his staple food of late.

But lack of well-made tea wasn't his real complaint. Truth was, he envied the closeness his servants had and regretted when their true nature separated them from him. He missed their companionship during the full moon when they needed to be free and left him alone.

But he wasn't alone now. He had Stella.

Sebastian perked up at that thought. The fact that Rebecca and Harold were running the hills tonight in search of fresh game instead of keeping to their usual diet of raw meat from the butcher shop meant that Stella would also be on her own for dinner.

Perhaps this could be a good time to introduce a new full moon tradition, one just for him and his new companion. For one thing he could take her for a flight over the vineyard. That would be romantic in the full light of the moon.

In the meantime she needed to eat. Sebastian wondered if he or either of the shape shifters had mentioned their full moon holiday to her. Possibly not...she'd been intensely curious about them and had asked him what kind of parafolk they were. He hadn't felt comfortable telling her, but if she knew about their need for this monthly night off, she might have guessed the answer to that question.

Sebastian sighed. Keeping her in the dark so that she wouldn't be tempted to use his people in one of her books had become more trouble than it was worth. Maybe it was time he eliminated the problem.

Tonight he'd get her promise not to get specific with her writing and eliminate that risk altogether. Then perhaps he could explore their relationship more fully and even take advantage of having her here.

For one thing, it had been ten days since her coming and was very likely time to feed from her again. In the week and a half since she'd become his companion, her body had changed to produce more blood than usual, and he suspected she could support a good feeding tonight.

In fact, she might even be strong enough to allow a more intimate feeding — if she was in the same mood he was in.

His cock woke again at that suggestion and this time Sebastian didn't discourage it as fast as he had before. He headed out of his bedroom with a jaunty step. The night was looking up.

Chapter Eight

"You mean we're on our own for dinner? Where are Rebecca and Harold?" Stella looked about the empty kitchen with surprise. For the first time since she'd come, there was no sign of the small Asian woman or her British husband.

For the first time, it looked like she might have to cook her own food.

Oddly enough Sebastian seemed almost smug. Well, that suited him...after all he wasn't going to have to actually prepare a meal or clean the kitchen afterwards. His dinners came pre-packaged without any need for dishes.

"Harold and Rebecca are off tonight...doing something..." The nightwalker definitely looked close to saying more then apparently changed his mind. It probably had something to do with their parafolkness, but she knew from the look on his face she wasn't going to get more information out of him without a battle she didn't feel up to waging.

She had better things to waste energy on. With a sigh, Stella began opening cupboards and searched the refrigerator, looking for dinner ingredients. Her usual breakfast had been waiting for her in the afternoon but she hadn't seen the servants at all. Sebastian's explanation confirmed that they were gone.

So it was the first time she'd cooked for herself in a while. She was hungry. Surely there was something easy to fix. Unfortunately, outside of several boxes of dog treats and a couple of boxes of her favorite cereal, there was actually very little in the cupboards. Rebecca must do the shopping daily.

"I was thinking I could take you into town tonight."

Stella paused in the middle of examining a package of raw chicken parts. Odd, it wasn't a whole chicken the way they were usually packaged. There were several pieces missing and the rest wasn't particularly appetizing. She threw it back into the meat bin and closed the refrigerator.

"You want to take me out for dinner? Do they have good Chinese places here?"

Sebastian laughed. "They do, but you might enjoy something more in keeping with the region. I know a couple of great places that serve the best Northern Californian cuisine."

"You mean the folks who eat there taste great?" Stella took a stab at where he'd been dining when he went out late in the evening. Her guess was confirmed by his sheepish expression.

"Let's just say that no one leaves these places unsatisfied…including me. Are you interested?"

She looked down at her jeans and sweatshirt, chosen thinking that they would be staying in, and sighed. Once again she wasn't dressed for the evening's activities. Sometimes she thought Sebastian did it on purpose.

"I'll change and be right back."

When she came back downstairs she found Sebastian waiting for her in a black leather jacket, standing before the mirror and apparently adjusting something in his mouth. When he turned she stared at his face, unable at first to understand what was different.

Then she realized. "Your fangs are gone!"

He muttered something that sounded like a curse.

"It's a prosthetic," he said with a slight lisp. "Artificial teeth that cover my own. At the place we're going they don't know me and I prefer to keep it that way."

She stepped closer. The new teeth were somewhat larger but not unnatural-looking. It actually wasn't a bad look for him. "I like it."

He growled. "Don't get too used to it. It's uncomfortable and I don't like wearing it."

The place in town that Sebastian drove her to for dinner was as good as he'd promised. Stella had an excellent roast duck with very light citrus sauce, roasted red potatoes with rosemary and steamed-to-perfection baby vegetables. Even the bread was wonderful, although she had to admit that the wine, while pricy, wasn't nearly as good as what Sebastian had given her to taste the night before.

Being with him was certainly becoming an education and if she weren't careful she'd be spoiled for the lesser things in life, like inexpensive wine.

Throughout dinner, Sebastian kept her company with a martini followed by a cup of coffee.

"Are you planning on eating before we leave?" Stella whispered to him.

He grinned at her with his abnormally normal teeth and she found herself missing his usual fangy smile. "No. I had other plans for tonight."

In the dim light of the restaurant, she saw a brief glow in his eyes. Taking a chance, she opened her mind and tried to speak mentally with him.

So, just who is on the menu tonight?

She knew she'd made contact when he startled. Then he leaned forward. *Actually…I thought we could be together tonight.*

Together… you mean you want my *blood?*

His expression turned particularly smug. *I want all of you, little star.*

Oh so that's how it was. Sebastian had decided to have sex with her, and feed from her as well, and just now he'd decided to tell her about it. *Wasn't that special,* she thought privately.

Fuming inside, Stella grabbed the rest of her glass of wine and took another sip. It wasn't at all good but she withheld her grimace. "When were you planning on letting me know?" Even though she kept her voice sweet, Sebastian must have realized she wasn't pleased with his high-handed approach to seduction.

"It isn't like we haven't discussed it," he said. "You were quite willing to go to bed with me earlier."

Of course she was. But a man shouldn't think he didn't need to ask. "That was then and this is now. And the answer is no."

Sebastian's good humor faded away. "What do you mean, no?"

"I mean no. No, I'm not going to bed with you. No, I'm not going to bed with someone who seems to think he makes all the rules."

He put his hands on the table and glared at her. "Don't be ridiculous, Stella. Of course I make all the rules. After all, I'm your master!"

There was a sudden hush in the conversations around them and Stella realized that Sebastian's voice had carried to the nearby tables. Someone snickered and she turned her head to see several people staring at her, the men with amused speculation, the women with outrage. Everyone seemed to be waiting to see how she was going to handle the situation.

Never had she'd been put into this embarrassing a situation before and she was furious.

All things considered, there really wasn't any choice—Stella tossed the remaining wine in her glass into Sebastian's face and leapt to her feet.

"Get this straight. You do not own me, I am not your slave, and you most definitely are *not my master!*"

Eyes wide with astonishment, Sebastian stared at her with his jaw dropped, the wine dripping into his open mouth. A smattering of applause following her, Stella went out the door as fast as she could, more than a little scared as to what he would do to her.

But when she reached the parking lot, there wasn't the pursuit she'd been afraid of. Apparently she'd managed to stun the mighty Prince Sebastian into immobility. She'd probably pay for it later, but at the moment it felt pretty good to stand up to him.

As she slowed down, she recognized that while she might have been willing to put up with his attitude in his home, there was no way she'd accept it out here. Sebastian had to understand she was a modern woman and wouldn't be a slave to anyone.

If that meant she couldn't be his companion anymore, then so be it. No man was going to call himself her master and get away with it.

Once in the parking lot though, she realized she didn't have a plan for what to do next. They'd taken Sebastian's car, the keys for which were in his pants pocket, and her car was back at his house. Even if she could find a phone, she couldn't call the servants since they were out for the evening. She'd have to find a place to stay in town for the night.

She had her purse and credit cards, and the town of Napa was crowded with hotels. She'd look for a room and return to the house tomorrow. Once they'd both calmed down, they'd discuss this "master" business and either she'd straighten him out, or she'd be straight out the door.

Several blocks later, though, she was footsore and discouraged. There was a flaw in her plan that she'd been unaware of…the popularity of Napa as a tourist destination. In spite of the multitude of small hotels, there was literally no room at the inn at any of them.

After being told no for the tenth time, Stella wandered into a small corner tavern to rest her feet and come up with a better plan. Maybe she could save some walking by getting someone to call around and check on availability.

Not for the first time, she regretted not having gotten a cell phone. Right now one would be a really handy thing to have.

The inside of the tavern was refreshingly quiet. The lighting was dim and the music subdued, perfect for a place to hole up for a while. Only a few people populated the inside, mostly sitting in clumps of two or three at the tables, and there were a couple of what were probably regulars sitting at the bar itself. They had half-consumed drinks in front of them but their attention was riveted on a game show playing on the television.

The bartender gave her a welcoming smile as she snagged the stool in front of him. "What can I get you?"

"Something cold."

"White wine?"

Wine did not sound good. "A martini. Vodka, with two olives."

"Ah, been one of those kinds of nights."

She reached down and eased her shoes off her feet. "You wouldn't know of any vacancies in town, would you?"

"You came to Napa without reservations?"

This wasn't the first time tonight that question had come up. Stella rubbed her aching toes through her stocking and replayed the excuse she'd come up with to explain her situation. "We had reservations, but then I had a fight with my jerk boyfriend…"

"And now you need your own room," a new voice completed her sentence. Stella turned as a man joined them. Like Sebastian, he was a lot taller than her, but instead of blond hair, his was brown that fell in waves around his thin pale face. As he smiled, she noticed his teeth—big, even and very white. For some reason they reminded her of the false teeth Sebastian had been wearing.

Then he came closer and she saw his bright blue eyes glow briefly.

Oh shit! Another vampire!

His smile broadened into a grin. *That's nightwalker, little psi—and I'm glad to meet you too.* "Donald Morgan," he said aloud then took her hand and shook it. But instead of releasing it right away, he pulled it to his mouth. For a moment she wondered if he was going to kiss it, but instead he simply held it to his nose and sniffed the skin lightly. Stella saw a look of disappointment appear and quickly disappear.

Donald leaned over and whispered into her ear. "Now what can I do for our illustrious prince's companion?"

Another nightwalker…and one who might be open to talking about what he knew? The opportunity was too good to pass up. Stella pulled one of her business cards out of her purse and handed it to him.

He stared at it. "You're a writer?"

"A novelist. I write romance stories about parafolk."

"Really?" A grin took over his face. "So how can I be of assistance?"

"Well, you can start by answering a few questions."

* * * * *

Sebastian was beyond angry. *Stella was gone!*

It had taken a few moments to clear things up at the restaurant. He'd spent a few moments reaming the proprietor for the glass of bad wine that had been served to his companion, after which he'd paid the now much-reduced bill. He'd hoped to find her waiting near the car, but there was no sign of her in the parking lot.

He took to the sky, flying along the rooftops to avoid notice. Sebastian was on the hunt now, for Stella, the only woman in four hundred years to throw wine in his face. What he was going to do with her when he caught her he wasn't sure, but she was damn well going to know that this was not proper behavior for a companion.

He doubted she'd left with any plan other than finding a place to hide for the night, so he tried several of the small inns in the neighborhood. Sure enough, she'd been there. He'd known even before the night manager at each place had told him—her sweet scent still lingered in the lobby air.

Her smell was strongest in the last place he tried, like a trail suspended in the air, so as he went out the door he followed it, turning the corner until he realized the scent led him to one of Napa's smaller taverns but did not go past its front door. Obviously she was inside.

Part of him wanted to rush through the door and haul her away, but prudence dictated another approach. It was unlikely she'd be alone in there and he didn't need another scene like the one in the restaurant. Modern times required modern methods of dealing with a woman. Much as he wanted to, he couldn't just grab her and take to the sky.

After a couple of deep calming breaths, Sebastian opened the door and stepped inside. With his enhanced sight his eyes didn't need to adjust to the darkness within. He spotted her immediately at one of the small tables, but the man sitting with her stopped him from rushing to her side.

Instead Sebastian took a moment to size the other man up and when he did, he grew angrier than before. Another nightwalker was here in Napa Valley, and without the courtesy of letting him know of his presence.

What was the world coming to? As he came closer he learned other things about this new nightwalker, and he didn't like any of it.

"Stella," he said when close enough and was gratified to see her startle. She cast a wary glance at him over her nearly empty martini glass, almost as if she expected him to strike her. That look offended him more than he'd anticipated. Surely she didn't expect he'd really harm her...she was his companion for heaven's sake!

The man with her didn't startle or look surprised, even when Sebastian took the seat next to him. Clearly he'd been expecting Sebastian to show up.

Any nightwalker worth his blood would be able to tell just whom it was she belonged to—just as Sebastian could tell who'd sired this new vampire. He was a young one, just a few years old, barely more than a youngling but strong in spite of that. This one would bear watching—if he survived the next few minutes.

Something Sebastian wasn't certain could be counted on.

Sebastian kept his tone light, but neither of the pair at the table was fooled into thinking he wasn't angry. "Stella, you should introduce me to your young friend."

He'd emphasized the word young, and the other man narrowed his eyes. "Donald Morgan. I was just keeping your lady company. No harm done."

He lifted his arm, turning his wrist upward and holding it out. Sebastian stared at it, then at the man, and shook his head. The homage was appreciated, but he couldn't feed in an open bar even if he wanted to and he wasn't sure he wanted to anyway.

"I don't know you...you're new, and your turning wasn't approved."

Donald tensed but pulled his arm back without an outward show of anger over the rebuff. "My maker doesn't necessarily follow the rules."

"That I'm well aware of. Where is Vanessa anyway?" he asked bluntly. Vanessa Hind had been a fugitive ever since trying to kill his friend Jonathan Knottman. She was suspected in the deaths of several other nightwalkers, and their companions, in her megalomaniacal attempt to seize control over the nightwalkers in the parafolk community.

Vanessa apparently felt that nightwalkers should be in charge and that all others, parafolk and norms included, should be subservient to them. Her ideas were dangerous and actions worse, necessitating the death sentence he'd put on her.

Sebastian didn't necessarily hold Donald responsible for her actions, but since he was new and she was his maker, he suspected she wouldn't be far from him. Having Vanessa around was very bad news, particularly since he had a new companion to worry about.

"I don't know where she is. Me, I'm here on vacation."

Sebastian tried to break the man's mental wall, but Donald managed to hold his stare and keep his mind closed to the probe. Finally he had to give up and instead took Stella's arm.

"Are you ready to leave?" he asked, hauling her to her feet without giving her a chance to argue.

Donald raised his hand. "Don't worry about the bill. The drink is on me."

Sebastian pulled out a twenty and threw it on the table. "No one buys anything for her but me," he growled, putting as much menace into it as possible. Then he started for the door, Stella somewhat meekly in tow.

But when they had gone just a few steps she wiggled her fingers at the nightwalker they left at the table. "'Bye, Donald. Nice talking to you."

"Nice talking to you, Stella. Keep me in mind for later, okay?"

Sebastian turned to the other man, all pretense of civility gone. "There will be no *later*," he ground out through clenched teeth. "I keep what is mine."

Donald watched them go, turning Stella's business card over and over in his hand. The little author had been enticing company, and he'd enjoyed talking to her. He'd enjoyed feeling the strength of her mind too. That was new since he'd become a nightwalker, being able to touch the mind of a woman that way.

Stella was the first female psi he'd met and he liked her a lot. If she wasn't already taken...

He rubbed a finger across the lettering of her card. She had an email address and website—he'd check those out when he got back to his computer.

The vibration of his cell phone caught his attention, but when he opened it, he sighed when he realized who was calling. He pushed the connect button.

"Yes, Vanessa."

"Where are you? Steve called—he's already out there with the bait and he's waiting for you." The female nightwalker's voice sounded way over the edge...which given the circumstances wasn't surprising.

Donald grabbed his glass of vodka and tonic and drank it empty. "I was just leaving."

"Good. Don't take your car. You'll have to fly out there. We don't want to leave too many tracks—"

He winced. As if he didn't know the plan. "I know what to do, Vanessa," he said, interrupting her.

She was silent for a moment. "See to it nothing goes wrong, Donald, or it will be your neck at risk."

Another thing he already knew. He tucked Stella's card inside his wallet. "I'll call when it's done."

* * * * *

After they got outside, Stella looked up and down the street. "Where's the car?"

"Still at the restaurant," Sebastian told her and was surprised to see the crestfallen look on her face.

"So I guess we have to walk back." She was clearly not looking forward to that and as he glanced down, he realized she was wearing a pair of sexy boots that, while they made her legs look long and graceful, didn't seemed to be much use for walking. Since she'd walked here, her feet were probably hurting.

It would serve her right for throwing wine in his face to make her walk back. But she was his companion even if she didn't understand the full ramifications of what that meant. Sebastian decided to take pity on her poor feet.

After leading her into an adjacent quiet space away from the street, he lifted her into his arms, eliciting from her a surprised squeak.

"You can't carry me all the way to the restaurant."

"I could, but that's not what I had in mind." He opened his mind to the moon's light and his feet lifted off the ground. Stella stared at him, her arms suddenly thrown around his neck.

"You can fly?"

"Not really. It's more like levitation and I can only do it when the moon is full." He reached the roofline of the building next to them and began gliding smoothly over it. Stella clutched his neck more tightly.

"I am sorry—about what happened—before. You just—made me—so angry." Her words came out fast and jerky, and Sebastian realized she was truly frightened.

"Don't you like heights? That's a strange thing for a star to be afraid of." He hugged "Not to worry, my companion. I have no intention of letting you fall."

"It's just that I didn't know," she continued to say. "Donald explained…"

"What did he tell you?" Sebastian still wasn't happy that this new nightwalker had been with Stella when he found her. He didn't like anything about that situation, including the jealousy that had swept through him.

"Donald told me that 'master' is what a companion sometimes calls his or her nightwalker. It doesn't mean you regard me as a slave."

"Oh." That was a good explanation and one he should have given a while ago. Donald had actually done him a service. "It's all right, Stella. I should have known better than to say such a thing to you when you didn't know what it meant."

He could feel her relief, as she seemed to melt into his arms. "Thank you, Sebastian."

He halted and hovered in a dark shadow above the street and let his lips press against her forehead. She tasted sweet and salty and he knew he had to have her in his bed tonight no matter what. He could just take her there without allowing further discussion but modern women and modern times required a modern approach.

He'd seduce her tonight, starting now. Slowly he lowered them to the ground just steps away from the car. As he set her on her feet, he tilted her chin up so she had to look into his face.

"Stella, I will ask two things of you. First of all, please avoid throwing things at me when you are angry and making a scene in public. It is undignified."

She had the good grace to look guilty. "Okay, sure. What's the other thing?"

"The next time someone serves you a glass of bad wine, do not hesitate to send it back." He shuddered. "Life is too short, even for me, to drink bad wine."

Chapter Nine

It was close to one a.m. by the time they got back to the house. Sebastian drove the car into the enclosed garage and the heavy lightproof doors slid shut behind them. When he killed the engine, the sudden quiet seemed to fill the car.

Stella was curious about what she'd seen when Sebastian had confronted the other nightwalker. "Why did Donald offer you his wrist?"

"It's a ritual feeding. Shows respect...although he knew I couldn't take advantage of it in a bar populated by norms."

"So you think he didn't mean it?"

"I don't know. He's new and I don't trust his maker." He gave a short laugh. "Although since I made her and she made him...I suppose I could think of him as a grandson."

The thought of Sebastian being a grandfather, given how young he looked, was too funny. Stella burst into laughter. "I'm sorry, I just can't think of you as even being a parent, much less a grandparent."

He didn't look pleased at her laughter. "Nightwalkers don't have children in the normal fashion, so of course I wouldn't be a parent. But that doesn't mean I can't be parental. I take great responsibility for my people and their welfare."

Stella tamped down her amusement. "I didn't mean that you didn't. If there is one thing I can say about you is that you have a sense of responsibility." She waited a few seconds. "Oh master of mine," she said and again burst into laughter.

Sebastian's eyes narrowed. "You are not nearly as funny as you think you are."

"And you are way too serious, Sebastian. Don't you ever think about just having some fun?"

"I have fun. I had fun recently."

"Oh when? What did you do?"

"I..." His voice trailed off and she could see he really had to think about it. He straightened. "It doesn't matter."

"Of course it matters. All people, even parafolk, need to do something they enjoy. You need to have fun. What do you enjoy doing?"

"What do I enjoy?" He seemed to think about it then he grinned at her. Turning in his seat, he slid his arm around her back and moved closer to her. "For one thing, I enjoy eating. I also like making love." His lips closed over hers and Stella was swept away by his taste, the feel of his tongue sweeping deep into her mouth. She reciprocated and his teeth felt strange until she realized he still wore the prosthetic that hid his fangs.

She leaned back from him and studied his face, the want there, and the determination to have her. Hunger was in his eyes, in his very attitude, both for the nourishment she carried in her veins and the satisfaction he would find in her body.

But he wouldn't force her to go with him. He was every bit the gentleman when it came to her. She could say no to him—that was true.

But why would she want to?

"Maybe we should go upstairs," she told him.

The heat in his eyes fired to incandescent. "Good idea. I've been wanting to show you my bedroom."

Sebastian had a very nice room and an even nicer bed. Stella had a brief moment to admire the dark masculine colors of the comforter and plush pillows before he pulled her to him and pressed her hard against the wall. His kiss had gone from tentative and experimental in the car to intently possessive. She'd teased him about being her master. Now he seemed bent to prove himself exactly that.

She couldn't seem to help encouraging him either. For some reason his tendency to take control only made her more open to his aggressiveness. All this time she'd thought she liked quiet, unassuming men. Sebastian was proving her wrong as the more forceful he was, the more her body cried out for more of the same.

While she'd always written about "alpha" males, she'd done so knowing the market for them was better, telling herself she'd rather write about the kind of man she thought attractive. What a surprise to find that she actually liked being dominated by a big, strong man. At least she liked the way this particular man used his strength to hold her against the wall and kiss her into submission.

On the other hand, maybe she just liked Sebastian.

He slid his fingers down her front and Stella experienced a sudden chill as the buttons parted, but that was short-lived after he covered her breasts with his hands. They imparted a warmth at odds with the fact she knew he was a few degrees cooler than she was.

Maybe it was just that at his touch she heated in response. Certainly he had the most talented hands of any man she'd known before. They gently cupped and massaged her through her lace bra, teasing her nipples into pinpoints.

Stella was glad she'd thought to wear some of her more decorative underwear tonight—not that she'd been thinking of Sebastian undressing her when she'd selected them. Well, maybe he had crossed her mind when her hand had fallen on the turquoise lace demi-cups and the matching thong, but she'd never admit it to him. At least not tonight.

Whether or not her choice had been deliberate, Sebastian's smile as he pulled off her clothes was appreciative. "So beautiful you are," he said in a dark whisper that sent shivers up her spine.

Soon the rest of her clothes were on the floor. Stella worked to make sure Sebastian's followed close behind.

As she helped him tug off his shirt, she noticed the smell of wine that permeated the front...her wine, where she'd tossed it at him. He really had been surprisingly nice about that. She'd expected some kind of retribution but he must want to make love to her more than he wanted to get even.

Either that or he was biding his time on exacting revenge for her actions, and she wouldn't put it past him to do exactly that. At the moment she didn't care a whole lot. Right now she was more interested in his lovemaking.

He could punish her later if he really wanted to. In fact, it might even be fun. A man with as many years spent loving women as he must have should have some *very* interesting ideas about punishment—disturbingly sensual ideas.

She liked the way he touched and caressed her, even if he did dominate the situation at the same time. It reminded her of when he'd made love to her the first time, in her hotel room in San Francisco. There was never an issue of choice. No hesitation, no need for her to do more than lie back and enjoy.

Sebastian had known that she wanted him and knew how to make it happen.

Same thing tonight. All Stella needed to do was give over all control to him and she'd have the sexual experience of her life. He bent his head and his lips closed on her nipple, still encased in the lace covering of her bra. Drawing fabric and nipple into his mouth, he suckled her while his hand carefully tweaked her opposite nipple. Sebastian could have left it at that, but instead his free hand slipped into the front of her underwear, unerringly finding her most sensitive spot. A few strokes later and Stella couldn't help her whimper at his skillful multi-front assault.

Her senses reeled under it. She rested her hands on his shoulders and gave him no resistance. Seemingly recognizing her capitulation, Sebastian lifted her and carried her to the bed. The comforter was plushly soft beneath her as he laid her across it. With a practiced move her bra was snapped open, her breasts falling into his hands. With a quick jerk he slid her panties down her legs and then she was naked on the bed.

Sebastian slid onto the bed on hands and knees, caging her with his arms and legs but not lying on top of her...not yet.

He stared down into her face. "The last time we were like this you did not know what I was or what it would mean to be with me. Now you do." He took a deep breath. "I have not changed, little star. If I make love to you, I must drink of you as well."

One hand played along the vein in her throat. "Will this be all right with you?"

In spite of him being a pure alpha hero, he was asking permission. Stella smiled at the incongruity. He might be a four-hundred-plus-years-old vampire, but Sebastian really was trying to be a modern man.

"I understand, Sebastian. Just be careful," she added, remembering how that incident in San Francisco had ended with her needing a transfusion.

"I will, I promise. I will never risk your life." He dipped his head and captured her lips, and again she realized he still wore his prosthetic.

Trying hard not to grin, Stella touched his lips. "I think you probably need to take that out if you're going to bite me."

With a grimace, Sebastian reached into his mouth and pulled the covering free, tossing it to the side. Stella smiled as his natural teeth appeared, complete with his dual fangs. Funny how his teeth no longer bothered her...they gave an extra level of sensation when he ran them along the curve of her neck. He teased her skin with tiny nibbles while his hands delved into the juncture of her thighs and stroked her with unerring skill.

In moments Stella was moaning her pleasure, ready for more of him. Sebastian wasted no time. His knees spread her wide and he sank down between them, his cock now poised just outside.

"This feels so right, my star. I'm glad to be with you again."

Stella stared into his face, inches from hers. She stretched her arms up to him. "Make love to me, Sebastian."

A look crossed his face that she didn't immediately recognize, softening his stern features. He seemed…pleased.

He entered her slowly, taking his time and drawing out the process until her body nearly screamed for completion.

Once he was inside he smiled down at her, his expression possessive. "Mine," he said, and she felt his mind echoing the sentiment. *Mine, mine, mine.*

Yours? She responded in amusement.

But Sebastian wasn't amused. *Mine. My companion, my woman. Mine to take and keep, care for, and use to both our pleasure. Mine.*

The forcefulness of the sentiment stunned her. He wasn't kidding, he really meant what he said about her belonging to him. Again she was reminded of what he'd said about being her master and she wondered if he didn't see her less as a person and more like some kind of possession. A convenient source of nutrition.

Without thinking about it, Stella's mind reached out to his. Like a bright silver ball it seemed to appear before her. Her own thoughts combined with his, darkened with passion to a deeper shade of pink. In his mind she saw his need and his hunger.

Feed, Sebastian. That's what we are here for.

The bright silver darkened as he read her discontent. *That is not my only purpose with you,* he protested. In spite of that she felt his hunger rise to the surface, harsh and unrelenting. His mouth descended onto her neck and she felt him nuzzle her.

Between her legs, he moved in a particular way and she had a quick climax that overshadowed all other sensations. When it faded she realized he was now sucking on her neck, his fangs having made the needed holes while she was distracted.

No wonder she hadn't realized before that he'd bitten her. That was how he did it, waiting until she was in the midst of an orgasm. Even now she barely felt any pain, only the rhythmic pull of his mouth, drinking what he needed to survive.

After a few moments she began to feel faint and so pulled on his arm to get his attention. But he seemed oblivious so she tried again, this time sending a mental command. *Stop, Sebastian. You've taken enough.*

He slowed, both feeding and in the wild possession of her body. For a moment he stopped, his body quivering at the effort needed to stop, then he drew away. His tongue lashed out, sealing and removing the signs of his feeding from her neck. His breath was hot against her skin.

Rising over her, he stared down at her, the heated anger in his glowing eyes nearly scorching her.

"As I said, that was not my only purpose with you," he snarled. He took up pistoning into her again, over and over again and harder than before. Now it was all Stella could do to keep pace with him.

His hands reached down to capture hers, pulling them high over her head and securing her to the bed. Now there was no question of it…she couldn't move and had to give in to his pleasure. He stared down at her as if willing her to come again, daring her not to, and she couldn't help giving in again to his will.

Even so, she opened her mind as her orgasm crested, sending the sensation to Sebastian, and caught off-guard, he too lost the fight for control. She almost didn't recognize his capitulation at first until he stiffened and cried out in unison with her as they came together.

Afterward he lay across her, breathing hard. A moment later he pulled himself to the side and tugged her deeper into his arms. His grasp felt like iron—Stella doubted she could have broken his hold even if she tried. It was like he was making a point, but she wasn't sure what that point was.

What did possessiveness mean when the man was an ancient vampire? What did he really want of her? He hadn't wanted her here in the first place and had only agreed to keep her from telling others what she knew.

But things had changed and she wasn't sure why that was. She wished she could reach out to his mind and read his thoughts but she didn't dare. Even if she could do it without his knowledge, she wasn't sure she would like what she learned.

"We should talk," Sebastian said, his voice a deep rumble behind her.

Isn't that what some men said right before they broke up with you? But if that was his intention, why did he hold her so close? Stella held her breath, waiting for his next words.

But he didn't get a chance to speak again. Instead there was a furious pounding on the bedroom door.

"My lord, please! We need you," came a cry from the hall. Stella almost didn't recognize Harold's voice. It had a gravel tone to it, as if forced through an inhuman mouth.

Sebastian was on his feet and at the door before Stella could react. Still naked, he flung open the door. Stella climbed from the bed and wrapped the sheet around herself, stumbling over the length as she followed him.

In the meantime two figures staggered into the room. They were both roughly man-sized but their skin was covered in coarse hair that barely hid the fact neither of them wore any clothes. Torsos were vaguely those of a man and woman but their limbs were oddly proportioned, hands and feet twisted into paws. Each face bore the stamp of humanity but was marred by a mouth and nose elongated into what could have been a muzzle.

Only their eyes kept true to their innate humanity.

They looked in part like humans who'd changed into wolves, or vice-versa, but the process had been interrupted somehow. Stella's jaw dropped as she realized who they were, mostly from those still too-human eyes.

It was Harold and Rebecca, and they were shape shifters, although she couldn't imagine why they would appear in partial form.

Then she realized that Rebecca, the smaller of the pair, with black fur and a female figure, was bleeding, a steady flow from her shoulder.

Sebastian snatched her away from Harold and carried her to the bed as Stella ran to the bathroom. She returned with towels just as Harold collapsed against the doorway.

"What happened?" Sebastian said, his voice sounding murderous as he used the hand towel Stella handed him to wipe away the blood.

"We were attacked, up near the ridge. Shot at...a couple of times," Harold gasped out. "Silver bullets, I think. Must be—hurts too much for lead."

Stella turned to the shape shifter leaning heavily against the wall. "You were hit too?"

"Yes. Bullets of silver—and something else." He stared at his partially formed hand. "They must have been coated in something. I'm not sure what, but it forced this...a partial change."

Stella grabbed his arm and helped lower him to the floor. "Where is your wound?"

"Here." He held up his arm and showed her the wound through his upper arm, still seeping bright red blood. It wasn't as serious as Rebecca's but Stella used another towel to help clean it away and bind it off.

"I must have bled enough to eliminate most of the poison. Only one bullet and it passed through." His eyes turned to Rebecca's limp form. "I was hit first and she jumped in front of me. Took at least one meant for me."

To Stella's amazement, Sebastian lifted Rebecca into his arms and began licking her shoulder.

"What are you doing? That's disgusting." She tried to get to her feet but Harold grabbed her arm.

"It is all right, Miss. His saliva will stop the blood flow and heal the damage. That's why I brought her to him."

His grip felt as firm as the nightwalker's and Stella realized as a shape shifter he probably was much stronger than she'd have expected. Suddenly she remembered Rebecca helping her to her room her first night here and how she'd wondered that the much smaller woman had managed the job. Now she knew.

Harold and Rebecca had much more strength than she had, but they'd been laid low by bullets someone had fired at them. Unexpectedly, she felt a surge of anger, even stronger because of how helpless she felt.

Stella said nothing but pressed the towel firmer against his arm.

Long minutes passed with almost no sound but Harold's heavy breathing and a few low moans coming from Rebecca. Sebastian's treatment made no noise and Stella found herself holding her own breath.

Then she realized that Rebecca's foot, which hung off the end of the bed, was changing, the hair retreating and the shape becoming that of a human foot. Sebastian turned her a little and began working on the other side of her wound.

Harold staggered to his feet and with Stella's help made his way over to them. In amazement she watched as the rest of the black fur disappeared from Rebecca, leaving behind smooth naked skin and a striking female torso. Rebecca was a very beautiful woman.

Stella could also see that she was more than a little pregnant. After a few moments Rebecca opened her almond-shaped eyes and blinked at Sebastian, then her husband and finally Stella. For an instant she seemed confused. Then her eyes widened as she realized her state of undress.

"Your lordship!" she cried and grabbed the edge of the comforter beneath her to wrap it around her nude body. "You're naked!"

Sebastian let out a laugh that sounded forced but relieved. "Now I know she's going to be fine." He left them to head for the closet and when he returned he was wearing a black silk robe.

He beckoned Harold over. "Let's get you fixed up as well, then you can tell me again what happened."

Ten minutes later both shape shifters were sitting on Sebastian's bed, wrapped in blankets since their clothes were in their room and Sebastian wouldn't let either of them leave until he had all the details. While Sebastian had cured Harold's wound Stella had grabbed her clothes and dressed in the bathroom, but she'd returned to hear their story.

Both Harold and Rebecca were back to their normal appearance, if paler than usual, most likely from the blood they'd lost. Even so it was clear they still felt the effects of whatever poison had coated the silver bullets. Neither could move quickly and when Rebecca tried to stand she nearly fainted.

Silver bullets coated with something designed to harm shape shifters. Clearly someone had been gunning for them tonight, within Sebastian's territory, and that was not a good thing at all.

"We'd just reached the top of the ridge. Were having a good run—enjoying ourselves," Harold paused and smiled at his wife, whose cheeks reddened, and Stella understood what enjoying themselves meant. Given that they'd caught Sebastian and her in bed together, she had to smile at the other woman's discomfiture.

"When we reached the top, we smelled something. Not like rabbit—better than that and larger. We went to investigate."

"Curiosity killed the werewolf," Rebecca said quietly. "Should have known better…should have hunted elsewhere…it was a trap."

"A trap?" Sebastian said.

"Ambush." Harold shook his head. "We did find an animal, but it was dead and staked to the ground. When we got close, they opened fire. Two guns, one on either side, shooting across the clearing. We were both hit but we managed to get out of there before we started to change."

Rebecca caressed her husband's arm. "He carried me close to five miles in that halfway state. I kept saying he should put me down and go for help but he wouldn't leave me."

Harold tugged her closer, ignoring how his blanket slid off his shoulders. "I would never leave you alone. Not out there where *they* were. I had to get you to safety."

For a moment he watched them, but then Sebastian stood and headed for his closet, a dark look on his face. Moments later he was back, dressed all in black, including a tightly knit cap that hid most of his face and all of his bright-colored hair.

Harold tried to get up but Sebastian stopped him. "I can fly faster than you can run and you need to be here…" His glance took in both Rebecca and Stella. "I need you to stay here."

He left the room and Stella turned to Harold. "What does he intend to do?"

The shape shifter shook his head. "Go after those who shot us, I suspect." He looked worried. "I wish he wouldn't go alone."

She stood and headed for the door. "Don't worry, he won't have to."

Quickly she grabbed dark clothes from her bedroom then headed downstairs. When she arrived, Sebastian was pulling magazines for one of the M-16 rifles from a secret panel in the fireplace.

He startled when she came up to him. He took in her appearance with one long look. "What do you think you're doing?"

Stella grabbed the rifle from him and shoved one of the magazines into place. She checked the sight then made sure the safety was on. "I'm going with you."

"The hell you are!"

"Yes—the hell I am." She matched his glare. "You aren't going alone. You can take me with you or call in the authorities—or I will once you are gone."

"No. I won't take you."

From the stairway, another voice broke in. "She's right, sir. Either she goes, or I do."

Both of them turned to see Harold, blanket still clutched around him. He stood as best he could but Stella could see the effort it took for him to stay upright.

"You need someone with you, sir. Stella, me or the police. It would be foolish to go alone and you didn't get where you are by being foolish."

Sebastian stared at his servant then turned to Stella. He pointed to the rifle in her hand. "Can you use that?"

She let out the breath she hadn't realized she was holding and nodded. "I once was going to write part of a series on military women—kick-ass heroines and such, so I took some training at the local National Guard. The publisher cancelled the series so I didn't get to write the book, but I qualified as a sharpshooter."

Sebastian looked dubious. "On targets."

"Yeah, on targets. But that doesn't mean I can't fire on a human being if I have to." She set her jaw. "No one shoots a friend of mine and gets away with it."

Sebastian stared a moment longer then grabbed a second rifle off the wall and another magazine. He showed the latter to her. "This one and the one in your gun are loaded with silver bullets. Shape shifters are sensitive to the metal, as are nightwalkers, but these bullets will kill humans too."

"Silver is bad for nightwalkers?" Their adversaries were using silver bullets too. Suppose Sebastian got hit.

He answered as if he'd heard her thought. "Companion blood cures silver poisoning." He gave her a hard look. "Keep close and don't get hurt. I may need you."

This was a bad idea. "Maybe we should just call the police."

He shook his head. "The authorities know about me, but they also believe me to be law-abiding and mostly harmless. I'll call them in if needed but I need to look into this myself. If nothing else, we need to find the bullets that hit Harold and Rebecca so we can analyze what they were coated with."

That she understood. "Otherwise we don't know how to treat them. And with her pregnant…"

Sebastian nodded grimly. "That's why this is so important. If nothing else we need one of those bullets and if we wait or call in the authorities we might not get them." He gave her a sardonic smile. "Besides, as you put it, no one shoots a friend of mine and gets away with it." He pointed to the door with his weapon. "Let's go."

They were halfway to the door when he suddenly turned around, pulled her into his arms and gave her a rough and passion-filled kiss. The intensity knocked the breath from Stella and she stared after him when he released her.

"For what it is worth, I'm glad you're with me, little star. Let's go find the bad guys."

Chapter Ten

Again Sebastian flew with Stella under the full moon, only this time their journey held an urgency the previous one hadn't. While he'd hoped for a romantic trip across the vineyard, he couldn't do it at the slower speed he'd intended. He worried that by the time they got to where the shifters had been attacked there would be no clues left of their attackers.

In some sense he even regretted the time it had taken to heal Harold and Rebecca, but their wounds had been too serious to delay treatment.

Inside, Sebastian shook with barely controlled fury over what had happened. It had been nearly half a century since anyone had dared harm anyone under his direct protection and now he couldn't imagine who would have been so foolish as to test him this way.

The means used worried him as well. The villains had used weapons designed to kill parafolk and that meant someone on the outside knew far more than he—or she—should about them. Either that or it was a threat from within, and in that case they were even more in trouble.

The mysterious substance that had been on those bullets was a particular concern. He'd never heard of a poison that could force a shifter to change into a half-human form. If nothing else, he wanted one of those bullets for analysis. While the fact the bullets had passed completely through had probably saved his servants' lives, it was a shame neither of them had been able to collect one at the scene.

Not that either of the pair had probably been thinking overly straight at the time. The shifters had been married for many years and were expecting their first offspring. Seeing his mate hurt and nearly killed must have made Harold near insane.

Except for his maker he had never felt that way about a woman, but he had to admit, if it had been Stella who'd been injured— No, he didn't dare let that thought finish. Stella was a problem at times and an indulgence much of the rest but he didn't think of her the way he had the one great love who'd eluded him.

Stella was his companion…simply that, and frankly, that was enough to justify his wanting to protect her.

Which was what he intended to do, even if she had forced him to take her with him. It was to satisfy Harold and keep him home with Rebecca that Sebastian had given in to Stella's insistence on going with him. That didn't mean he intended to take her anywhere near danger.

From the house, he chose a circuitous route to the ridge, one that anyone looking for him wouldn't expect him to take. He had no intention of flying into an ambush. It took longer but he was well on the other side of the ridge before he flew close enough to the ground to land.

Stella looked confused as he lowered her down and released her. They were within the vineyard, long rows of grapes on either side, heading up and down the hillside like a set of waist-high fences. The height would provide cover for him as he proceeded up to where the shape shifters had been attacked.

"Why have we stopped?" Stella asked in a whisper, as if she expected someone to hear them. Her eyes followed the lines of vines up the hill. "Isn't the place they were up there?"

Sebastian hoisted his weapon. "You're going to stay here. I'll come back for you when I know it's safe."

"The hell with that!" Stella clutched her rifle tighter. "I didn't come with you to sit in the field!"

"I'm not taking you further." He glanced at her feet and was amused to see she was still wearing the boots she'd been in earlier in the evening and that had hurt her feet. "You can always follow me, I suppose."

She glanced down and her eyes narrowed dangerously. "You don't believe I can shoot, do you?"

"I don't think you'll shoot me...at least I hope you won't. If you did you'd have to walk back to the house," he added with a grin. "Stay here like a good girl and I'll be right back."

As he moved quietly up the hill he heard her mutter behind him. "You are so lucky I wore these stupid boots...or I might shoot you."

He picked up the scent of the bait when he was within a hundred yards of the top of the ridge. Whatever it was, he could imagine to a pair of werewolves it must have smelled like a rich cabernet smelled to him. Sebastian hovered even lower to the ground, maybe a foot above it, and moved as a shadow between the vines until he reached the path at the top of the ridge.

Now he walked, cautiously, moving slowly and listening to every sound. There weren't any, and that concerned him. It was rare for the world to be so quiet, but something had silenced the normal nocturnal inhabitants of the vineyard.

Slowly he came to where he could see what had attracted the shifters. It was a small deer, freshly dead and tied to a stake just as they'd described. The stake was to keep it from being dragged away easily.

He smelled the blood, both from the animal and then also the shifters, the peculiar scent of werewolf blood that had fallen in scattered spots on the ground. Even now he tasted that same blood on his tongue from where he'd healed them.

He'd rather still taste Stella's blood instead. Werewolf blood always made him a little jumpy, but Stella was like a fine wine.

So far he hadn't found any signs of their attackers. Either they were staying very quiet or they were gone.

Must be gone…no one could be that quiet. In the silence he should hear them breathing or at least feel their mental signatures. Casting out and scanning, he sensed nothing. Sebastian shook his head. It had been too much to hope that they'd have hung around and waited for him to be stupid enough to let them trap him.

Maybe he could still find one of the bullets though. Carefully he searched the ground using his enhanced vision, hoping to spot the flash of silver.

He'd covered about half the path when the sound of something…or someone stumbling in the dark caused him to turn his weapon in that direction. "Who are you?" Sebastian challenged.

"Don't shoot!" At Stella's voice, even sounding as annoyed as she was, he lowered his weapon. "It's just me. I tripped over something."

He heard her fumbling in the dark and then a bright light erupted from her direction. "Oh shit!" she said. "Sebastian, I think you better see this."

Just a few yards away, Stella stood with a small flashlight that she must have been carrying in her pocket. A good idea to have brought that, he thought, even as he realized what she was training it on.

The beam from it illuminated a body on the ground.

Sebastian stepped closer. A man, human from the smell of him, with pale blond hair and twin marks on his neck. Fang marks that Sebastian knew very well. While he didn't recognize the man, he knew Vanessa's teeth marks when he saw them.

The marks had come close to being obliterated by the deep slash across his throat, which was the most likely cause of death. Sebastian examined the body closely. The dead man's eyes were wide and he looked surprised. Hadn't expected someone to kill him, for certain. He wasn't armed, nor did he have any identification on him. That had probably been taken to keep anyone from identifying him.

So the man was Vanessa's. The questions were, why was he dead and had she killed him? The shifters had said there were two attackers firing from the sides. Perhaps the other had slain this man to keep him from talking.

The slash across his throat had caused him to bleed out—not even a companion could suffer that much loss of blood, and this man hadn't been a companion for long enough anyway. The place was saturated in blood…only Sebastian's preoccupation with the deer and the place where the werewolves had been hurt had kept him from smelling the body earlier.

A sound from Stella caught his attention and when Sebastian looked up he noticed her looking pale. She swallowed convulsively. "Is…is he dead?"

He pointed to the slash across his neck. "Oh I think so."

"I think…I think I'm going to be sick." Dropping the flashlight, she stumbled away and moments later he heard her retching.

He couldn't help feeling a surge of pity. Must be her first dead body. Sebastian gave her time to recover while he used her small light to verify that nowhere nearby was the man's weapon or any of his other belongings. Whoever had killed him had made sure to leave no evidence.

Most likely Vanessa had selected him recently and made him her companion to bind him to her before pulling this one job. He'd never known her to be so ruthless before, but if she were behind the attack on his servants she was already playing in very deep waters. Killing a temporary companion wouldn't be that big a stretch for her.

Unfortunately, he still didn't have what he'd come here for, one of the bullets that had hit the shifters. Frustrated, Sebastian returned to where the deer was and again began searching the ground, this time using Stella's flashlight in the hopes it would find what his low-light vision had missed.

Eventually Stella limped into the clearing and sat down heavily. She looked so miserable that Sebastian almost felt guilty for having left her behind.

"You didn't have to follow me," he told her. "I was going to come back for you."

She lifted her rifle and for a moment he wondered if she really was going to use it on him but she kept it trained on the ground. "And suppose you'd gotten into trouble?"

"I would have still come back. I'd never abandon you, Stella. You have to trust me."

She pulled off her boot and examined her foot. Even from a distance Sebastian saw how red it was. He pointed to it. "The good news is that should be fine in a few hours. Companions heal faster."

"Doesn't stop it from hurting now, unfortunately," she muttered, rubbing her foot. "So have you found anything? Other than the dead guy that *I* found."

He hated to admit defeat. "No. Whoever was here must have made a point of picking up the spent bullets. They didn't leave a one."

Standing, Stella limped over to where the deer was tethered. Her face scrunched and she looked like she was going to cry. "Oh the poor thing."

The "poor thing" would have made his friends an excellent dinner, but Sebastian decided not to point that out to her. He thought about flying it back to the house for exactly that purpose but couldn't really carry both it and Stella. Better to leave it for the scavengers.

Dawn would be coming soon enough. They should get back.

She leaned closer and pointed to the side of the animal. "Sebastian, is that a bullet hole?"

In an instant he was next to her. Could it be possible that in spite of all their efforts to leave nothing behind, their attackers could have used the same ammunition to kill the deer?

He handed her the flashlight. "Here, hold this." Barely daring to breathe, he grabbed the skin around the small hole and stretched it, then with one sharp pull, ripped the animal apart.

Stella gasped and he felt her tremble beside him, but she held the small flashlight steady. And there in the middle of the animal's chest, shining in that bright beam of light, was a lone silver bullet in nearly perfect condition.

* * * * *

The first cramp struck Sebastian about halfway back to the house. A deep shooting pain, and it was all he could do to stay focused on being airborne.

Stella clung to his back and she must have felt the deep shudder go through him. Immediately she linked minds with him.

What's wrong?

Not sure. Dismayed, he realized his mental voice was weaker than it should have been. He didn't want to alarm her but knew better than to hide something from her. *My stomach...hurts.*

Are you hungry?

No. Shouldn't be. He grimaced. *It might have been something I ate.*

Like me? Stella didn't sound amused.

No. Not you...

Abruptly he broke off the connection as another pain ripped through him. This one was long and hard and he didn't want her to feel it with him. He moved lower to the ground and sped up as soon as the shuddering stopped, working to make it back to the house before the next cramp began.

Stella spoke aloud. "Something you ate but not me. Poisoned werewolf blood?" she spoke directly into his ear.

He nodded, distracted by the thought of when the next spasm would begin. The answer was, not long enough.

"I may have to land," he said through clenched teeth.

Stella pointed. "Over there. Near that building."

It was a shed used to store equipment for the remote part of the vineyard. Not perfect but it beat setting down in an open field with dawn coming. He made for the spot and landed just as another serious cramp hit him.

He bent over, clutching his stomach as a pain as intense as fire spread through his torso. He tried to breathe through it, barely managing to maintain control. When it finally passed he looked up to see Stella's anxious face.

"Not to worry, little star. I don't intend to die."

Her teeth worried her lower lip. "But I know you're really hurting. I can *feel* it, Sebastian."

He didn't have an answer for her. Instead he leaned against the side of the building. In addition to the cramps, his limbs were starting to feel numb, which worried him even more. This was similar to the symptoms Jonathan had reported when Vanessa had poisoned him, more evidence that the female nightwalker was responsible for their current set of troubles.

He really should have taken the threat she represented more seriously and have organized a hunt for her. This was his fault for not having made certain she was dead.

How much time was left before sunrise? A couple of hours, but without flight and in his current shape he'd be hard-pressed to get back to the house before then, particularly if the paralysis continued to affect his limbs. At least the shed would provide some protection…if he could get inside the locked door. At this point he wasn't sure he had the strength to break the lock.

"You think it was the blood from the werewolves that's the problem?"

"Has to be. I wasn't exposed to anything else."

"Why didn't it hurt you before?"

"Not sure. Maybe it takes a while to affect the stomach. Or…" An idea struck him and he stared at Stella. "Or maybe it's because I'd just had a good drink of companion blood before healing them."

A hopeful look crossed her face. "You want to take blood from me again and see if it helps?"

Sebastian took her hand and turned the wrist to him. "Join minds with me, Stella."

Again her pinkness seemed to surround him. He was actually beginning to like that shade of pink. He bit down and she made a small gasp but when he let her see how much he appreciated her help, she quieted. *Take what you need,* the soft pinkness told him.

He didn't dare take too much but the cramps eased and his legs and arms grew lighter with each mouthful. Finally he pulled away and licked her wrist clean, erasing the signs of his feeding.

Sebastian leaned back against the wall. He was better, but for how long he couldn't say. He didn't dare go up in the sky again and risk a fall, particularly with Stella in his arms.

He couldn't and wouldn't risk her.

Meanwhile, she stared intently at the door to the shed. "It's locked," she said.

Yes, it was, and he didn't have the key and he couldn't break down the door. The poison really had taken too much out of him. Maybe he'd be able to do something once he'd rested a moment.

Stella was fiddling with the lock and after a moment there was a click and it swung open. She replaced a set of hairpins back into her hair.

At his curious look she shrugged. "I once studied lock-picking. For that same book I was going to write."

"You were going to write about a woman who can fire a rifle and pick locks?"

Stella's grin looked forced. "You'd be surprised what you have to know to be a romance writer."

Actually, he was beginning to not be surprised by anything Stella told him. Instead he moved into the cool darkness of the shed. There were places he was sure he could lie safe and sound during the daylight hours.

Stella studied his feet for a moment. "Take off your boots. And socks."

He blinked at her in surprise but lifted his feet to comply. "What do you need them for?"

"I'm going for help but I can't walk in what I'm wearing so I'm borrowing your boots for the trip. The extra socks will help fill in the space."

He finished undoing his boots and handed them over to her. With a grim determination he hadn't seen on her face before she changed her fashionable footwear for his.

"Fortunately," she said, "your feet aren't all that much bigger than mine."

"The result of growing up so long ago. I'm fortunate that I'm tall enough to be considered normal for this time."

Standing, Stella tried a few experimental steps and smiled with satisfaction. "This will do." She hoisted her rifle over her shoulder. "I should be back before dawn, but if I'm not…"

"I'll find a place to sleep, away from the sun. Not to worry, little star, I've been alive a long time. I can take care of myself."

"I know," she said, her voice suddenly quiet. "But I kind of like worrying about you."

He was surprised. Both by what she said and how much he liked hearing her say it. "Take great care, Stella. No telling what is out there." From his pocket, he pulled her flashlight and handed it to her. "You'll need this more than I will."

She paused before exiting. "I'll be back for you." Then she swung the door shut and it was quiet and dark.

The small amount of blood he'd taken from her kept the cramps and deadening of his limbs away for close to an hour. After that they began again, slowly increasing in intensity.

In between cramps he thought about the dead man in his vineyard, the silver bullet and the fact someone had dared attack his servants on his land. That made him furious but it also made him very worried.

For a long time he'd lived a quiet and peaceful life and he had to admit that even given the circumstances of her blackmailing him, adding Stella to his life was one of the best things that had happened to him.

But his was no longer a quiet, peaceful life and having Stella in it put her into danger, which was not acceptable to him. Once they'd gotten through this immediate emergency he'd have to do something about it…even if that meant removing the marks and all her memories of him.

Assuming he could still do that, given how strong she'd grown in her mental powers.

He was clutching his knees to his chest during a particularly bad set of cramps when the door swung open. Outside the sky held just a hint of light, the false dawn that told him the sun would be rising within the half-hour. Silhouetted in the doorway stood Stella's curvaceous frame, with Harold in the background.

The shape shifter carried what Sebastian recognized as one of their special lightproof blankets. Quickly he stepped forward and wrapped it around Sebastian as he struggled to his feet.

"The cramps are back?" Stella asked as she and Harold took opposite sides of him and helped him walk to the van parked just outside.

"Just a little. They'll be better once I'm asleep."

"You'll need to feed a little more before then," she told him and looked at Harold. "Can you drive?"

The butler still looked shaky but he nodded. "The distance to the house, yes. You get in back with him."

It wasn't more than a ten-minute drive but it was comforting to have Stella with him in the back of the van. Equipped for long journeys, the van had a long bed-like couch for him to lie on. Sebastian stretched out on it now, Stella beside him.

He sipped from her wrist, less than he wanted but he needed to avoid draining her. No telling how long he would need to drink from Stella to keep the poison from conquering his body.

Finally he stopped and leaned back on the couch. Dawn was approaching, he could feel it in the depths of his bones. "We'll need to get that bullet down to Los Angeles," he told her. "There are labs there and people who can analyze it."

"Does Harold know where to take it?"

"Yes, but he couldn't drive that far right now. I'm not sure Rebecca should even be traveling in her condition and I can't ask him to leave her."

Stella stroked his head. On her face was an intent determination. "Don't worry about it, Sebastian. We'll find a solution. You rest and by the time you wake up there will be a plan."

The thought of giving over control to his companion even though she was the least affected of all of them didn't sit well. "Rest is what we all need now. Plans can wait until later."

Sebastian closed his eyes just as he felt the sun's rise over the vineyard to the east. He wished he could see it, but could not any more than he'd been able to see it rise during the last several hundred years. For now he would rest.

There was nothing else he could do at the moment.

* * * * *

Stella continued to stroke Sebastian's hair as he went still, lying on the bed in the back of the van. She stared at him for a moment. So this was what the big-bad-vampire looked like when he was asleep. Like a sweet-faced angel, his hair a golden halo around his head, his features lapsing into perfection without his habitual scowl to mutate them.

He really was a beautiful man...and that man had made love to her just a few hours ago. Stella wasn't used to having the attentions of a man like Sebastian, an alpha hero of the "first water", as one of her Regency heroines would put it. She rather liked it.

She wasn't sure she liked how much she liked it though. She was occasionally way out of her depth when it came to him.

The back of the van was windowless, designed to be a refuge from daytime sunlight, so Stella couldn't see where they were. But she heard the sound from the tires change as they turned off the dirt road from the shed onto the paved road leading to the house. Moments later the van paused and waited for a moment with the motor running, then proceeded slowly until it came to a complete stop.

When the back doors opened, Stella saw Harold and the artificially lit interior of the garage, well-sealed against the sun's rays. The shape shifter looked worn but not completely dead on his feet.

She indicated Sebastian. "What should we do about him?"

"Leave him here for now. That's a comfortable enough resting place." The shape shifter sighed. "We may want to move before it gets dark and it will be easier if he's already in the van."

Stella followed Harold into the house. The door led into a hallway leading to the living room, off which was the kitchen and pantry. The place seemed unusually quiet. Most likely Rebecca had finally gone to bed.

When she'd arrived at the house in her borrowed boots, Stella had been surprised to find both shape shifters dressed for action and waiting for Sebastian and her return even though both clearly needed sleep after their ordeal. She'd taken Harold with her but had insisted that the pregnant shape shifter retire.

"You should get some rest."

Harold nodded wearily, barely suppressing a yawn. "I'll recheck the locks and windows first and make sure the alarms are set. I'm sure Rebecca did it before, but we can't be too careful."

Stella headed for her own room. This was the latest she'd been up since coming into Sebastian's world of darkness. She released the lock on her window shades and opened them to see the vineyards that stretched in all directions from the house, the early morning light detailing the fall colors—green and red leaves, and the darker brown of the vines.

It took her a moment to realize that her computer, which she'd left on, was signaling that she'd received an email while she'd been gone. Stella sighed. Probably her agent wondering where she was with her latest book, but it could be something else. She opened the mail.

"*Dear Ms. Robertson. The house is the next target. You must leave.*" It was signed "A Friend" and had been sent around five a.m.

Moments later she was running down the stairs into the great room. "Sebastian," she screamed, just before remembering he was dead to the world in the back of the van.

Harold answered her instead, entering from the kitchen. "What is it?"

She grabbed his arms. "We need to get out of here. Now, today. They plan on taking the house."

Even if it looked like a fortress, the place wouldn't hold up to a serious attack, particularly if those involved used fire rather than bullets. With both Sebastian and the shape shifters still suffering the effects of the poison, they were in no shape for a serious fight.

Even so, Harold wasn't convinced until he saw the email and with some surprising hacking skills examined the headers to find from where it had been sent. "A Friend" was working from a computer somewhere nearby.

Harold shook his head. "Sebastian isn't going to like our making a decision like this without him."

"I'll take responsibility. We've got to get to Los Angeles as soon as possible." She chewed on her fingernail. "In fact, that's one thing we have on our side. They'll assume we have to wait until Sebastian rouses to make any move."

"Possibly. It could be a trap, meant to drive us out of the house."

"Maybe. But I don't think so." She thought about the young nightwalker she'd met the evening before. She'd given him her card, and it had her email address on it. She could think of no one else who could have sent her that message and Donald hadn't struck her as being a bad guy, even if he was associated with the mysterious Vanessa, someone Stella resolved to learn much more about.

A troubled look still covered the shape shifter's face. "We could drive today and be in Los Angeles tonight but I don't like making Rebecca sit that long in a car. She needs rest."

Stella thought about the action novel she had been going to write and remembered all the research she'd done on how someone could go on the lam and disappear from public view. She smiled. All that work was suddenly coming in very handy.

"Okay, Harold, here's what we are going to do."

Chapter Eleven

At sundown Stella was driving the van down California's Central Valley on I-5, heading toward Bakersfield. She watched with no little apprehension when the light grew dimmer, the sun disappearing over the hills to the west.

Harold had warned her that Sebastian wouldn't be pleased that she'd taken the initiative to load the van and head for L.A. without his explicit approval. Besides which, she knew he'd be equally bothered to discover that while he'd slept she'd driven the nearly seven-hour trip by herself. Given that she'd only had a very few hours of sleep, she hoped he wouldn't yell at her too much. The last thing she wanted right now was a scene.

Light faded from the sky and then from the back of the van she heard a thump. It repeated, then there was silence.

Moments later the lightproof door that separated the back of the van from the front seats opened and Sebastian's head poked through.

Mostly keeping her focus on the road in front of her, Stella gave him a quick glance. He didn't look happy and she steeled herself. How was he going to react to being taken for a ride he hadn't approved? Not well, she could tell.

He said nothing but his head disappeared and she heard the sound of the cooler she'd stowed in the back open and close. He reappeared and moved into the passenger seat, fastening his seat belt with one hand.

The other hand held a bag of blood from the cooler. Sebastian bit off the end and began to suck down the blood with gusto. In a surreal way it reminded Stella of a man popping the top off a can of beer and slugging down a few gulps.

"How are you feeling?" she asked.

He stared at the bag. "Better." He watched the scenery outside the window, not looking nearly as surprised as she'd thought he'd be. She reached out to him with her mind only to find that it had become a silver dome, impenetrable. With her fledgling control over her powers she couldn't move past it.

"Sebastian..."

He turned to her and now she saw his anger, his silver-gray eyes near molten with it. "Didn't I say we'd discuss a plan later, after I woke up?"

"There wasn't time..."

His hand sliced the air in furious denial. "There was plenty of time. Where is Harold? Rebecca?"

"In a safe place. I drove them to a hotel near the San Francisco airport. They checked in and will rest in the room until they can take a plane to Los Angeles tonight." She glanced over at him. "Rebecca wasn't up to a long drive today, but by evening she should be able to deal with a short flight. You can call them if you're worried."

"Call them?"

"They have a cell phone. We bought three prepaid phones. Yours is in there." She indicated the van's glove box with her hand. "There's a sticky note on the back with all three numbers, the shifters', mine and yours."

He opened the compartment and took out the phone. In a moment he'd connected to Harold and a brief conversation ensued. A few minutes later Sebastian closed the connection, looking visibly relieved.

"They've reservations on a flight to LAX at eleven tonight." He smiled. "It seems everyone is taking initiative now. They already called Jonathan and told him what was going on. His people will collect them from the airport and if anything goes wrong they'll check into a hotel nearby and call us from there."

"How are they?"

"Rebecca is no worse but no better," he said carefully. "She didn't have much of an appetite today."

Before leaving the shape shifters at the hotel Stella had provided another small cooler similar to the one in back with the blood but holding uncooked hamburger patties to keep the shifters fed until later that night. Room service wouldn't have raw meat on the menu.

That Rebecca hadn't eaten was worrisome. It wasn't good that a pregnant werewolf wasn't hungry. They had to get the bullet Sebastian still had in his pocket to Los Angeles and get some answers.

Sebastian stared at the phone in his hand. "These are very convenient, but why three?"

"Three what?"

"Three phones. Why'd you buy three phones?"

"Just in case we get separated. Harold won't leave Rebecca's side, but…"

"But you think I'll let you leave mine?" He gave a short, unamused laugh as he slipped the phone into a pocket. "Stella, I have no intention of letting you out of my sight. I'm better but I'm in no way healed. I still need you."

Reaching over, he grabbed her arm and pulled it to his mouth and she realized what he meant. He needed her blood, companion blood, the universal cure-all for nightwalkers. Not her, Stella, the woman, but what was in her veins.

"Keep driving, Stella," he said. Then she felt his teeth bite into her wrist.

Oddly enough, it didn't hurt. She felt his mind brush hers and while she stayed focused on the road ahead, she still felt him drink from her.

But he didn't drink very much. Just a little, like a man taking a dose of medicine or a shot of whiskey. Not enough to be a meal, just enough to do the job.

He finished and erased the marks from her wrist. Her hand released, Stella put it back onto steering wheel and tried not to think about what had just happened. Sebastian licked his lips and fangs clean and returned to the subject.

"So what was the urgency in leaving before I even woke up?"

Conquering her dismay over the impersonal way he'd taken her blood, Stella told him about the email message. Sebastian listened, his jaw tightened. "You believe they would dare attack me in my own home?"

"I believe that after last night it is wise to presume that no place is safe from attack. Someone intended to kill the shape shifters, or at least make them seriously ill. I wonder if they may have intended to poison you as well... They must have known you'd try to save them and that the poison would work on you as well."

Stella took a deep breath. "This may have been a carefully orchestrated attempt to assassinate you."

Sebastian sat back and contemplated her for a long moment. She felt his anger ease a little as he considered. "This could just be your writer's mind, imagining a dastardly plot where there isn't one."

"Sure. Special poison-laced silver bullets must be a part of every hunter's kit. And all hunters have fang marks on their necks when they go out to shoot werewolves."

That earned her another short laugh, this one more wry than humorless. "Point taken. There is definitely something going on." He gave her a sharp look. "Do you think you can trust this 'friend' of yours?"

"I think it might be someone who is caught up in all this and doesn't want to be."

"A spy in the enemy camp? Possible. Someone who might want to acquire favor with me."

He seemed like he was going to say more but was interrupted by the brief burst of a siren coming from behind. Startled, Stella looked in the side mirror to see flashing lights behind her.

"Are you speeding?" Sebastian looked over at the dashboard but she answered him anyway.

"No. At least not enough to catch their attention." Trucks and cars had been passing her at high speeds all afternoon as Stella stayed within five miles of the speed limit. With what would look at first glance like a dead body in the back of the van, she hadn't dared get pulled over for any reason.

Sebastian set his jaw. "Pull over and let's see what the officer wants."

Stella eased to the side of the road while the cruiser followed her and stopped behind. She rolled down the window and prepared a "who me, officer" smile as he came up on her side.

The officer, a young man with sandy blond hair, sunglasses and a serious expression, didn't smile back. "License and registration."

Stella fumbled in her bag for her wallet while Sebastian pulled the registration from the glove box. "What seems to be the problem officer? The van is registered to me and she wasn't speeding."

"Just a routine stop." He took the papers and went back to his vehicle.

Sebastian opened his door. "Stay here, Stella."

Curious, Stella watched through the side mirror on that side. She saw Sebastian move to the rear tire of the van and lean over as if looking at it. The officer immediately moved toward him, hand on his weapon.

"Sir, please return to the car!"

Sebastian leaned back on his heels and looked at him intently, holding his hands up. "I thought I heard something wrong back here. A funny noise."

The officer froze in place and an odd blank look took over his face. His hand moved away from his gun and he moved slowly toward Sebastian. "What sort of noise?"

When he came close enough Sebastian took his arm and pulled him to the side of the van, away from the road. They both knelt, huddled by the side of the van. Stella wasn't sure but it looked like they were discussing something very intimately.

Then she realized what Sebastian was doing and gasped out loud. He was feeding from the officer! He didn't take very long and in a moment he leaned back. The young man was smiling and he tapped the side of the tire. "It could be a nail. You should get that looked at."

"I will, as soon as I can."

The young man stood and started to walk away, but Sebastian held out his hand. "The papers."

"Oh yes, sir!" Still sporting a slightly goofy smile, he handed back the registration and Stella's driver's license. Sebastian thanked him and came back to the van but crossed in front to Stella's side.

"I think I'll drive, Stella. You need a break."

She couldn't argue with that...not after the seven hours she'd spent on the road with the very little sleep she'd had. She moved to the other seat and Sebastian climbed in. In moments they were on the road. The officer passed them a few moments later, eyes fixed to the front.

At the next off-ramp, Sebastian left the freeway. Concerned, Stella watched as he headed for the opposite side and then got back on heading north.

"Where are you going?"

"You may have a point about a conspiracy, Stella. That officer was looking specifically for us. There is an all points bulletin out on me and, apparently, you, and it included a description of our vehicle. They are seeking us for questioning in the investigation of a man found with his throat cut in my vineyard."

"He told you that?"

"It was in his mind."

"I thought you had a good relationship with the authorities in Napa? Can't you just explain you had nothing to do with the body?"

"I could but it would take time. The bullet we have needs to get to those who can investigate it and we just don't have time for a lengthy discussion with the authorities."

"What about the police officer? Didn't he report that he'd spotted our van before he stopped us?"

"Don't worry. I erased our encounter and all memory of us. He's now reported that the vehicle he saw had a different license plate than what they are looking for."

"Is that what you were doing while taking his blood?"

Sebastian shot her a surprised glance and even grinned. "Taking his blood made him more susceptible to mind control. And besides, I needed a snack." His grin broadened. "Why, little star…you almost sound like you are jealous."

"I'm not," she said, although she wondered if perhaps she wasn't a little upset that he'd fed from someone else.

Sebastian contemplated her for a long moment then returned his attention to the road. When he spoke his voice was softer. "I need blood to survive, Stella. That's what I am and I can't change it. While I can feed from you more now, I'll still need others, always, unless…" He stopped suddenly and Stella wondered what he'd intended to say but thought better of.

Finally he went on. "I can survive somewhat on bagged blood but it isn't that healthy for me. Rather like a steady diet of fast food would be for you. I need fresh blood daily if at all possible. At the moment things are a little different in that I need frequent small amounts of yours to counteract the poison in me. It might not cure it but companion blood at least reduces the symptoms."

"So you'll keep me nearby if only for that."

"That and…" he gave her a sideways smile, "there are other compensations for having you as a companion that I haven't fully appreciated before now."

"Like last night?"

He didn't deny it. "Indeed. Last night was—quite enjoyable. But more to the point, you did well today in getting us out of danger's way. No doubt the authorities would have been at my door this morning when I couldn't respond, and with the shape shifters hurt it was far better that we weren't there."

She hadn't really expected him to admit it. Stella felt the blush rise in her cheeks. Also, she'd thought in terms of a frontal attack, men with weapons, but really all someone had to do was call the police. For the first time Stella realized what a tightrope Sebastian and the others had to walk to stay out of the authorities' official scrutiny.

"So if there is an APB out on us, where are we going to go?"

"First of all, we need to get off the main highways. We'll take smaller roads from now on to avoid notice." Moments later he took another off-ramp and headed west on a farm road that led across the valley toward the hills.

Stella couldn't help a yawn. It had been a long day and she was so tired. "We're going to take surface roads to Los Angeles?" That could take all night.

"We'll get to L.A. eventually but first I have a stop to make." He looked over at her. "Go ahead and sleep for a bit,

Stella. You did well getting us out of Napa, but now it's my turn. I have a plan for where we can go."

Only planning to sleep a little while, Stella leaned her seat a little farther back and closed her eyes.

*****

It was several hours later when she woke back up. The world outside the car had changed from the open fields and orchards of California's Central Valley to close-set trees and darkness. There were houses too, some close to the road, others behind high gates. Through the fresh air vents, Stella smelled eucalyptus and the scent of the sea.

"We're in Santa Barbara," Sebastian told her. "I have some old friends here."

Old friends. "Other nightwalkers?"

"Another nightwalker. And her...companion," he said, but Stella wondered if he wasn't going to use another word instead.

"Oh." A female nightwalker, and from the pleasure in Sebastian's face a very good friend indeed. Stella fought another losing battle with jealousy over the blond man sitting next to her. Of course he'd have had other women in his life. Probably thousands given his age, and some of them would have been of his own kind.

Two nightwalkers would have so much in common. How could she compete with a woman of his own kind?

Depressed, Stella watched as Sebastian turned into a narrow driveway with a gate across it and slid open the cover of a control box. He reached for the buttons then stopped and turned to her. *Pay close attention, Stella.*

Startled by his suddenly speaking mentally to her, she watched as he pressed a series of buttons. *Remember the code — one, two, two, eight, five, nine. Someday you may need to come to them for safety.*

Aren't you worried I'll take advantage of this?

As the gate slowly opened, Sebastian turned to stare at her. "I trust you not to do that. Whatever else happens between us, little star, I believe that we won't hurt each other. Agreed?"

She nodded, for once wordless. Sebastian had never said he trusted her before. From him it seemed a major concession.

Once the driveway was clear he drove slowly up it until they reached the house, a low building, built partially into a hillside. Stella wondered if perhaps some of that building was underground…like the nightwalker's bedroom.

Two people were standing in the doorway to the house as they climbed out of the van. The man, tall and blond, stood with a protective arm around the dark-haired beauty at his side. When they grew close enough, Stella saw the small marks on his neck and realized he must be the companion.

The woman smiled as Sebastian approached, proffering her wrist when he grew close enough. Stella wondered if he would bite her but all he did was take her hand and kiss the back of it gently. "No need for formalities, Natasha. Your and Daniel's loyalty I've never questioned."

"Nor should you, darling." She gave a quick glance to Stella. "And you are?"

Sebastian slapped his forehead. "My manners. Forgive me, Natasha, but it has been a long few nights. This is Stella Robertson, my companion. Stella, my old friends Natasha and Daniel."

"Your companion?" Natasha broke into a delighted smile that revealed her dainty fangs. "This is indeed a surprise."

Her expression looking at Stella, who was still rubbing sleep from her eyes, was sympathetic. "You've had a long journey. Come inside and I'll offer refreshments suitable for everyone."

Once in the house the lady nightwalker led the way to a vast living room decorated with understated and comfortable furniture. Large glass doors to the back gave a view of a hillside leading down to the sea. With the moon still large in the sky, it was well lit outside and beautiful.

After taking drink orders—serum for Sebastian and a Diet Coke for her—Daniel headed for the kitchen. Natasha sat on one end of a long couch and Sebastian took the armchair closest to her. They looked like the best of friends sitting so close together.

Trying not to feel left out, Stella took the chair on the opposite side of the couch. When Daniel returned he delivered their drinks and sat next to Natasha, one arm casually around her waist.

"I recognized your code at the gate so we came to meet you," Natasha said once they were settled with drinks in hand. Sebastian sipped his glass of cold serum with appreciation. "What brings you to Santa Barbara so unexpectedly?"

"There has been a problem." Sebastian filled them in on the attack on Harold and Rebecca. Interestingly enough, Stella thought, he left out that he himself had been affected by the poison.

Even so, Natasha clucked in dismay and Daniel's genial expression grew serious as they heard about the body left in the vineyard.

Natasha gave the tall blond man next to her a nervous look. "A companion was killed? How terrible!"

"I don't think he was a full companion, Natasha. I think he was very new and most likely only bore the marks to make him loyal. The marks were Vanessa's, I'm almost certain."

For the first time, Daniel spoke, anger burning from him like an explosion. "Vanessa! That bitch—she's responsible for this?" he spat out. "I thought we'd seen the last of that little monster of yours, Sebastian. Didn't you order her execution after she tried to kill Jonathan?"

"Even so...I don't think she'd kill a companion, particularly not with a knife. That's really not her style."

Natasha looked worried. "There has to be someone else involved."

Sebastian nodded slowly, his face impassive. Yes, impassive, but Stella suddenly knew that he felt much more than that. Deep inside he mourned over the necessity of the decision to order Vanessa's death. He had strong feelings for this woman. Obviously he still felt something.

Feelings? Or maybe misgivings. Stella reached for him, opening her mind to his and reading the emotions foremost in his mind. Regret was strongest of what he felt. Regret for...making Vanessa a nightwalker? Or for having failed to keep her from the heinous path she'd taken?

There was more to this relationship between her nightwalker and the infamous Vanessa than she'd been told. Stella didn't like ambiguity in her relationships, or those she was in a relationship with. Somehow she needed to find out the truth of what was between Sebastian and Vanessa.

In the meantime, she relaxed about Natasha, seeing that what was between her and Stella's nightwalker, as she'd begun to think of him, was friendship and nothing else. She caught nothing but warm vibes from both Daniel and the lady nightwalker as Sebastian continued to tell them about the anonymous email message warning her to get the others out of the house.

They turned downright admiring when he told them how she'd organized the escape, hiding the shape shifters near the airport and getting the cell phones to keep them connected.

"An excellent idea!" Natasha beamed at Stella. "How did you ever learn so much about going into hiding?"

"Well, it was for a book I was going to write..." she began, but Natasha clapped her hands and laughed delightedly.

"I knew there was something familiar about you! You're that writer our prince has been so fond of! I recognize you from that picture on the back of your books." She glanced mischievously at Sebastian. "So you finally found a way to meet her! I thought you'd have to resort to heading to one of those romance writing conventions."

At the look of consternation on Sebastian's face, Stella broke into laughter. She could almost see what would happen if he dared show his face at a convention of that sort, twenty women to one man, and that man more often than not a cover model. Sebastian would get no end of attention given that he, in truth, was actually more attractive than the handsomest cover model she'd ever met.

Besides, those women wouldn't be able to ignore how totally straight he was. It would be like a catnip ball thrown in the middle of a herd of cats. Scary.

As if anxious to deflect the conversation, Sebastian brought up the bullet and their need to get to where it could be analyzed. That turned the conversation serious again and he, Natasha and Daniel fell into an in-depth conversation about what was going on in Los Angeles and how best to get there.

In spite of the caffeine in her drink, Stella grew sleepy again. It had been a long day, even with the nap she'd taken in the car getting here.

A poke on the arm roused her. Daniel's friendly face smiled at her. "I understand you drove all day today and you were up all last night. Did you get any sleep?"

"Once Sebastian took the wheel I got some rest," she yawned. "On the way to here. And I took a nap in the van outside the hotel."

"The hotel?"

"Where the shape shifters are. We packed up and left as soon as we could, made a few stops to get the phones and other supplies, and we took a couple unobvious routes to make it hard for anyone to follow. After I dropped Harold and Rebecca off at the hotel reception, I drove around the parking lot and found a quiet place under a tree. I figured we were safer there than anyplace else for a while so I climbed in the back and took a nap. I slept a couple hours before starting to drive."

"You slept in the van? The shifters would have shared their room," Sebastian's voice broke in.

"I didn't want to leave the van alone. In case...well, in case something happened to it."

"There is only one bed in the van," he said, a grin on his face. "Did you share it with me?"

"Uh, yeah." Stella felt her face redden. Silly, really. After all, they'd already shared a bed far less innocently than when she'd curled up next to him in the back of the van. "You weren't using the whole thing."

She could swear the blood-sucking jerk was laughing at her although he didn't dare do it to her face. Also looking amused, Natasha tapped Sebastian on the arm.

"Even so, it would be better for you both to be on your way. I suggest we transfer your belongings to one of our cars and then you take off down the coast. No one should be looking for you." She grinned at Sebastian. "The Mercedes, I think. You can leave the van here until things have calmed down."

Sebastian's smile broadened until his fangs showed. "I was hoping you'd suggest the Mercedes."

Natasha stood up and pointed a finger at him. "Now, Sebastian, I expect to get it back without so much as a scratch on it!"

Chapter Twelve

෪

Stella settled back into the butter-soft leather of the bucket seat beneath her and gave in to a heartfelt sigh. So *this* was why someone bought a luxury car. It wasn't just the prestige or the powerful engine a car like this commanded. The truth was the darn thing was actually really comfortable to sit in. Her seat might have been an easy chair in a living room.

A living room on wheels—that's what this car was, with a folded-down top and a windshield that would keep the wind off her face as they headed to Los Angeles. Stella smiled, imagining how the trip down the Pacific Coast highway was going to be in a car like this.

Fun. It was going to be more fun than she'd had in years. Being a writer was mostly a solitary job, spending long hours at a computer, but since she'd been with Sebastian it had been one adventure after another and she had to admit—she was enjoying every minute of it.

Standing by the side of the car, Natasha handed her a colorful scarf. "You'll need this to keep your hair from blowing all over the place."

As Stella reached for the scarf, Natasha grabbed her hand. She held onto it for what seemed to be a long time then released it, smiling at Stella.

"Take good care of him," she whispered, her gaze fixed on Stella. "He's waited a long time for you."

More than a little spooked, Stella wanted to ask what Natasha meant, but before Stella could question her the lady nightwalker broke eye contact and stepped back. Left with the scarf, Stella slowly wound it around her head, tying it firmly on the side, trying to subdue her now frantically beating heart.

Was Natasha psychic or something? Could she see the future? If so, she certainly seemed to be seeing Stella with Sebastian for a long time to come and that was more than Stella normally envisioned.

The subject of Stella's speculation opened the door on the driver's side and almost jumped into the seat in his enthusiasm. Sebastian growled happily as he caressed the steering wheel. "I've always wanted to drive one of these."

"Why haven't you bought one then?" Natasha asked pointedly. "It isn't like you couldn't afford it."

He gave her an unconvincing shrug. "Well, you know. It isn't that practical to have a convertible in Northern California."

"Like those planes of yours are so very practical!" Daniel laughed from the driver's side of the car. He handed Sebastian a Dodgers baseball cap, which the nightwalker took and stared at in dismay.

"Couldn't you lend me a Giants hat at least?"

"Giants!" Daniel grimaced. "That's a San Francisco team. This will make you fit in better down here."

"But I like the Giants and they have a great ballpark." Sebastian sighed and with an air of outraged dignity fit the cap over his blond hair.

Stella glanced over at the dark blue cap with the white L.A. at the front. "Oh it suits you, Sebastian."

He growled something she was pretty sure she was glad she couldn't interpret and started the engine. Natasha and Daniel stepped back as one, his hand wrapped tightly around her waist again. They stood together, facing the world as a couple, united in a way Stella had written about so many times before but had rarely seen in her real life.

Seemingly oblivious to everything else, Sebastian gunned the engine, a look of supreme masculine pleasure on his face at the deep purr the car made. "I promise I'll return it in one piece."

"Just be careful, Sebastian," Natasha said. "I sense there is more danger here than you expect. We don't really know what—or who—we're up against."

For an instant a look of deep age and seriousness took over Sebastian's face. "I'm always careful of my responsibilities, Natasha. Very careful," he repeated in a low tone. "No one and nothing that I'm responsible for comes to harm on my watch, no matter whom I'm up against."

* * * * *

Erasing the narrow wounds she'd made on the young man's neck, Vanessa pulled back with a satisfied smile. His eyes were still glazed with expended lust, his erection just now fading inside her.

Rolling onto the mattress next to him, she lay contented, well-fed and sexually fulfilled...life just didn't get much better than this. "You may go and tell your masters that I am pleased."

Unable—or unwilling—to acknowledge what she'd meant to be a dismissal, her dinner didn't budge from the bed. Apparently Alex wasn't ready to leave yet. His eyes danced merrily as he sat up and pushed her back onto the bed. She let him, enjoying the feel of his powerful arms around her.

Strong. She liked them strong, and this young man's body surged with health, even after the blood she'd taken. He was a "gift" from the local San Francisco underground movement, someone's distant cousin she'd been told. His masters thought she was working for them, an assumption she would disabuse them of when the time was right. But not quite yet, so she didn't feel inclined to simply kick the boy out.

"I didn't...expect it to be like that. I thought I'd be weak, but I'm not."

"I don't drink as deeply as some do. I've never had control problems."

"I feel like I could stay in bed all day with you. Or night," he whispered seductively.

"Tempting...but I have too much to do tonight." She patted his face. "You need to go."

"Can I come back? Tomorrow?"

Regretfully, Vanessa shook her head. To feed from him tomorrow would be too soon, even with his stamina. To her pride, she'd never killed someone while feeding...unlike some she could mention. No one died by accident around her. Otherwise, yes, but not by accident.

"We should wait at least a week."

His mind read such strong disappointment that she nearly laughed out loud. He was a strong psi, but with no control and very little shielding, again, just the way she liked them, strong in the body and weak in the head. He had real promise.

"I'm not dizzy at all."

She patted him again. "Maybe I could take a little more tomorrow. I could use someone like you...for protection...as well as other things." Maybe she'd even make him a companion...

That thought dimmed her mood. Unfortunately she needed a new companion, something she wanted to have a little chat with her partner about.

Speaking of whom, she could feel his disapproving presence outside the door, preceding a strong rap on the wood. "Vanessa, are you done with dinner?"

Barely allowing her guest time to head for the bathroom with his clothes, Vanessa rose and headed for the door. She pulled on a robe, merely for effect. It wasn't like Donny-boy hadn't seen her without her clothes before.

Sometimes she wondered if he wasn't just jealous of her sharing her body with her meals. But when she opened the door he barely glanced over the body her robe concealed. No, he wasn't interested in her anymore that way.

Or many other ways, she knew. Sometimes she wondered just what she had sired when she'd turned Donald Morgan into a vampire. She'd thought she was making a partner in her plans for leading their people into the next century but now she wasn't so sure. Much was wrong with the way Donald behaved sometimes.

She wished she could read him, but unlike Alex, her would-be companion, since his turning Donald's mind had a solid wall around it.

"So have you found them?"

"No," he said, his voice showing all the frustration she'd come to expect from him. "Apparently they left the house early this morning and there's been no sign of them since then."

"You're sure they were all gone?"

"It took our people nearly an hour to get inside and they checked every safety place they could find. No one was in the house."

"So you alerted the authorities?"

"There is an APB out on Sebastian about Steve. The police are looking for them and have a description of the van...no sign of it so far."

Vanessa leaned closer to Donald. "You haven't really told me what happened to Steve—how he died?"

No sign of nervousness showed on Donald's face. "I told you—it must have been Sebastian or the woman. They must have been in the field and heard the shots then jumped him while he was alone."

"And you were?"

"I'd followed the shape shifters back to the house and by the time I returned Steve was dead."

The story was a good one. Plausible, even fit the facts. "The only thing is, I've never known Sebastian to use a knife to kill anyone. A gun or his teeth, yes. But never a knife."

She grabbed his belt and pulled him forward, then fingered the switchblade she knew he kept in his front pocket. If she smelled it, would she recognize the scent of her former companion's blood?

"You, on the other hand…"

Donald pulled away, breaking her grip on his pants, and it bothered her how easily he did it. "If you have something to say to me, Vanessa, say it. Don't accuse me by implication. As for what kind of weapon our prince might use, there is always a first time for everything."

"I suppose so." She had her suspicions but this wasn't the time to voice them. Perhaps he had killed Steve but that didn't mean he was working against her. There hadn't been any love lost between the vampire she'd sired and her companion.

The pair had always been oil and gasoline, an explosive combination, and anything could have happened on that hill last night. She had more important things to worry about. Like a missing pair of shape shifters and a nightwalker prince who seemed to have a mysterious woman working for him.

Not that she was too worried about their quarry. There was only so long they could remain hidden.

Agitated now, the younger nightwalker paced the room. "We're never going to find them on the road," Donald said. "There are too many routes Sebastian could take and too many places for him to hide. They could have even changed cars by now."

Vanessa sat on the bed. "They haven't gone into hiding. That's not Sebastian's way. If he knows he's under attack he'll head for a stronghold and muster an army to fight rather than go to ground. I'm sure he's heading for Los Angeles. My spies there tell me there has been quite a bit of activity around Jonathan's headquarters. We'll stake out the places he's likely to go and find him. Even so, it won't be easy now that he's been warned."

Alex emerged from the bathroom, fully dressed. He gave Donald a look that was pure masculine jealous dislike, clearly seeing the man as a rival for her affections. Little did he know that it had been over a year since Vanessa had been physical with the enigmatic vampire Don—and mostly at his insistence. He'd said he didn't feel comfortable being intimate with her since she was his sire…like she was his mother or something!

It was all Vanessa could do to keep a straight face when he'd told her that. He was a very strange young man, but being a child of the early twenty-first century he had his uses, familiarity with modern technology being one of them.

It made life so much easier to have a computer expert around.

"Donald, why don't you get on that computer of yours and see if you can't find us a flight down to L.A. tonight?" She turned to Alex. "You wouldn't mind driving us to the airport, would you?"

Alex grinned at her. "Hell, I'd be happy to drive you down there myself."

"That would take too long…but if you were willing to go as well…" She turned back to Donald. "Make that three tickets."

Donald gave the delighted Alex a long look then shrugged. "Sure. Three tickets to L.A. There should be a flight around eleven we can make." He glanced at his watch, apparently still not quite able to tell time using his innate sense, or unwilling to let go of his past life's reliance on such devices—she thought more the latter than the former. "We'll need to get packed quickly to do it, though." He gave her a sharp look. "We don't want to bring the guns in our luggage."

"The guns won't be necessary." Vanessa crossed to the room's desk and picked up a vial. "Only this and it can go into my bag. You handle getting us on the airplane and I'll deal with the rest." She smiled up at her new, besotted blood donor. "Alex can help me tell the local nightwalker association that we're leaving for a while."

* * * * *

Walking between Donald and Alex at the San Francisco airport, Vanessa was halfway down the concourse when she spotted Harold and Rebecca emerging from the members-only airline lounge. She grabbed Alex and Donald and herded them into the wall. Pretending to look for something in her carry-on, she made them lean in close to hear her.

"The shape shifters…the ones you were sent for. They are just ahead of us!"

"Sebastian's servants?" Donald lisped slightly on the S's. Even after a year he hadn't quite gotten used to the dental appliance that hid his fangs. "What are they doing here?" He took a fast glance around. "Is Sebastian or the woman here?"

"I don't see them." She reached out with her mind. "Or sense them, but there are so many people here. A lot of static." She turned to Alex. "You see the ones I mean?"

"The guy with the hat and the lady in the long-sleeved shirt and the scarf?" It was just past the full moon, Vanessa realized, and both shifters would still be in their "hairy" stage. Rebecca probably had dark hair covering her neck and arms, and even Harold's bald head wouldn't be completely smooth unless he shaved it. It was rare that shifters traveled this close to the full moon and they wouldn't be now if it weren't necessary.

Interesting that they'd be flying alone. What was going on, she wondered.

"Those are the ones. I need you to follow them and find out who they talk to and what flight they are taking."

"Will do!" Happy with his assignment, Alex trotted down the concourse.

"He reminds me of a German shepard," Donald said dryly.

Vanessa gave him a long sidelong look. "It wasn't that long ago you'd have been happy to do my bidding."

He stiffened. "It was long enough ago, Vanessa. I won't come to heel for you or anyone else anymore."

She pushed him hard against the wall, using all of her strength. Barely more than a youngling, he wasn't a match for her and his struggle against her was fruitless. Eventually he gave up and leaned against the wall, his face furious.

"Perhaps you aren't my 'dog' anymore, but you will obey me. You are in this scheme as deep as I am and if we're caught you'll get the same punishment. We can't fail. If we do, we're both dead." She stared menacingly at him. "You will follow my orders, if only to save your own neck."

Just then Alex returned. "They're in the boarding area for the eleven o'clock flight for L.A. Same one we're on, only they're in first class. As far as I can see there isn't anyone with them. No one even glanced their way when they sat down."

Exultation filled her. "I knew it. I knew that's where they would go. They must be meeting Sebastian down there. All we need to do is follow them after they land and they'll lead us straight to him." She glanced around. "Now we just need to make ourselves unobvious so they don't spot us."

Alex shook his head, looking disturbed. "Probably they won't notice. They were acting kind of sick. The woman had to sit down as soon as they got to the waiting area and he didn't look much better. I heard him tell the gate attendant that his wife was pregnant and that's why she didn't look that good."

"Pregnant?" Donald's voice caught on the word.

"Maybe she is and maybe it's just a ploy. What difference does it make if the animal is breeding?"

Alex stared at her in shock while Donald simply looked disgusted. Vanessa realized she'd stepped over a boundary line. It was all she could do to not roll her eyes. Oh for heaven's sake—two big strong men getting softhearted just because a woman was knocked up? It was enough to make her gag.

Still she had to live with them—best to keep the peace.

"Of course I didn't know anything about her being pregnant when I ordered them attacked," she said soothingly. "I wouldn't have done so otherwise. Now that we know, she and her husband won't be harmed any further—provided they don't get in the way," she added. "We'll just use them to find Sebastian. He's our real target."

At her reassurance a look of relief swept Alex's face but Donald continued to look at her as if she'd grown a second head.

Vanessa handed him her boarding pass and pulled a long scarf from her carry-on. "It would be better if I sat in the far back of the plane. You get us moved while I put this on in the bathroom."

Donald's eyes narrowed. "Okay. I'll take care of it—you're the boss." He added the last under his breath.

Vanessa turned back and gave him her most dangerous smile. "That's right—and don't you forget it."

Chapter Thirteen

As the Mercedes swept down Wilshire, Stella stretched her legs deeper into the warm air blasting from the heater. Sebastian had put the top up about an hour outside of Santa Barbara, after the novelty of being in a convertible had worn off. Fun as it was to speed along the ocean, late November was just a little too cool to drive with the wind in your face, even with the heat going full blast.

Snug in the leather upholstery, the purr of the powerful engine in her ears, she drowsed a little until Sebastian woke her. She glanced over at him, noting with amusement he still wore the Dodgers hat.

Even so, she decided it looked kind of sexy when he smiled over at her. "We're about an hour from Jonathan's. This is the first chance we've had to talk in a while."

Stella stretched and yawned but decided to stay awake. Probably Sebastian just needed something to distract him on the long drive. "What do you want to talk about?"

He seemed to think for a moment. "You've finally met some other nightwalkers. What did you think of them?"

"You mean Donald?" She laughed as he made a face. He still bore a grudge against the other male nightwalker for keeping her company that night. Or maybe it was his connection to Vanessa. She thought he was probably the reason she'd been warned to leave Napa this morning. But Sebastian probably meant his friends in Santa Barbara.

"So you mean Natasha and Daniel. I liked them a lot. They're like real people."

Sebastian smiled over at her. "Real people?"

"You know—not really all that different from anyone else. They're just...people."

He laughed. "You saw them as people. And me? Am I the same?"

Sebastian would never be just a person to her. "You're a lot more to me than that."

"Oh?" For a moment Stella wondered if he didn't want to know more, but he seemed to think better of it.

"Tell me why you like to write about vampires."

Stella laughed. "Other than the fact that the readers love to read about them?"

"You don't just write because you make money at it. You love it, I can tell."

She sighed and leaned back into the seat. "I do love it. I love making up a story, people and places that don't really exist. I love stepping into another time and then bringing the reader in with me."

"But you could do that and not write vampire stories."

"That's true." She thought for a moment, staring out the window at the nighttime world slipping by. "I guess I've always tried to see the human in those who aren't human. Vampires don't belong in the normal world, but that doesn't mean they are monsters. They are just visitors...and different."

"Visitors to the normal world. An interesting way to put it." He glanced at her. "Perhaps you don't belong in the normal world either. Your psi powers were latent when we met but were strong enough that I bet you've experienced them working from time to time. That would make your life interesting."

"What do you mean?"

"Odd things happening. For example sensing something wrong and deciding not to walk into a room, only to find out that there was someone you were trying to avoid already there. Flashes of insight about a person that turned out to be right. The kind of information you might learn from reading someone's mind, even without knowing that's what you were doing."

Stella laughed. "Now that you mention it…that has happened to me!"

"I'm not surprised. And when it did, how did that make you feel?"

"Weird. Like I was abnormal. If I said anything people would look at me like I was strange."

"Like you were a visitor to the normal world."

"I suppose that's one way to look at it."

"Is that why you like to write about the paranormal? You want other people to see it as you do…not monstrous, just different."

"So that I can accept myself? Maybe." She paused. "Does that sound strange to you?"

"Little star, I've been sleeping all day and drinking blood at night for over four hundred years. And yet you would cast me as a hero in one of your books. That seems strange to me."

"You stand up for your people and help them stay strong. I heard what you said to Natasha and Daniel, that no one you were responsible for would get hurt. You really meant that."

He seemed uncomfortable with that. "I'm prince of my people. They look to me to keep them safe."

"You take the responsibility of taking care of them. But I was told you'd never taken a companion before. Why not?"

"Why haven't you gotten married before now?"

His counterpoint took her by surprise. "What?" she gasped out.

"Why haven't you married? You've had lovers before but never committed to anyone."

And yet she had committed to him. Perhaps she was a little bit in love with him? "I hadn't met anyone I fell in love with…at least not long enough to last." She laughed. "Maybe you were right about my looking for someone like one of my heroes."

"Taking a companion is a little like marriage. It is a commitment and not one I was interested in making."

"Until I forced you into it," Stella said. "By threatening to expose you. I'm surprised you don't hate me."

"I admit I wasn't happy about that." Sebastian paused and his voice grew quieter. "When I said I'd protect those I call my own, I meant you as well. I've gotten used to having you around and I would miss you if you weren't here."

"I'd…miss you too," she said and she almost said more but couldn't. How could she tell him that he'd been right from the first? She'd wanted a hero like the men in one of her books and no one had ever measured up…until Sebastian had walked into her life. Instead she turned her attention to the world outside the window.

They were coming into town. The small shops and short buildings of Santa Monica had given way to tall office buildings. Sebastian made a few turns into the hills and then there was another of those gates with the security box that he typed into. This time he didn't share the number with her and she wondered if perhaps her reticence had been noted and if it bothered him.

Then, in her mind as they drove through the opened gate… *The number is seven, eight, one, nine, seven, one.*

Stella stared at him. "That's my birthday!"

He spared her a quick glance, his lips tweaking into a smile. "You were on my mind at the time and it was easy to remember."

The house and grounds were well lit, huge and imposing. The front of the house itself might have been a movie set for a southern mansion. Sebastian pulled into an open spot amongst the cars parked in front and stopped.

Stella stepped out and realized that over half the vehicles were well-kept luxury cars. "Who lives here?"

"This is the home of our City Chief, Jonathan Knottman, and his companion, Sharon. It operates as our headquarters in Los Angeles. We also have laboratories here, so we can get this bullet analyzed."

He must have noticed her counting the cars. "He's called a meeting tonight to discuss the situation, that's why there are so many cars."

"I guess money isn't really an issue for you folks," she said with a soft whistle.

"We get by," Sebastian admitted humorously. "Being able to read other people's minds comes in handy. Good investments and compound interest are our friends. Shortly after the crash in 1929 we got organized about finances and created a business to manage them. Almost everything is owned by that company and its subsidiaries, which makes it a lot easier to deal with the IRS."

He gave her a quick grin. "Yes, even nightwalkers have to pay taxes."

She didn't even want to think about what the property taxes on a house like this would be. "So most of you don't control your own money?"

"We all have some of our own but the bulk is kept communal. Why?"

"I was just wondering… Vanessa has been on the run for how long—two years? Where is her money coming from?"

Sebastian stood very still and his eyebrows rose. "That's an excellent question," he said quietly. "She must have funds, and that means she must have backing. Partners in whatever it is she's up to. Perhaps even an organization behind her."

"What she's up to is destroying you, Sebastian. I've been thinking about it. Why attack the shape shifters? What purpose did it serve, unless it was to get you out into that field, roaring mad and alone?"

Stella was gratified that he seemed to be taking her seriously. "You think it was an assassination attempt?" he said.

"I'm worried that it had to be. What other explanation fits the facts? The shape shifters posed no threat to anyone so why make them a target? I don't know much about parafolk politics but what I do know is that a lot depends on you being around to hold things together."

"Up north, not down here. Jonathan controls things here."

"So perhaps the threat is up there?"

Now Sebastian looked really troubled. "If so then things are worse than I thought. Let's go inside. I would like to discuss your theory with the others."

* * * * *

Sebastian watched as Jonathan, his oldest friend, welcomed Stella to his home. He noted the humor his friend exhibited at meeting his companion...the first he'd ever taken.

The last he would likely ever take. One lesson he'd learned from the attack on the shape shifters was that having someone like Stella gave those who were against him a target, and it gave him someone else to worry about. Part of him had wanted to free her earlier just to make her safe, and the only reason he hadn't was because he needed her blood for the sickness he still suffered from.

In the pair of long hours that he'd lain helpless in the shed back in the vineyard, he'd thought of releasing her as soon as he'd risen but Stella had removed that possibility. She'd taken the initiative to drive him from his home while he was still asleep, knowing or unknowingly binding her future with his. Those who chased them would likely by now know who she was. He couldn't very well tell her to go away once that had happened...it would only put her into danger.

Lovely, golden-haired Sharon came over and held out her hand to Stella. "I've read all your books and loved them. But I guess you hear that all the time, Ms. Roberts...or I guess that should be Robertson."

"Please, call me Stella. And I'm always glad to meet a fan." She gave Sebastian a humorous glance. "Which one did you like best?"

Jonathan gave him a knowing look as Sharon pulled Stella aside to talk about her books.

"So you finally met your favorite author. Interesting way of showing fandom, making her your companion."

"That wasn't entirely my idea. She rather insisted on learning more about the parafolk and when it turned out she was a psi it seemed like the right thing to do. It's only temporary."

"Of course it is. I would be surprised otherwise."

Sebastian shot him a suspicious look but Jonathan managed to give off an air of innocence and he decided to wait until later to set his friend straight as to how not permanent his relationship with Stella was going to be.

From his pocket, Sebastian pulled the bullet. "We need this analyzed as soon as possible."

"I know. We've been expecting it." Jonathan took it and called over a pair of psis, a man and woman who hovered nearby wearing lab coats. He handed it to them. "We need to know what it is and how to counteract it. In particular how to help a shape shifter who was in contact with it."

"A pregnant shape shifter," Sebastian added and all three of the others stared at him. Jonathan's eyes narrowed and his expression grew grim.

"Rebecca is pregnant? I didn't know that part. That is bad news." He turned to the others. "We'll need an antidote as soon as possible."

Without a word the pair in the lab coats grabbed the bullet, nodded and headed for the downstairs laboratory. Silent as they were, Sebastian sensed that their mental conversation was in full swing, discussing the best methodology to proceed and possible antidotes to test even before they hit the stairs.

They were the finest alchemists the parafolk had and for the first time in the past twenty-four hours Sebastian relaxed, knowing they now had the best chance of getting a cure for the poison in both him and his friends.

Just as he thought about it, a small twinge started in his stomach. It faded immediately but he was aware of just how much he needed that antidote too, or at least companion blood to reduce the symptoms. Fortunately he had Stella to keep him stable since even now he didn't want to tell Jonathan and the others he was affected.

"Harold and Rebecca will be in Los Angeles in a couple hours," he said. "We could have them come here."

Jonathan shook his head. "Vanessa will know to look for them here and if she has spies about they won't be safe. It is better they go directly to the safe house. I only told the ones picking them up where it is and I trust them completely...they'll be safe once they get there. So will you and Stella."

"I hope you're right," Sebastian said. It was time he told his friend about Stella's theory as to who might be behind the attack. "Let's go into your office. There is much I need to tell you."

Five minutes later, when he'd finished, Jonathan was leaning forward, all concern in his face. "You think it is a conspiracy of parafolk?"

"Not just any parafolk. I think it could be a group of nightwalkers. A few months ago a group of young nightwalkers from the northern California area came to talk to me about forming a separate group. They were complaining about our policies of treating all parafolk as equals. In particular they didn't like how shape shifters were allowed to compete for jobs."

Sebastian nearly smiled at how Jonathan grimaced over that last. Both of them were known for hiring whoever was best for the job, regardless of whether the person had mental powers, fangs or fur.

"So how did you respond?"

"This sort of thing comes up every decade or so. I did what I always do. I listened to the suggestions and explained that the parafolk were strongest when we stuck together. I said we needed each other and I wouldn't allow any group to go off on their own. The complainers went away and I thought the business was done."

He shook his head. "I'm beginning to think I was premature in thinking that."

Jonathan stared. "You think they would dare assassinate you for this?"

"I think they would listen to someone with ideas like theirs...in this case, Vanessa. And I believe she wouldn't mind seeing me dead. She could have convinced them it was the fastest way to get what they wanted—a separate nation of nightwalkers."

"Vanessa with backing." Jonathan shuddered. "That is scary. And if it comes out that this was a real assassination attempt on you, it could get worse. You are our most visible nightwalker, next to me. If the norms find out that you don't control all of the parafolk they could get nervous about allowing us as much freedom as we have. They tolerate us because they believe we keep the peace among our own kind."

"And if the peace is broken they may not tolerate us any longer."

Jonathan shook his head. "There are a lot more norms than there are parafolk. We're stronger, faster and we live longer, but we are mortal and can be killed. The norm authorities allow us to function because they don't think we're a threat, but if these separatists get their way then all of us may be in danger..."

"All of us, including the psis who are our companions," Sebastian finished for him.

A twinkle appeared in Jonathan's eyes in spite of the seriousness of the conversation. "Even our temporary ones."

Sebastian didn't comment. He didn't want to think about Stella being permanently in his world and permanently in danger.

Watching her sleep in the car tonight had brought forth feelings he'd thought long dormant. Caring and tenderness. The need to protect. The desire to take care of, coupled with the intense desire to hold. He intended that she would share his bed when he took his rest in the morning and he would wake with her in the evening.

That was an intimacy he hadn't known in so very long. He hadn't slept with a woman, worried how she would take waking next to his corpse-like body, but she'd shared his bed in the van this morning and not flinched away from him.

She would sleep with him tomorrow...or today, that is. His inborn sense of time told him it was after midnight now.

The shape shifters would be landing soon. "I'll need to get to the safe house. I don't want to leave Rebecca and Harold unguarded for long."

"You worry too much, Sebastian. Those with them are shape shifters and like us they protect their own. They won't leave them alone until you get there, and even then you might have to toss them out."

"I still think it would be better if I wasn't here. My presence is bringing too much danger to the door."

"Very well. I'll not try to talk you into staying. Let's go and see if your companion is ready to leave." Jonathan tilted his head and Sebastian knew he was listening to his bloodmate. "I have a feeling she and Sharon may have their own agenda."

Oh dear. Sharon and Stella together... What were they up to? Sebastian stifled a sigh. "Where are they?"

Jonathan licked his lips and grinned. "In the kitchen."

* * * * *

Sharon halted in her tracks and turned on Stella. "What do you mean you haven't eaten since this afternoon?" she said. "You must be starving!"

Now that someone had mentioned it, Stella was hungry. "I stopped for a hamburger on the highway around two o'clock but that was the last meal I had. I guess with all the excitement I lost track of getting anything else to eat."

The blonde put her hands on her hips and scowled fiercely. "That's just disgusting. Sebastian of all people should know better than to let a companion go hungry. We need more food than normal people. After all, we're practically eating for two."

"Eating for two?" Stella echoed weakly. Sharon made it sound like she was pregnant.

"It takes a lot of energy to make enough blood to feed a nightwalker. Hasn't Sebastian told you about being a companion?" She shook her head in disgust. "And he gave Jonathan a hard time. The man is simply incorrigible."

"He's not..."

"Don't waste your energy defending him. We need to get you something to eat now." Sharon grabbed her arm and pulled her from the small parlor they'd been talking in into a back hallway. In moments they were in a well-stocked kitchen. Sharon pulled several storage containers out of the refrigerator. "There is Peking Duck, rice, some leftover spaghetti and a little bit of fruit salad."

Suddenly Stella was starving. "I'll take the salad now. Maybe we could heat up the duck?"

Sharon handed her the container and a fork. "I'll cook — that is, I'll reheat while you eat."

Once the duck and rice was in the microwave, Sharon opened the refrigerator and grabbed an open bottle of white wine. Stella noted with amusement it was one of the few bottles of Chardonnay Sebastian's Nightflyer Vineyard produced. Pouring, Sharon put one glass in front of her, keeping one for herself.

She held the glass up in a kind of salute. "A toast."

Stella grabbed her own glass. "Toast? To what?"

"To Sebastian finally finding a woman willing to put up with him."

With a laugh, Stella drank but she shook her head afterward. "He's not that bad. He just doesn't like to be tied down." She put down her glass and, fork in hand, started on the fruit salad. Biting into a juicy piece of pineapple sent shockwaves through her taste buds.

"Four hundred and eighty years alone is more than 'not wanting to be tied down'."

"Four hundred eighty?" A surge of astonishment overtook her.

"That's how long Sebastian has been a nightwalker and he's never had a companion before. Never wanted one, I was told, which means every relationship he's ever had has either been with another nightwalker or short-term, and I suspect mostly the latter. I wonder when the last time it was he was with someone who actually knew what he was?"

"Other than me?"

"Well…yes. I'm guessing he slept with Vanessa, but otherwise…"

Horrified, Stella paused in the middle of forking chunks of fruit into her mouth. "What do you mean he slept with Vanessa?" Vanessa was their nemesis, the nightwalker responsible for attacking Harold and Rebecca, and who was trying to kill him.

Sharon's face showed her discomfort. "It was a long time ago, Stella."

"I don't care. He had sex with a homicidal maniac and he's afraid of getting too close to me? That's nuts!"

"I can't disagree with you."

Stella grabbed her wine and downed half of the glass. "How dare he say he doesn't want to get close to me when he once trusted her. He must know I'd never hurt him."

"I'm sure he knows that. It's just complicated."

"Yeah," Stella laughed. "Complicated. That's what they all say."

Just then the microwave beeped and Sharon went to retrieve the dish of rice and Chinese duck. She put it in front of Stella along with a fresh fork. Stella abandoned the rest of the salad in favor of this new offering.

"Oh this is so good," she said around a mouthful of sweet tangy meat.

Sharon picked up her glass and refilled it from the bottle. "So have you shared tastes with Sebastian?"

"What do you mean?"

"When you eat something. Can you show him what it tastes like?"

"Yes. But he doesn't seem to like it when I do. Except when I show him what his wine tastes like." Stella took another sip of wine. It really was excellent.

Sharon spun her wine around in her glass, watching the golden liquid swirl around the bowl. "But you *can* share tastes with him."

Stella shrugged. "Sure. That's part of being a companion, isn't it?"

"He told you that?" Sharon took a deep sip of her wine, swallowed and then put the glass down and stared at it. "He sure makes good wine...for an asshole."

Pausing in mid-bite, Stella stared at her. Jonathan's companion had called his prince an 'asshole'? "What do you mean?"

Sharon folded her arms and leaned across the counter and Stella felt the anger radiating off her. "Not every companion can do that, Stella, only special ones. Bloodmates can do it, and those are very, very rare."

"What's a bloodmate?"

"That's what the parafolk call a companion who can be all their nightwalker needs. They can provide almost unlimited blood, as often as needed."

Then Stella remembered that Natasha had called Daniel her bloodmate. "You're Jonathan's bloodmate?" she guessed.

"I'm not just his companion, if that's what Sebastian told you, and truth is you aren't just a companion either. You being able to share tastes means that you could be Sebastian's bloodmate and the fact he didn't tell you says a lot."

She shook her head in disgust. "He really is afraid of your being more than a temporary presence in his life."

The Peking Duck, which up to now had been extremely tasty, suddenly lost its flavor. Stella took a couple more bites before putting her fork down and again grabbing her glass. She drained it and then refilled it from the bottle, then stared at the amber liquid without drinking.

"You don't think he wants to keep me any longer than he has to. That's why he didn't tell me about being a bloodmate."

Stricken, Sharon stared at her. "Oh, Stella. I didn't mean it like that. He does, I'm sure. But he's…just a man after all. I really do think that he's scared."

"He isn't the only one, you know. This is at least as strange for me as it is for him."

Sharon grasped her hand and squeezed it. "I know it is. Maybe it's because it's his first time to care for someone like you. But you need to know the truth...that it could be more than just a temporary arrangement you have."

"Assuming he continues to dodge silver bullets."

"Yes. There is that." Sharon looked really worried. "This isn't really the time to be talking about permanent relationships. Let's get past the next few days. He's still drinking from you, right?"

"Yes." She knew why he needed her though. She had "companion blood" and he needed that after ingesting the poison the shape shifters had been exposed to.

Stella sighed. "He needs me...for now."

"He needs you for far longer than that, Stella. Maybe he just needs time to realize that."

"Maybe." And then again, maybe not.

She felt his presence before he actually came into the room, Sebastian's mind questing for hers even as he came through the door. There seemed to be an urgency about it that surprised her. Was Sebastian finally recognizing he needed her?

But no...she felt a spasm sweep through him, a remnant of the poison still circulating through him. He craved her blood to ease the pain—that's all it was.

"We should meet the shape shifters at the safe house," he said.

She held out her wrist. "Don't you need this first?"

Sebastian frowned and shook his head. "I can wait," he said and she saw his thoughts and realized he didn't want his friends to know how seriously his health had been compromised.

You didn't tell them the poison was in you as well? Don't you even trust these people?

He was startled that she'd read his mind and used her mental voice but he answered in kind. *It isn't that I don't trust them, but I don't want them to worry about me. As long as you are around the poison won't permanently affect me so it isn't like I'm misleading them.*

No...only lying by omission.

Now he was annoyed. *I do not lie to those I care about.* His eyes darted to the others in the room, who were watching them both carefully. "It is time to leave, Stella."

"I'm still hungry," she told him rebelliously. "And I haven't finished my wine." She took a deep sip and sent the sensation to Sebastian. He licked his lips in unconscious appreciation.

Jonathan and Sharon exchanged looks and Stella could see that they were having a silent conversation as intent as the one she and Sebastian had had. Jonathan looked positively smug as he smiled at his old friend.

"How the mighty have fallen," he murmured under his breath.

Sebastian cast him a dirty look before turning back to Stella. "We will get more for you to eat as soon as possible. Perhaps we can go through a drive-thru on the way. Please, Stella. I don't want to leave Harold and Rebecca alone too long."

More likely he just needed a quick bite. Even so, she pushed the rest of her glass away and stood, not completely steadily. Two glasses of wine on a nearly empty stomach had left her a little tipsy. "Maybe it is time to quit. There is a danger in too much of anything...including the taste of nightwalker wine."

Jonathan moved to Sharon's side and put his arm around her. "We'll get in touch with you as soon as the lab comes up with an antidote."

"You can call me on my cell phone." Sebastian pulled his from his pocket and rattled off the number. Sharon jotted it down as Jonathan stared at him.

"Wow, I never expected you to join the twenty-first century," Jonathan said.

"The influence of present company." He grinned at the phone in his hand. "But they are useful."

Just then it began to ring. Sebastian answered and as he listened his face grew grave. "Harold reports that there is a car tailing them from the airport. He doesn't want to expose the safe house."

"No choice for it then. Have them come here." Jonathan shook his head. "I guess we're going to have to turn this place into a fortress after all."

"I don't want to expose you and the others that way." Sebastian looked at Stella and then his old friends. "We'll leave now and head for the safe house…if we aren't here and they don't know where we've gone, we'll be safe."

"I really think you should stay."

"Harold and Rebecca need the antidote as soon as possible anyway. They should be here and it is too dangerous for them to be with me." He reached out to seize Jonathan's shoulder. "Keep them safe for me."

"What about Stella?" Sharon interjected. "Perhaps she should stay too."

"No." Stella broke in. "I'll go with him. He needs…" She was about to tell them that in the absence of an antidote he needed her blood but decided not to. Sebastian didn't want them to know so she wouldn't be the one to tell them.

"I'm his companion and I should to be with him," she said finally.

Chapter Fourteen

Ten minutes later they were driving down Wilshire again, with Sebastian keeping an eye out for a fast-food place to get something for Stella to eat. As he'd promised, he fully intended to buy her dinner. Trouble was, after midnight the number of open places was pretty small and they were almost to the safe house before Stella spotted a restaurant with an open sign.

"How about that one?" She pointed to the place and its colorful sign—Homer's House of Ribs. "I could go for some barbeque right now."

"Chinese food followed by ribs? Won't that give you indigestion?"

"I'll have you know that I've never had indigestion in my life. Owner of a cast-iron stomach, that's me."

Sebastian shook his head but he turned into the parking lot. "Let's just get it to go though. I don't want us more exposed than we have to be."

Inside, the place was cute and homey, with checkered tablecloths, red vinyl-covered benches and the smoky smell of truly great barbeque. Sebastian's mouth watered even though he knew he couldn't actually taste what he smelled.

I could taste it for you. What would you like – chicken, beef or pork baby back ribs?

He was still trying to get used to her being able to do that, talk to him in his mind…and even more, know what it was he was thinking about. He leaned over. "Baby back ribs sound fine."

Stella stepped up to the counter and smiled at the middle-aged woman behind the cash register. "I'd like an order of ribs to go." She peered at the menu. "With coleslaw, mashed potatoes and gravy, biscuits and a large Diet Coke."

The woman took the order and relayed it back to the kitchen behind her. Then she narrowed her eyes. "Don't I know you? You look familiar."

Stella shook her head. "It's Hollywood. Everyone looks like someone in this town."

"No, it isn't the movies. I'm not much of a movie fan." She continued to stare. Then her eyes glanced down and widened and she pulled a book from under the counter. Sebastian realized it was one of Stella's latest.

The woman opened the book to the inside back cover and snapped her fingers over the picture. "I know what it is. You look just like this picture. Are you Estelle Roberts?"

Stella's jaw dropped but she didn't deny it. "Why, yes. I am Estelle!"

The woman squealed, attracting the attention of the few people in the place. All of a sudden all Sebastian wanted to do was pick up Stella and make a run for it, but it was too late, particularly as the other woman grabbed Stella's hand and shook it.

"I'm Abigail Joseph, one of your biggest fans!" She shouted back to the kitchen. "Jerry, Doug, get out here. This is that vampire author I told you about!"

Immediately they seemed to be surrounded by people from the kitchen and the dining room. Lots of interested faces, smiling at Stella, curious about him. He tried to step into the background but couldn't with so many people around. What a ridiculous situation.

The next thing Sebastian knew the woman had an instant camera out and was pointing it right at Stella.

"Hold still! I've got to add you to my collection!"

Sebastian looked up to see that sure enough, there was a corkboard full of pictures of celebrities on the wall behind the counter. He was trying to make out who was there when there was a flash that momentarily blinded him.

"This is so exciting," Abigail said, shaking the picture after the camera spat it out. "We get movie types all the time in here, but this is the first time an author has come in!"

"Well," Stella smiled, obviously pleased by the attention, "even authors have to eat."

"So who is this?" Sebastian looked up to see that Abigail was staring at him. "One of your cover models?"

Stella laughed. "I'm afraid not. More like inspiration for the hero of my next book."

The big woman eyed Sebastian and nodded slowly. "He's inspirational all right. A real hero type. I'll have to be looking for that next one of yours for certain."

Stella dug her elbow into his side. "Hear that, honey? You're my hero!"

Resisting the urge to roll his eyes, Sebastian pulled out his wallet. "In the meantime, let's get your dinner and go."

Stella continued to exchange pleasantries with the restaurant staff but she didn't protest when he hoisted the bag of take-out and ushered her toward the door. She giggled on the way out.

"That's the first time anyone in a restaurant insisted on taking my picture. Imagine me on the wall, just like some big-name movie talent."

Sebastian's irritation over the incident melted away. Of course it meant a lot to Stella to be recognized that way and he shouldn't begrudge her the attention.

"The truth is, Stella, that you are way more talented than those actor types. They only act out someone else's character while you give life to everyone in your books. Yours is the much harder job."

She smiled and he found himself smiling back. "That could easily be the sweetest thing you've ever said to me. Thank you, Sebastian."

*****

"I can't believe we lost them!" Vanessa fumed in the back seat of the cab. Donald glanced at her in the rearview mirror and held his tongue. He didn't need to upset her any more than she already was.

The driver of the cab they'd appropriated was still in the trunk and at this point still breathing. Donald's ambition was to make certain the man lived past this night, something that might not happen if his maker got too angry.

Vanessa had a habit of taking her aggravation out on others and Donald didn't want to be party to yet another undeserved death. He had problems enough dealing with the ones that had been richly deserved.

"We tracked the shape shifters to the city chief's place," he said. "They must still be there."

"They were there, but Sebastian wasn't. I'd know it if he were. I'd recognize his mental touch even from outside the walls."

Alex spoke up from his place in the corner of the backseat, "Vanessa, we missed dinner and I'm kind of hungry. I don't suppose we could stop for something?"

Donald shook his head. "We shouldn't stop. We need to find out where Sebastian went to."

"We're not going to find him driving around like this," Vanessa grumbled. "We need to sit and think and, besides, I could use some coffee." In the rearview mirror, Donald saw Vanessa smile wickedly at Alex, who preened back at her.

"I didn't miss dinner and you were so delicious. I owe you something to eat." She looked around. "There's an open restaurant right over there. You like ribs? I bet you do. You'd look like a real caveman pulling meat off bones."

Alex slid closer to the female nightwalker and slid an arm around her back, stroking her side with his hand. "Yeah, I love ribs."

Suppressing the urge to roll his eyes at the shenanigans in the backseat, Donald pulled into the restaurant's parking lot. Five minutes later Alex was ordering at the counter while Vanessa wandered around the place with a steaming cup of coffee in her hand.

Donald smelled the overwhelming scent of smoke and roasted meat and once again wished he could eat solid food again. Blood was terrific once you got used to it but he did miss the flavor of barbeque sauce. Even the coleslaw sounded like it would be delicious and he'd never even liked coleslaw before.

With a sigh he found a seat at an empty table and sipped his coffee. Freshly brewed and hot, it was just what he needed. Vanessa had been right about that, it did do them good to stop.

At least he could still have coffee, even though he had to forego cream and sugar. Donald sighed. No sugar...and he had a wicked sweet tooth.

He'd been promised that he could seek a companion as soon as this job was finished...maybe even find one with mental powers strong enough to give him the taste of her food. A woman companion, for certain. But he'd have to wait until after he was free because with Vanessa around he didn't dare look for a woman.

The lady nightwalker wasn't good at getting along with other women...she barely got along with men she wasn't sleeping with. Sometimes she didn't even get along with the men who did share her bed.

She'd certainly never gotten along with him.

A companion of his own... Someone like Stella Robertson, beautiful, sweet-natured and strong mentally. Secretly he envied Sebastian having found the lady first. In fact, he hadn't even told Vanessa he'd met the woman who'd managed to gain the nightwalker prince's mark on that night of the full moon. As far as he knew, Vanessa still didn't know who wore Sebastian's mark.

"Donald, come here."

He kicked back in his chair. "I'm resting."

"I said, *come here*!"

Pushing aside his irritation at her summons, Donald joined Vanessa near the front counter. She stood near a bulletin board bearing a collection of instant pictures pinned in place. When he looked closer he realized many of them were autographed.

Vanessa pointed to one in the middle. "Do you see him?" She could barely control the excitement in her voice.

Donald looked and his heart dropped. It was a picture of Stella holding one of her books, a big smile on her face, but it wasn't the author who had caught the lady nightwalker's attention. Vanessa was pointing at Sebastian, standing in the background, looking blinded by the flash.

Donald leaned over and smelled the fresh emulsion on the print. Couldn't be more than an hour old.

"They were here!" Vanessa said. "And not that long ago. Had to be tonight." She headed for one of the tables in back and from her bag she pulled a map of Los Angeles. It was marked with small red dots at various locations.

"Where did you get that?" he asked.

"From some friends," Vanessa said absently. "You don't need to know who they are."

"People in Jonathan's organization?"

She ignored his question, which pretty much answered it in the affirmative. So she had spies even among those the other nightwalkers trusted. That wasn't good.

"These are the safe houses in the area. We know they were here," she pointed to the mansion they'd tracked the shape shifters to, "and now they were here." With unerring accuracy she indicated the location of the restaurant where they were now.

She examined the map and pointed to the single red dot in the area. "Unless I miss my guess, this is where Sebastian is headed."

"How can you be sure? Maybe they just wanted ribs and Stella knew about this place..."

"I read the woman behind the counter's mind and she was all excited about meeting one of her favorite authors. This was the first time she'd been here." Vanessa shook her head. "This place just happens to be on the way to where they intend to hole up and they spotted it just like we did."

Much as he wanted to, he couldn't argue with her logic. The red dot on the map seemed to mock him as Vanessa continued to stare in triumph.

"We'll go there and make certain he's there then I'll call our allies in town. They will organize the rest."

"We're not going to attack tonight?"

Vanessa laughed nastily. "You are a very young vampire, Donald. If you want to become an old one you will quickly learn that there is a right way to do things and a wrong way. The wrong way is to ever do anything when your opponent has an advantage. The right way is to always pick a time when they are most vulnerable."

"You mean after dawn? But we are vulnerable then too."

"We're vulnerable only if someone is out to get us, Donald, and at this time that isn't the case." She grinned at him. "We're the hunters, not the prey, and so we get to pick when and where to attack and the time will be tomorrow morning."

Chapter Fifteen

ಬ

There was no code box or gate blocking the driveway into the house on the hill and Sebastian drove up to the house without meeting any obstacles. Stella looked at the modest place in surprise. For once it wasn't a mansion but a normal home, even if there did seem to be a remarkable amount of lightproofing on the garage as they drove inside.

"This is meant to be a low-profile residence," he explained as he helped her out of the car and grabbed their suitcases from the trunk. "Not every nightwalker place can be elaborate or they would stand out. There are a few items they all have in common though."

He headed for the front door as Stella carried the bag of take-out. There was an alarm system on the front door, but Sebastian entered another code before ushering her through.

Leaving her food in the kitchen, Stella followed as Sebastian took her on a tour of the place, which was furnished in a style that seemed intended not to stand out. Sebastian pointed to the various features of the place that weren't standard *Better Homes and Gardens* furnishings.

"In this place, like all nightwalker homes, the windows are either blocked off or covered in lightproof shutters or curtains. In this place they are manual."

"As opposed to the ones at your home that close when they detect sunlight."

"Those are more expensive and harder to maintain, and you need backup batteries in case of a power failure." He grinned at her, revealing his narrow fangs. "We can remember to close the curtains before going to bed."

He headed off down the hall and she paused in his wake. For the first time Stella thought about going to bed and what that would mean. Did Sebastian want her to sleep with him? Did he even want to make love to her again?

He stopped at the end of the hall near the end door. "Don't you want to see the bedroom?" Sebastian said the words very softly but with great deliberateness, and suddenly Stella knew the answer to her question. He did very much want to have her in bed with him.

Slowly she moved down the hall toward him but stopped just short of where he stood. His eyes fairly glowed in the dim hallway. *Yes, I do want you, my sweet little star. Please come with me to the bedroom.*

She wasn't quite ready to go to bed yet. "I've still got dinner waiting for me," she said, although she wasn't nearly as hungry now as she had been earlier. Not hungry for food, anyway.

Sebastian shrugged and gave a low chuckle. "Never let it be said I left a woman unsatisfied—for food or anything else. We can see the bedroom later."

He ushered her back to the kitchen, where again the smell of hot meat and spice-laden tomato sauce assailed her nostrils. Sebastian found a plate and utensils for her in one of the cabinets and put them on the breakfast bar. Sitting on a stool, she opened the containers and dished out the contents.

From the refrigerator, Sebastian pulled a small plastic bag of yellow fluid and, using his teeth, tore a small hole before emptying it into a glass. He also found a bottle of good domestic beer, which he opened for her and poured into a mug.

Without preamble Stella grabbed a rib and began tearing the meat off, smoky-tart red sauce filling her mouth. She couldn't help a small moan of satisfaction. "Oh these are so good," she murmured around a mouthful before washing it down with a slug of beer.

Sebastian shook his head and grabbed some paper towels off the roll, handing them to her. "I've never quite understood the reasoning behind eating the meat off the bones that way. It's incredibly messy." He reached over with one of the towels. "You have sauce on the end of your nose."

Stella snatched the towel from his hand and dabbed at her face. "You would have to try it to understand. Eating with your fingers is fun."

An odd look crossed his face. Curiosity, interest? Did he really want to know why she enjoyed the experience of eating ribs?

Apparently so. *Very well, little star. Show me what you mean.*

Stella opened her mind and reached out with it, seeing the silver of his thoughts open and waiting for her. It was their easiest linking yet outside of when they were engaged in sex and it suddenly felt very natural to have her mind linked with his. When the link was fully in place Stella took a small bite of the tender meat and tore it off the bone, sending not only the flavor but the sensation of tearing the meat to Sebastian. She felt his mind jerk at the primal nature of the act just before he too moaned at the rich flavor of the sauce.

After chewing slowly she washed her mouthful down with beer and by then Sebastian was grinning at her. "So primitive! It is a way for civilized man to pretend to be a caveman, right?" He laughed. "How absolutely marvelous!"

"Rather like biting someone and taking their blood—isn't that primitive?"

He stopped laughing then nodded with a grin. "In a way it is. It is so basic to what we are…to what I am, that I hadn't really thought of it that way. I take blood from normal humans because I must. It's the only way for me to live…"

"Unless you found a bloodmate like your friends did."

Now Sebastian's grin faded back to a wary smile. "Sharon told you what she was."

"And about Daniel and Natasha." Stella picked up her beer and considered the amber fluid without drinking. "I've learned many things since becoming your companion, Sebastian. I was told since I could share tastes with you, I might be a good candidate for becoming your bloodmate."

He leaned his long frame against the counter next to her. "The thought of you becoming my bloodmate is not a stranger to me, Stella. I've thought of it many times in the past month…and in the last couple of days. That I haven't told you about it doesn't mean it has not been on my mind."

"So why wouldn't you tell me? Why did I have to find out from others what I could be to you?"

He hesitated. "All of this has been so sudden, Stella. You came into my life without warning…"

It was that same tired argument and she was weary to death of it. "You came into mine first," she interrupted him. "And believe me, what you did to me, the way you changed my life, far exceeded what I did to yours." She took a deep breath. "I didn't know anything about what I was or that your people existed, and you in one night turned everything I thought I knew upside down. You proved to me that those odd times I thought I knew someone's thoughts were real. And then there was what happened between us in bed…"

Her voice trailed off. "That was more than sex, Sebastian. When we came together it was like a grand plan was finally under way. We were meant to be together. You know that even if you aren't willing to admit it."

He was silent a while, his mind a silver wall she couldn't penetrate. "One of the luxuries of having so many years behind me is that I've experienced so many things. I've known joy and hate, war and peace, and love…oh yes, I've known love." There was bitterness in his laugh that nearly broke her heart. "You write stories about lovers, Stella. You should know this one."

Not certain she wanted to hear, Stella listened anyway.

"I once loved a woman beyond all reason, enough to change my entire life for her... I thought we would live together forever, as that's how long we had on this earth. There was only one problem. She did not love me—or a least not quite enough to stay."

"She left you?"

"In a way. She died. On purpose, leaving me to face the centuries without her."

The ribs she'd eaten suddenly rested uneasily in her stomach. "You mean she committed suicide?" Stella asked in horror.

"You sound surprised. We don't die under normal circumstances, so my kind does that when life becomes too much of a burden. When we are no longer pleased by the duration of time we spend alive and when each sunset becomes something to dread and all we wish is to sleep and never wake up."

"I can't see you doing that, Sebastian."

"No, I would not, at least not now. But I understand why others might."

"Like this woman you are talking about? The one you loved?"

There was world of hurt in his expression. "She is much harder to understand, little star. You see, she had her own reasons for dying and they were very hard for me to accept. The reason my maker took her life was that she had no one to love. And yet there I was with her, loving her. I would have hoped she could have seen what I gave her was enough—but it wasn't. It isn't enough to love someone...they must also love you back. Without that, you have nothing."

He pushed away from the table. "I'll leave you to the rest of your dinner. I'm feeling the need for a shower right now."

Stella considered the beer in her glass for a moment. "Sebastian."

He paused in the doorway. "What is it?"

"I'm sorry you lost the woman you loved."

He stood very still. "It was a very long time ago."

"Not long enough apparently. I wonder if there will ever be enough time for you to forgive her."

"Forgive her?"

"For not falling in love you."

His eyes flashed but then another look crossed his face and she realized she'd hurt him and that made her feel worse than ever. He turned and headed for the back of the house and a few moments later she heard water running.

She'd hurt Sebastian. The tin man had a heart after all? He'd hidden it from her, made it difficult for her to see him as a man with an emotional center...someone who needed a lover, but it was there anyway. He desperately needed someone to love him, to make him whole.

If she couldn't do it then who would?

The ribs no longer held the appeal they'd had. Stella bundled them up and put them into the refrigerator. With everything else topsy-turvy in her life, why not have ribs for breakfast—which wasn't really breakfast but a meal she ate in the morning before heading for bed.

Heading for bed...alone...

All of a sudden Stella didn't want to go to bed alone. Not tonight...not if other possibilities still existed.

She followed the shower noise to the bedroom and through that to the master bathroom. As she moved through the bedroom she noticed that both of their bags, hers and his, had been left on the otherwise empty top of the dresser. He hadn't moved her bag to the spare bedroom. Apparently there was still some chance she could mend things between them.

Good thing she was good at rewriting...she needed some serious editing to make this situation work.

Stella started by removing her clothes before entering the bathroom. He'd closed the door and the room was steamy as she slipped inside, dressed only in her underwear.

In the shower Sebastian turned, staring at her through the clear glass door. Stella stood firm although inside she quaked with uncertainty.

"Want some company?" she said.

In her mind came his answer. *The shower is big enough…if you are willing to put up with my presence.*

Well, I do need to get clean and I want to be sure you don't use all the hot water.

He actually laughed and she felt it deep inside her. It was an honest laugh…and one that seemed slightly relieved.

I have heard we should conserve water. Shower with a friend, they say.

Or a lover, Stella responded.

Through the glass she saw his expression clear, even as she saw the acceptance in his mind.

If you can still see me that way come to me, little star.

Stella left her underwear on the countertop next to the sink and opened the shower door. The moment she did his hand reached out and pulled her inside and immediately she was surrounded by steam, followed closely by Sebastian's arms. He held her so tight she felt like she might break.

"I need you," he whispered into her hair, already becoming soaked under the shower's spray. He kissed the back of her neck, pulling her into his chest. "Don't leave me, Stella."

"I know you need my blood."

He crashed one fist against the wall, cracking the tile. If he hadn't a death grip on her she would have jumped away but that was impossible.

"No! Not just that! I need *you*, Stella. I need…your comfort. Your wisdom. I need you with me."

For tonight, she knew. It was just for tonight, or for the time being. Not forever because she was certain he didn't want that. But for tonight and the time being she could make the promise he needed. She'd leave it up to him when their relationship would end.

"I promise, Sebastian. For however long you want me, I'll love you."

His eyes flashed molten silver and his mouth descended onto hers in a kiss that was almost punishing in its intensity. She moaned and opened to him and his tongue swept in, taking possession as easily as he pulled her into him.

Warm as the spray was, their bodies seemed hotter, until she could almost believe that the water superheating on their bodies generated the steam in the enclosure.

Stella closed her eyes and gave herself up to the experience of having a hot male nightwalker making love to her in a shower. He pressed her hard against the tile, lifting her to bury his face between her breasts, taking deep breaths as if filling his lungs with her scent.

In her mind his voice came through loud and clear. *I do love your smell, my star. It makes me feel so alive.*

But you are alive, Sebastian. And you are my lover.

Of that, have no doubt!

His mouth covered the nipple on one breast, his hand fingering the other, the twin motions leaving her breathless and wanting. *Yes, Sebastian!*

I love it when you say that.

Still holding her up, he turned so her back was to the shower spray and he wedged himself into the corner. She felt his cock hard and ready against her. "I know I should wait until we're out of here," he said into her ear. "But somehow I just can't bear to wait."

And so he didn't. Sebastian lifted her higher, his hands cupping her bottom, and plunged into her at full force. It might have been painful if she hadn't been so ready for him, his cock filling her even more than before.

He knew just how turned on she was, just how much he could do to her without causing her harm. It was strange to have someone that in tune with her.

Strange and exciting at the same time.

She wrapped her arms around his neck and braced her feet against the tile. Using her legs, she rose off his cock and then back down on it again. Sebastian groaned his approval and leaned back, letting her set the pace.

That too was exciting, that he allowed her to make love with him, giving her control. Stella reveled in the realization that he was now treating her as an equal partner in their lovemaking at least.

She moved until she felt him stiffen. She also felt the hunger in him and noticed how he bit down on his lip, not wanting to bite her. But why would he do that? Didn't he need her blood?

Or was it just that he wanted her to feel like she was completely in charge this time? Whatever it was, she didn't want him biting himself when he could be biting her.

She caressed his face with one hand, gaining his attention. *Take what you need, my love. Drink from me.*

His eyes flared silver and hot and then he tilted his head and bit down on her neck. The pain was miniscule, incidental to how satisfying it felt to give him what he needed, to be such a source of satisfaction to him. No one else could do this for him.

She could so get used to that...being what this man needed.

All too quickly he groaned and she felt as much in his body as his mind how close he was to orgasm. She too was close. All she needed was to close her eyes...

Come with me, my star. Join minds with me.

She did and then there wasn't just her or him but the two of them combined and the rising tide of their mutual climaxes, orgasms hot and immediate. Stella screamed something…maybe Sebastian's name, she couldn't tell. He didn't seem all that certain of what he was saying either but in her mind she felt such acceptance that she could barely believe it.

He did want her in his life, and that was the thought that pushed her over the edge and into an orgasm so intense she barely recognized her name when she heard him whispering it over and over in her ear minutes later.

Her name she had problems with but one thing was completely clear. "Sebastian," she murmured back at him.

"What is it?"

"We've run out of hot water. The shower is cold."

With a chuckle, he pushed away from the corner and turned so that it was his back being drenched in icy water and not hers. "Never let it be said I didn't protect you, my companion." Reaching behind, he turned the knobs until the water stopped. "No need for a cold shower for either of us."

Later she lay in bed with him, dried and warm between the sheets. She nestled into the crook of his arm. The clock showed a few hours until dawn but even so he didn't leave the bed. Apparently he wanted to be in bed with her even though he wasn't tired the way she was.

Stella yawned, only belatedly remembering to cover her mouth with her hand. "Excuse me," she said.

He smiled at her. "The intimacy of being able to forget proper manners. I don't mind watching you yawn."

"Watching me yawn? How about sleep? I really need to get some."

"I don't mind that either. What about you? Do you mind sharing my bed?"

"I didn't before. In the van."

"But I didn't know then. And you didn't have much choice. What about now? You will likely wake when I'm in my daytime state."

"I know, Sebastian. I've seen you like that. Barely breathing, very quiet and still."

He caressed her arm some more. "You meant what you said. About loving me for as long as I want you."

"Yes."

"What if what I want doesn't meet with your expectations?"

Stella didn't want to think anymore. "I guess we'll deal with that when we come to it, Sebastian."

"How is your book coming?"

Her book? Since when was Sebastian interested in that? "I'm doing all right. Pretty much done with the research on it."

"Oh," he said, and she thought she detected a little disappointment in her answer. "I thought it would take longer."

"I'm pretty good. It doesn't take me long to get what I want."

He laughed but it sounded almost sad. She yawned again and snuggled into his side. "I'm sorry, Sebastian, but it has been a long day and I'm really tired."

He kissed her forehead. "Go to sleep, Stella."

For a long time he watched her sleep. His companion…his first one, and probably his last. It would break his heart when she left.

For her own good he shouldn't keep her longer than necessary. Once her research was done and he didn't need her blood anymore he would have to let her go.

He should be pleased that she'd agreed to stay this long and love him the way she did. But he wasn't pleased and he didn't want her to stop loving him. Not when he was coming to realize how much *he* loved *her*.

She'd asked if he could ever forgive the Countess for not loving him. The answer was that maybe he could…if he could somehow gain Stella in exchange.

Not that he'd tell her that yet.

Once he'd given a woman that kind of power over him and it had nearly destroyed him. He wouldn't do it again until he was certain of her, and that she would stay with him.

Stella sighed in her sleep and smiled as he put his arm around her and hugged her closer. There were a couple of hours left before dawn but he didn't mind just lying there for a while. He had his lover to keep him company.

Chapter Sixteen

With a jerk, Stella woke up and at first didn't know where she was. Two days of barely any sleep, trying to doze in a car, and a different bedroom every night...she might as well be back on her book tour.

But then she recognized the room in the safe house and the bed, and more important the man lying next to her, Sebastian. She looked at the clock—just about six-thirty. Her nightwalker was sound asleep, his breathing nearly stopped, an inert mass. If she hadn't known better she might have actually thought he was dead.

But she did know better. Nightwalker sleep was a near hibernation-like state, using less oxygen, a sluggish heartbeat and almost no digestion, slowing down the body's need for fuel. Like this a nightwalker could exist almost indefinitely. They all went into this state when the sun was up, the better to survive.

But she didn't need to be asleep right now. She'd napped so much the evening before she was hardly tired and staying in bed held little appeal.

She pulled herself to her feet and dressed in fresh clothes from her bag. It felt good to have something on that she hadn't been wearing for two days and after brushing her hair and teeth she began to feel relatively human.

She wasn't particularly hungry yet, and to her dismay she couldn't find any coffee in the house. Maybe she could get someone to buy her some later. There was a television in the living room but it was her computer that beckoned to her. She hadn't worked on her book in a couple of days and she missed the writing. In particular she missed the control she had when writing a book.

All this adventure without end was getting to her.

She set up the laptop on the kitchen breakfast bar and grabbed a stool. Maybe she could use the phone to connect to the internet and download her email.

When the screen cleared and showed her desktop there was a pop-up window with a message, "Would you like to join wireless network T-REX?"

Stella grinned. One of the neighbors was running a WI-FI router and hadn't password protected it. She clicked "yes", and sure enough got four bars in her network icon. She rubbed her hands in glee and got down to business.

The first was checking email, and sure enough a bunch of messages downloaded to her inbox. Two were from her editor, three from her agent, so she looked at those first. Both of them wanted to know more about this next new book she was writing and when it would be done.

When she knew how it was going to end was the answer but she typed a nominal response, giving her a month's time to come up with a better one. As far as her editor and agent were aware she always knew how her stories were going to end and to admit she didn't have a clue about this one was likely to throw both industry professionals into shock.

Once that mail was done she looked through the rest, dismissing most of it into her junk folder. She was down to one message without a subject header and was about to file it the same when she noticed the sender was nightwatch@eoel.com, the same "Friend" who'd emailed her the day before.

Heart pounding, she opened it. Again, it was a warning.

"Get yourself and your friend out of the house. They know you are there," it said, then listed the name of the street outside the house as if to prove the sender did know exactly where she was. "The attack will be during the day."

The warning had been posted around five-thirty, close enough to dawn to make Stella wonder if the sender was a nightwalker. If so, it must have been posted just before he or she had gone to bed. But she didn't have time to debate the issue.

Grabbing her phone, she ran to the front window and dialed the shape shifters' number. "Hello?" a weary-sounding Harold answered the phone.

Stella quickly filled him in and the sleepiness vanished from his voice. He gave a curse that seemed at odds from his ever-proper butler persona. "Damn his stubborn pride! Sebastian should have taken some bodyguards with him. I'll have someone there as soon as possible but in the meantime see if you can find a place to hide Sebastian and then get out of the house yourself. No reason to risk your life."

Stella ran back to the bedroom and stared at the two-hundred-pound inert male lying on the bed. She tried shaking him, but he was completely unconscious.

Hide Sebastian? How was she supposed to do that? It wasn't like she could throw a bedspread over him and pretend he was a pillow. There was no way she was going to be able to carry him, and dragging him over the carpet would only give him a rug burn without moving him very far. Even if she were able to somehow move him from the bed, where was she going to hide him?

If she could get him to the car she could drive away, but she couldn't possibly drag him that far or lift him into the trunk, and he'd burn from the sun in the backseat under the heaviest blanket they had. It sounded impossible.

Too bad there wasn't a large trunk or cabinet, or even drawers under the bed...

On the other hand... Stella looked at the bottom of the bed. It was a platform bed made of wood, solid on all sides, and when she lifted the mattress at one corner she noticed that a plywood board to support the mattress topped the frame's sides. If it was made in two sections, which given the width of the king-sized bed seemed likely, then she might be able to lift one section out and roll Sebastian into the space underneath.

What she needed was a lever to lift the mattress and slide it out of the way. Stella ran back to the kitchen and opened the tall closet, pulling out a broom and a mop. She stuck them under the mattress on the side farthest from Sebastian and used towels to cushion them against the bed frame. No point in leaving marks that would clue someone in to what she'd done.

Pushing and shoving with all her strength, she managed to get the mattress onto the poles and nearly halfway off the bed. As she had hoped, the wood under the bed was in two sections.

When she tugged on the section she'd uncovered it slid up to reveal a cavity easily big enough to accommodate the sleeping nightwalker. She worried a little about how little air would be inside, but then he didn't breathe much when asleep. He should be fine.

Rolling him into the space was easier than she'd thought it would be. Stella winced as his naked body hit the floor but the wall-to-wall carpet seemed soft enough. She grabbed one of the many pillows off the bed and stuck it under his head, then tucked an extra blanket from the linen closet around him. Her eye fell on his bag… She could take it with her but she had her own stuff to carry, so she stuck it at his feet. When she was done he was all tucked in, almost cozy, she decided.

Even so, she cringed when she pushed the wooden platform back into place. It really did have the feel of sealing him into a crypt. But this was to keep him alive. She pushed the mattress back into place and once the bed was made there wasn't the slightest hint of Sebastian in the room at all. She threw the towels into the bathroom laundry basket and put the mop and broom away. All seemed in order.

Now to make her own escape. Carrying her laptop case and overnight bag, Stella was halfway into the garage with the keys to the Mercedes when she heard a car pull up in the driveway outside. Several car doors opened and closed and there was the sound of feet scuffling on the front porch. A peek out though the door's peephole revealed several men, none of whom she recognized. For a moment she hoped they were the bodyguards Harold had promised, but when she reached out with her mind several of the men had thoughts of finding and destroying the vampire they'd been told was in the house.

Nothing to do now but run! Stella took off out the back door of the house only to find two men climbing over the side gate. She ran but they caught her before she got to the back fence, one holding a cloth across her nose and mouth that smelled sweet. The world went fuzzy and then dark.

* * * * *

A damp washcloth on Stella's forehead roused her and when she opened her eyes, she was back in the house, lying on the living room couch. The men from the front porch were running throughout the house, opening closets and cabinets, obviously searching for something—or someone. From the back of the house she heard similar sounds and hoped that no one would think of checking the inside of the bed frame.

Given that they were still searching, she knew they hadn't thought of it yet.

Stella pulled the cloth off her face and used it to wipe the residual chemical they'd used to subdue her away from around her mouth and nose. Immediately she felt better, which was good. She needed her wits about her now.

An extremely tall man with shoulders the size of a football player's and a shiny bald head seemed to be directing the others. Funny how on some people a naked pate looked elegant, like Harold's did, but on this man it just made him look mean.

He noticed she'd regained her senses and came over, towering over her with a face full of anger. "Where is he?" he said menacingly.

Stella decided innocence would be the best game to play. "Where is who?"

"The vampire you were with. Where has he gone?"

Stella crinkled her nose and looked at the man like she thought he was crazy. "*Vampire?* Is this a joke?"

"No it's not a joke. There was a vampire here with you last night."

"There was a *man* with me," Stella said, a plan forming in her head. "He left just before dawn…went to get coffee and donuts, he said. I fell asleep for a while but he hadn't come back when I woke up." She put a look of disgust on her face. "I guess once he got what he wanted he didn't feel the need stick to around for breakfast."

"Got what he wanted…you mean you had sex with him?" Baldie, as she'd decided to call him, looked horrified.

She forced her mouth into a rueful smile. "Not that it's any of your business."

"Why would you do that?"

"I met him in a bar last night and we got to talking. Had a lot in common, it seemed at the time." She shook her head. "I probably did have a little more to drink than I should have and, well, he was pretty gorgeous and seemed like a gentleman."

She made a noise that she hoped sounded like a suppressed sob. "Serves me right for believing it meant something to him."

"You met a guy in a bar and came with him here to have sex. Why this place? Is it yours or his?"

Stella shook her head. "He said it belonged to some friends of his who were on vacation and that they'd lent him the key. It was cheaper than a hotel. Since he hasn't come back

I was just about to leave myself when you folks broke in." She opened her eyes wide. "You don't suppose he did the same thing, do you, and that it doesn't belong to friends? Oh man, I could get arrested for breaking and entering." She tried to make it sound like that was the worse thing that could happen to her.

One of the other men came into the room. "No sign of him, boss. The towels in the bathroom are wet and the bed was used..." He glanced over at her and Stella's blush didn't need to be faked. "But there isn't anyone else around. She's the only one here."

The big guy turned his attention on her. "So you were here with some guy who told you he had permission to use the house and he took off and then you were about to leave. Why'd you run out through the backyard?"

"Are you kidding? The way you were coming into the house like an invading army? You scared me." She looked around and shrank back into the couch cushions to show she was still frightened. It wasn't nearly as hard to pretend as she'd thought it would be.

The fear in her face must have been convincing and the big guy put up a consoling hand. "Don't worry. We aren't after you. All we want to do is talk and if what you're saying is true you can leave."

"Why should I talk to you? Are you with the police?"

A look of disgust came over the man's face. "No. The local police don't work with us most of the time. They say we're nuts because we believe that vampires and werewolves exist. I think they get bought off and that's why they don't investigate, even when we bring them proof."

"So if you aren't with the police?" she prompted. "Who are you?" She tried pushing on his mind, and to her surprise it worked. He opened up to her and she read his mind even before he began to speak.

"We're with the Paranormal Watchers Society and we're dedicated to protecting normal humans from these supernatural freaks of nature…with or without the authorities' help."

Stella considered planting in his mind that they had no business breaking in here or questioning her but decided instead to simply play along. If she knew Harold, there was a rescue party of parafolk well on the way and the longer she could keep these folks busy the more likely it was they'd arrive before anyone could get hurt—including her.

She tried placing in Baldie's mind that she was a poor innocent victim of a one-night stand and that the big bad love-them-and-leave-them man she'd slept with had run out on her early this morning. Even if they believed he was a vampire, they'd think he had gone someplace else to sleep and wouldn't look for him here.

Another man came in. "There's a Mercedes convertible in the garage. A real nice one."

The big man picked up a set of car keys off the coffee table and tossed them to him. "Check it out. Maybe the vampire is in the trunk."

Stella recognized them as the ones she'd had in her pocket. She checked and sure enough the rest of her stuff was on the table as well.

"You searched me?" She put all the outrage she was feeling into the question.

"We had to make sure you weren't carrying a weapon. Or anything else." He nodded at her neck. "Also wanted to be sure you weren't one of their companions."

"A companion? What's that?"

"A human who has sold his or her soul to the devils. They have marks on their necks." He pointed to his own neck with two fingers. "Fang marks."

Stella touched her own unblemished skin and said a quick thank you that Sebastian had marked her in a less obvious spot. "If the man I was with was a vampire, wouldn't he have left marks?"

"Not necessarily. They've got some spooky talents, like being able to erase the wounds they make. Did this guy bite you at all?"

"Not that I can remember." He looked at her skeptically and she shrugged. "I told you, I'd had a little bit too much to drink."

"What did he look like?"

"Tall, blond. Really good-looking."

"Yeah, they usually are. It sounds like the one we're looking for."

"Really?" She opened her eyes wide and wondered where the cavalry was. It must be over half an hour since she'd called Harold and traffic couldn't be that bad this early in the morning.

"Listen," she told him. "I'm telling you the guy you're looking for took off before dawn. If he's a vampire he's probably hiding out in a cemetery or coffin store or something. I know you don't want to get in trouble with the police, and the way you folks barged in here, one of the neighbors might have called 911 already."

She leaned over the coffee table. "Assaulting me like you did and keeping me prisoner could get you into a lot of trouble. Why don't we all admit to making a mistake, me by going home with a strange guy and you by coming here, and we'll just go our separate ways?"

The man he'd given the car keys to returned. "Nothing in the car, but I found this." He handed her interrogator a small piece of paper and with sudden worry Stella recognized it as the registration of the car. If they knew who owned the car…

The big guy's gaze suddenly turned intense. "You said this was your car?"

"Actually it isn't really mine. I borrowed it from a friend up in Santa Barbara."

He held up the registration. "You have interesting friends. This car is registered to a company we know is a front for the parafreaks."

"Oh? Wow." Again she tried pushing her innocence into his mind but this time he wasn't buying the idea.

"Yeah. Wow. Quite a coincidence. You have a car registered to the parafreaks and got caught running from a house owned by parafreaks. If it wasn't for the lack of marks..." A sudden gleam went through his eyes. "Maybe I should give you another little look, like under that blouse."

Oh no. "You are not going to touch me!"

Stella screamed and got up to run but at their leader's curt "hold her" two of the bigger men grabbed her arms and held her still while the big man unbuttoned her blouse and shoved it off her shoulder. The twin scars on her upper shoulder revealed, he snarled at her, then backhanded her and sent her crashing back onto the couch, her head reeling.

"She's a companion. Search this place again!" he yelled. "Tear it apart if necessary!"

Stella felt sick to her stomach, from more than the blow to her head. *She'd failed and they would find him now.* She was barely conscious when someone called from the front porch. "Boss, the lookout down the street just called. A big black van like the ones they use just turned the corner and is coming this way fast. We should get out of here."

"Not without the vampire," the leader said.

"We haven't found him and have no proof he's even here now." The other man pointed to Stella. "Let's take her with us. If she really is his companion he'll come after her. We can set a trap."

"Bait for a trap. That's a good idea. George, you take her. Someone else get her stuff." In moments Stella was thrown over someone's shoulder and was outside. Like so much meat, they tossed her into the back of their van, her bags tossed carelessly in afterward. Stella cringed as she imagined the beating her poor laptop was taking and hoped the case would protect it. On the other hand, given the situation, she could use some protection herself.

They pulled out of the driveway and drove away at high speed, but not so fast that they'd probably attract a police car. They also didn't seem to be worried about pursuit, so Stella knew that the black van must not be following them.

She tried to rise but one of the men held the same cloth to her nose as before and then she felt a needle slide into her thigh. The world twisted, turned and went black, and this time when she closed her eyes they stayed closed.

Chapter Seventeen

Sebastian opened his eyes and confusion filled him. The world around him was close and black. He was lying naked in a box...a wooden box with a padded surface below, a pillow under his head and he was wrapped in a blanket. The box was small...too small. He gasped, opening his mouth to take in more air, and there wasn't any.

Wooden walls and a ceiling—someone had stuck him in a casket! The claustrophobia that had plagued him since childhood attacked and a cry tore from his throat. He pounded on the wooden ceiling and it bounced upward, revealing a lighted area above, but fell back into place, obviously weighted down. Encouraged at the brief taste of fresh air, he shoved harder and it flew off with a crashing noise. The lid lifted off, he could see he was lying on the floor. The weight had been a mattress, the wooden box he was in the base of a bed.

Sitting up, he saw the bedroom he'd fallen asleep in last night, but then he'd been on top of the bed, not inside it. A chuckle caught his attention and he turned to see Harold sitting on a chair, trying hard not to give into full-fledged laughter.

"You should see your face, my prince," he said. "I don't think I've ever seen you so terrified. Given the circumstances you really should get over this fear you have of small places."

Wrapping the blanket around himself, Sebastian reassembled his shattered dignity and stood up. He glared at the disassembled bed around him, the mattress balanced against the opposite edge, pillows and sheets scattered everywhere. The crash had been the bedside lamp falling over, the lampshade askew. Harold walked over and picked it up out of the way then went to Sebastian and helped him out of the platform.

"Here." Harold handed a small vial to Sebastian. "Drink this."

"What is it?" he started to ask but then realized what it must be. "The antidote?"

"Yes and it works fine, at least on shape shifters. They tell me it should be even more effective on you, but we had to wait until you were awake to give it to you."

"That's why you left me inside the bed?"

"I didn't see any reason to move you. You were safe in there."

"Besides, you wanted me to wake up where I was."

"I have to admit it crossed my mind. I thought it would do you good."

"Being ill hasn't cost you your sense of humor. I think I'm happy you are better. And your lady?"

Harold's smile broadened. "Even with her pregnancy it worked on Rebecca. She spent much of the morning eating everything in sight...although I have to admit she's developed a strange fondness for vegetarian lasagna." He hesitated. "We'll have to see about our cub, but so far she seems all right."

Sebastian caught the gender-specific pronoun. "She? You're having a little girl?" It would be fun to have a baby girl shape shifter around. He felt almost as proud as a grandfather.

Harold shrugged. "We were going to wait to find out, but with this it seemed prudent to do as many tests as possible. Now we know what color to paint the nursery."

"That's one good thing at least." Sebastian sipped from the vial and made a face. It was nasty stuff, but as it slid down his throat he could feel the warmth spreading and in moments the lingering malaise that had plagued him for the last couple of days released its hold on his arms and legs.

He wouldn't need any more of Stella's blood to keep the illness at bay…but that didn't mean he didn't need Stella. Speaking of whom.

"So would you like to tell me what I was doing in the bed and what the hell is going on?"

Harold shook his head and gave a heartfelt sigh. "Not really. You aren't going to like it and will just yell at me."

Sebastian closed his eyes and counted slowly to ten, first in French, then German and finally English. Most of the time Harold was the perfect butler, but when he was in this kind of a mood it only meant one thing…that there was trouble and a lot of it. Even the normally calm and collected shape shifter was perturbed and that just didn't happen too often.

"What happened here?"

"The Watchers broke in this morning. Someone emailed Stella again to warn her and she was able to call us before it happened. I told her to hide you and get out of here and sent troops over at once."

"She hid me in the bed?" Sebastian broke into a grin. "Clever!" He looked around and noticed his bag in the base of the bed. "She even left me my clothes."

Grabbing the bag, he headed for the bathroom. "So where is she?"

"Well, that's the problem. They were gone when we arrived and we thought she'd gotten away. None of her stuff was here. But then the car was here and when we searched the neighborhood with a couple other psis there was no sign of her. Then this showed up in the mailbox."

He handed Sebastian a note. Written on a torn sheet of cheap printer paper it read, "The vampire should come to St. John's Church tonight at nine, alone, or you'll never see her again." A lock of Stella's distinctive red hair was taped to the paper. Sebastian sniffed it and caught her scent, plus the scent of chloroform. For the first time in centuries he felt anger build to the point of a murderous fury and all he wanted was to put his hands around someone's neck, preferably the person who'd dared to touch his little star's hair.

"You were right, Harold," he said softly, but there was more than a bit of a snarl in his words. "I really don't like it."

*****

Stella stared at her butchered hair in the mirror and felt like strangling someone. Did they have to have taken it from the front? When she got her hands on the moron with the trigger-happy scissors she'd cut something off him a lot more important than his hair.

She bet it was that bald son of a bitch from yesterday. The man probably had it in for anyone who wasn't follicly challenged.

She fingered the three-inch length left on one side and tried pulling it over her forehead. Maybe she could make bangs...or maybe it was time for a whole new hairdo.

Her hairdresser would have a conniption fit over it though, and Mario wasn't someone you wanted mad at you. He'd blame her, she knew it, and how was she going to explain that a madman had cut her hair while kidnapping her from her nightwalker?

The man would simply freak. She didn't want to face him. Maybe someone could do something with it before her next appointment, or perhaps she could just avoid seeing her hairdresser until it grew out.

Stella dropped the hair and pushed back from the mirror. Truthfully her hair was the least of her problems. When she'd woken from her kidnapper-imposed nap she'd found herself in this windowless room with the door locked and unfortunately not a hairpin around to unlock it. Her laptop and bag were missing and she had no idea where she was — other than it was a place she definitely didn't want to be.

Her watch said it was well past dusk, as if the state of her complaining stomach wasn't enough to tell her it had been far too long since she'd eaten. That was one thing about being a companion she'd yet to become comfortable with, the fact that she was hungry most of the time.

Unexpectedly the locked door clicked open, and Stella grabbed the bedside lamp and hid behind the door. She raised it, preparing to use it against whoever came through.

The door opened and Stella tried to throw her makeshift weapon as a figure came through the door.

Faster than she could move, he did, and grabbed the lamp out of her hand. "What are you, suicidal?" a familiar voice asked. He brandished the lamp under her nose. "What would you do if you had brained me? How did you plan to get out of here?"

Stella stared as she recognized who it was and her heart plummeted. Of all the people she might have expected to find allied with the Watchers, Donald Morgan hadn't been on the list.

She stared at the nightwalker who'd once offered loyalty to Sebastian, not even trying to hide her disappointment. "Wow. And here I thought you might be one of the good guys."

Donald's mouth turned downward into a frown. "Don't be so quick to judge whose side I'm on."

"All I know is what I see. You're a parafolk, so what are you doing working with these cretins?"

"At the moment, I'm trying to rescue you. Haven't you ever heard that the best place to watch the enemy is from inside their camp?" He glared at her and she could see in his mind how he really felt about her captors. It was funny in a way, to see his thoughts so clearly that they might have been written on his face.

What she read made her believe him when he said, "I'm not your enemy, Ms. Robertson, and all I want to do is get you to safety. Do you want to get out of here or what?"

"Of course I want to."

"Then come with me."

"Wait a minute. What about my things?"

"Things?" Donald visibly rolled his eyes. "God save me from women and their things. Here." He thrust her handbag at her. "Your other stuff was locked up but I was able to get this."

Stella brightened and grabbed the bag, rummaging around in it for her cell phone. Maybe she could call Sebastian and tell him where she was. It was there, but when she tried to turn it on it registered a dead battery. "Dang it, I knew I should have plugged it in last night."

"Where is the charger?"

"In my laptop case."

"Figures. Unfortunately that's up in the suite with Vanessa. You'll have to do without it." He turned to leave and after a moment's hesitation Stella followed him. He led her down a long unguarded hall and to a stairwell that led upward. She suddenly understood that the lack of windows was more because they were in a basement than for security reasons.

They began climb the stairs, Donald in the lead, listening carefully as he proceeded.

"So where are you taking me?" she asked.

"Someplace safe."

"How do you know what's safe? I was safe before and look what happened."

Donald turned to her and blew out a breath of frustration. "You weren't supposed be in that house when they got there. Don't you ever read your email?"

She stopped. "You're Nightwatch?"

"Who else?" Donald truly looked annoyed. "You mean you got the message and were still there?"

"I didn't get it until it was after dawn and I couldn't leave then. I had to make sure Sebastian was safe first."

"You risked your life to save him? Why?"

Now it was Stella's turn to be annoyed. "I'm his companion, Donald. That's what we do."

Donald stared at her. "I didn't think you were that close to him. It sure didn't look like that in Napa."

"Napa was a while ago."

"Two nights!"

Stella stared at him. "I guess it was only that long ago. So much has changed since then and...the way I feel has too. I couldn't leave him in danger."

He shook his head. "If I ever have a companion, I hope she's got sense enough to run when she should. Not that I'd ever let her get put into danger in the first place."

"No one looks for danger, Donald. But those who hang out with the bad guys often find it."

Turning, he glared at her. "Listen, Stella. This isn't one of your books where you get to pick the bad guys and make them nothing but evil. There's more than one side going on here. I don't go along with what the Watchers advocate. Why would I when I'm one of those they want to destroy? But there are some real problems among the parafolk and there are those who want to solve those."

"You mean like killing off pregnant shape shifters?" Stella taunted him. "Is that part of the plan?"

If she hadn't been so mad she would have been impressed by how deeply the man flushed. "That wasn't supposed to happen," he said awkwardly. "We were only after the male and we didn't know she was pregnant."

Stella poked him in the chest, hard. "That's the dumbest excuse I ever heard. You knew she would be with him that night. Besides, he'd done nothing to hurt you any more than she had, whether or not she was pregnant. Attacking them was just wrong, no other way to look at it."

"We just wanted Sebastian to hear us out, and all he did was dismiss us like spoiled children."

"So you decided to kill his servants? Oh that's mature all right."

"I honestly didn't know that was going to happen. I thought we were going to take them prisoner and make Sebastian listen. Now they've taken you for the same purpose."

"The Watchers took me to trap Sebastian, and I don't think that making him listen is what they have in mind. They want to kill him."

"Vanessa won't let that happen," Donald said, but she didn't think he looked that certain.

"Vanessa wants Sebastian dead, just like she wants Jonathan dead, and anyone else who doesn't approve of her plans for a new parafolk society." Stella was fighting mad now and she let all of her frustrations of the past few days descend on Donald.

"You think you deserve special respect because you're a nightwalker now and you resent the fact that others have positions you don't have the experience or qualifications to fill. But rather than get that experience or find a way to learn how to do your own job better, you make up an excuse to deny them the place they earned."

"We've never been given a chance!"

"From your actions, you haven't earned a chance. You really don't get it, do you? Nightwalkers need the other parafolk. Who will protect them during the day if not the shape shifters and psis?"

"I have nothing against the psis! In fact..."

"I know. You want a companion for yourself some day, someone other than a volunteer to feed you." Stella laughed a little at his startled expression. "You forget I can read your mind pretty easily now. I know you want someone for more than food."

She shook her head. "But, Donald, we need each other to survive and making a deal with those who want nothing more than to destroy all of us makes no sense."

He stared at her a moment and then to her astonishment actually nodded. "I've been more than a little worried about the direction the NorCal nightwalkers were taking. Vanessa isn't all that stable and sometimes the things she does…"

"Like slicing the throat of her own companion?"

Donald gave her a sidelong look that sent chills down her spine. He cleared his throat. "Actually…she didn't do that."

"Oh?" Stella looked at him with sudden suspicion. "Oh…" she said finally when his gaze stayed fixed on her face. There was something oddly calm about him and she knew something else about Donald that she wouldn't have expected.

He could kill if he had to protect someone.

Finally he nodded and let that intense gaze drop. "He was going to kill Sebastian, and you if you got close enough. I couldn't let him do that." He turned to her. "If you tell Vanessa, she'll kill me for certain."

"Like I'd do that," she said.

He took her hand and held it for a long moment, and Stella read much in his face and mind and knew why time after time he'd risked his life to warn her. He was younger than she was, physically, but he was attracted to her anyway…but then again he was a nightwalker now and age had become more than the number of years a person had.

He recognized just how long his life was going to be and even as young as he was he felt those years ahead of him. Already, mentally, he was years older than his physical body, which would never age.

If she weren't committed to Sebastian… Stella saw in his mind his thoughts about her.

But she was committed to the nightwalker prince, and she saw Donald recognize that fact, react to it and then, finally, accept it. He dropped her hand.

Donald's shoulders slumped for a moment then he stood taller, even more determination in his face. "I'm getting you out of here, Stella, because taking you was wrong. What you've said, much of it I've thought myself but didn't dare admit it. I'm not happy about what I've done, particularly with respect to Sebastian's servants. If I could do all this over, I wouldn't have anything to do with Vanessa or her plans, and I'll never go against another parafolk again."

He gave her a very small smile. "You can tell our prince that after I take you to him."

She mused over what he'd said the rest of the way up the stairs. Donald was going against his maker and that was pretty dangerous, she knew. But even more so if Vanessa figured out just how much Donald had betrayed her.

They'd reached a landing marked first floor and there was a painted metal door with a push bar marked "emergency exit only". Donald started to open it when Stella grabbed his arm, remembering what would be left behind.

"Once we leave, we can't get back in?"

"No. This leads to the parking lot. I've got a car waiting there for you."

"But my computer! We have to get it back!"

"Your notes for your next book?" Donald practically sneered and that made her angry. Yes, she was only a "romance novelist" but she had a right to write what she wanted. Even so, there was more at stake than her next novel.

"Actually I was thinking about those emails you sent me. If your maker reads them she'll know I had help and I'll be willing to bet she'll guess you gave it to me."

Now Donald looked worried. "She might not find them... In fact, she might not even figure out how to turn the thing on."

"Or she might be smarter than you are giving her credit for. In any case I think we should get it back."

Donald held up his hands. "Okay, okay. I'll see what I can do. Give me a moment."

He went through the door marked "ground floor" while Stella waited behind nervously. Ten minutes passed and he still hadn't returned, and Stella began to wonder if she shouldn't go ahead and leave without him. Perhaps he'd run into Vanessa or the others and couldn't get away. If so, he wouldn't be able to guide her to safety.

She moved to the door leading out of the building and pushed it open, hoping it wasn't alarmed. It didn't seem to be and she looked out into a dark and empty parking lot. The outside air smelled sweet and inviting. All she'd have to do would be to head out there and find a phone to call Sebastian and she'd be safe.

Even so, she paused before exiting. Could she really leave Donald alone to face their enemies after all he'd done for her? Without his warnings she, Sebastian and the shape shifters would have been captured or worse by now. In particular, she'd been able to save Sebastian's life just this morning. She had no illusions that Baldie and his men wouldn't have staked Sebastian as he slept if she hadn't been able to hide him.

Besides, Donald would be safe right now if she hadn't insisted on his getting her computer. All and all, she owed him.

Even so, walking back into danger wasn't that great an idea, particularly if she ran into anyone who recognized her. But maybe she could find a way around that. She'd seen in Donald's mind that the Watchers were providing volunteers to him and Vanessa so they could feed. Perhaps she could use her mental powers to convince one of the guards that she was Donald's dinner. They would take her to him and she'd be able to help him escape.

Of course the first plan would be to avoid looking like she had when they'd brought her in here. Fortunately Donald had given her back her purse so she had something to work with.

First she took off her sweater, revealing the lightweight tank top she wore underneath. She also tugged off her bra, giving herself an overall appearance of "loose womanhood", exactly the kind of woman she would expect to allow a vampire to bite her. The skimpy top along with her jeans gave her a completely different look, and knowing men they'd be looking more at her cleavage than her face.

But even so, the next step was makeup, just in case someone did look higher than her now-substantial front. Fortunately she carried an emergency supply in her bag. Stella pulled out her makeup and a small mirror and went to work. A heavier-than-usual application of mascara as well as liner, plus some very red lipstick, and she barely recognized herself in the reflection. Finally she piled her hair on her head and covered it with the scarf she'd gotten from Natasha, to cover how red it was. Popping a stick of gum in her mouth, she started chewing to make her voice sound different, and the change was complete.

Stella Robertson the author was now Susie the airhead, walking blood source. All she had to do was convince the first guard she found that she was Donald's designated dinner and she'd be led right to him.

She folded her sweater and stuck it into her bag and eased the door open to the hallway. There was no sign of anyone so she carefully slipped through and headed in the direction she thought Donald had disappeared toward.

Chapter Eighteen

Stella hadn't gone more than twenty feet before she found someone hurrying in her direction. A tall blond man, he stopped and stared as if not quite sure of what he was seeing. Then he grinned.

"Hey, babe. What you doing here?"

Stella decided to try out her excuse, reaching for the man's mind while she did. "I'm Susie...looking for one of the vampires. I'm supposed to be his dinner."

"Dinner?" He snickered and his grin broadened. "Oh yeah, I can get into that. I'm Alex, the companion of Vanessa." He pointed to the barely healed fang marks on his neck and Stella read in his mind how proud he was of them. "I know all about the care and feeding of vampires. You're here for Donald, right?"

"Uh...yeah." Stella found it easier than she expected to be uncertain. "Donald is the one I'm looking for."

With the air of a man with a sudden purpose in life, Alex grabbed her arm. "Look no further, you sweet little thing, just come with me. I'll see you get to him safely."

Alex pulled her past a number of doors and around several groups of men and women who stared after them in barely disguised disgust. One thing about it, being someone attached to one of the Watchers' pet vampires wasn't going to get her any awards for popularity. She wondered if Alex was simply oblivious to them or if he just didn't care what they thought.

As it turned out, it was the latter. "Don't let the stupid norms here get to you, Suzie. These folks wouldn't recognize a good thing if it sat on them." He directed her into an elevator and pushed the button for the penthouse, which she read in his mind was the nightwalkers' location. Of course, Vanessa would live in style even if a basement apartment would make more sense for a vampire.

"A good thing?"

"Yeah." A bemused smile took over his face. "It is really great being with Vanessa, being her main man and all. She's..." His voice trailed off for a moment and Stella got a mind-full of sensual activities that left her cheeks red with embarrassment. Vanessa was an inventive and acrobatic lover...although that one position did look rather interesting...

"She's really something," he said finally.

Yes she was, but not for the reasons he thought. Still, Stella was in no position to give her real thoughts on the matter. "You've been with her long?"

"Just a couple of days, but I know already that she's what I've been looking for in life. Someone special." Alex had that funny off-balance look that she'd always written about but had rarely seen on a man's face. Dang it if the man wasn't more than a little bit in love with the female nightwalker. Well, at least with Donald's confession to the deed Stella knew that Vanessa wasn't responsible for killing her own companion.

Alex might live long enough to know what kind of mistake he'd made—assuming Donald didn't decide to kill him as well. The nightwalker had an odd sense of justice. He was willing to attack the shape shifters when he hadn't realized Rebecca was pregnant but he'd killed his partner rather than let the man hurt her or Sebastian. Add to that the warnings he'd given her and she could almost trust him.

The elevator doors opened and they were on the top floor of the building. Alex directed her to a set of double doors that most likely led to the penthouse suite the nightwalkers were occupying. As Alex fumbled for the card key to open the door, Stella took a moment to take in her surroundings. Through the window at the end of the hallway she saw the evening sky and the partial moon just rising. Too bad it wasn't full, she thought. Then maybe Sebastian could fly to her rescue.

All she could hope was that Donald didn't inadvertently give her away when he saw her. As far as she knew Vanessa had never laid eyes on her, so she wouldn't recognize her.

Alex opened the door and ushered her into a large living room. One wall was taken up with glass and overlooked a huge outdoor patio, beyond which was a glamorous view of the city.

A slender dark-haired woman sat on a couch talking to Baldie, the leader of the group who'd stormed the safe house in the morning. She cringed inwardly, hoping he wouldn't see through her flimsy disguise.

Fortunately he did nothing more than give her a passing glance. It was the woman who stared at her long and hard as a small smile formed on her face. Very small, but Stella saw the tiny tips of her fangs as she drew back her lips. Stella got the distinct feeling she'd been spotted and waited for Vanessa's denouncement, but instead the dark-haired woman turned to Alex. "Is she for Donald?"

"Yep. I found her downstairs and brought her up for him. I figured that was better than letting him go down."

"Very good thinking," she told him and Stella watched Alex preen under her praise. The female nightwalker rose and walked over to her. "Come with me."

She seized Stella's arm and nearly dragged her across the room, her gentility fading away. Vanessa leaned over and whispered in her ear, quiet enough so that the others wouldn't hear.

"This is no time to be shy, Ms. Robertson. You've got a hungry nightwalker to feed after all. He doesn't bite… Well, he does, but not too often."

The door was quickly opened and Stella was shoved through. She was now inside an elegant bedroom, one side of which was a sliding glass door that led to a patio. Very dark window shades had been rolled aside to reveal the outside sky.

Entering behind her, Vanessa closed the door and stood observing Stella with the air of a cat watching a canary, waiting to pounce.

Sitting on the bed with silver handcuffs on his wrists sat Donald, staring morosely out the uncovered glass doors. When she and Vanessa came through the door he turned to them and then groaned aloud. "What are you doing here?"

Stella looked at Vanessa, who clearly knew who she was and shrugged philosophically. "I thought I'd try to rescue you."

Donald stared at her and then at Vanessa and gave a short ironic laugh. "Great job so far!"

Stella just shook her head. "I take it that they were on to you when you got back up here?"

He lifted his bound wrists. "Yeah, you could say that."

Vanessa broke in. "I was on to you for some time, Donald, but I needed proof of how you were doing it." She pulled Stella's laptop case out from under the bed and removed the computer from it. "Once I figured out you were warning her, it was only a matter of figuring out how you were doing it. That was clever of you, using electronic mail to get information to her. I wouldn't have thought of that."

"How did you know?" Donald asked.

"Sebastian eluding me once or twice might be a coincidence, but three times? That's got to be a conspiracy." She opened up Stella's laptop and turned it on. "You've been telling them all along when we were going to strike. You even killed Steve rather than let him attack Sebastian." Vanessa gave a curious look at Stella. "Or was it Ms. Robertson you were trying to protect?"

Stella decided this was a good place to jump in. "So what do you plan to do with us?"

"With him?" She indicated the bound nightwalker. "I've got special plans for Donald. There are some new formulas I've been dying to try out and Donald will make an excellent subject for my experiments. As for you..."

She eyed Stella carefully. "There are a couple of possibilities. For one thing there is that letter you sent to your editor. The one to be opened if you disappeared for any length of time?"

A deep pang of fear crept through Stella. "How did you know about that?"

"I looked on your machine. All sorts of interesting things were on it. If you don't return then a lot of people will be asking questions of Sebastian and the others... That would make the Watchers happy and probably leave me in a better position to do what I wanted."

Stella could see that happening. "So you're thinking of killing me? Just to force that letter to go public?"

"Maybe." The nightwalker woman laughed and it wasn't a pretty sound. "On the other hand, I also read the notes for that new book you've got started. The one about real vampires living today? Maybe I'll just see to it that you get out of this all right on the condition that you finish that book. That would also force people to take notice."

She smiled at Stella. "You see, I win either way. But first we have to find out whether Sebastian cares enough about you to meet us tonight at the church."

"He'll know you're planning a trap."

"Of course. But he's too noble to leave you here with us. Even if you did plan to betray him by publishing a book about us." Vanessa turned to leave. "Now if you'll excuse me, there are still plans to be made." She left the room, leaving Stella with dark thoughts.

Once the door bolted shut, Stella examined the door behind her while Donald watched her. "You were planning a book about the parafolk?"

"I was...but I wasn't sure how it was going to end. I'm not happy with how it was going."

"That's all we need, to get more publicity."

Stella sat back from examining the door and blew out a frustrated breath. "It's bolted on the outside. Not much I can do about it. Still, at least things are a bit better."

"They are? How?"

She threw her bag on the bed and began rummaging around in it again.

Donald watched in clear consternation. "What are you looking for?"

"A hairpin."

Donald rolled his eyes. "Why? Haven't you done enough with your hair?" He shook his head. "That is not a good look on you."

"Very funny." She found the small bag where the rest of her hair accessories were and pulled out one of the pins. She then sat next to him on the bed and grabbed his wrists, raising them higher so she could see. The end of the pin went into the handcuff lock and she jostled it around a little until she heard a satisfying clicking sound and the cuff fell open.

Donald's stare turned into a look of respect. "That's a handy trick."

"Amazing the stuff you learn being a writer," she told him and grabbed his other wrist. "Let me get the other one."

In moments he was free of the cuffs and rubbing his wrists. A nasty rash had broken out on the skin just from exposure to the silver.

Stella slipped the cuffs into her bag. No telling if they'd turn out useful later. "Now the next step." She grabbed the laptop case and pulled out her cell phone recharging cord, plugging the phone into the wall. In seconds the phone showed power and then the distinctive beep that meant she had voicemail sounded. Holding the phone carefully so that she didn't unplug it, Stella entered the code for her mailbox.

Sebastian's voice came through the phone. "Stella, if you get this message, please call me as soon as possible."

He sounded angry, but never had Stella been happier to hear him, mad or not. She dialed his number and waited for him to pick up.

"Sebastian?"

Through the phone she heard a loud high-pitched noise then her nightwalker's voice came through, loud and clear over the background sound. "Stella? Where are you?"

"I'm in a building on the top floor." She looked at Donald and he quickly supplied the address, which she relayed back to Sebastian.

"Just as we thought. And you're in the penthouse suite? Excellent, I know where that is." There was a grim satisfaction in his voice. "Just hang on, we'll be there in a moment."

Stella stood and walked around to the window. She stared at the emptiness beyond. "You will? But how?"

Her question was answered when moments later a black helicopter came up alongside the building and landed on the rooftop patio. Looking like parafolk marines, several large men and a few women jumped out of the side of the helicopter, partially shifting to animal form as they landed. In addition to fangs and claws, they were armed with automatic weapons. They rushed the glass doors into the living room next door and Stella heard the sound of breaking glass through the door.

Soon afterward there were screams and a couple of short bursts of automatic gunfire. Stella was glad not to be in that room. It must have seemed like a nightmare, seeing a pack of armed half-shifted werewolves charging in that way.

A familiar form exited from the pilot's seat and headed unerringly for the bedroom where she was held. She heard in her mind Sebastian's voice, his silver thoughts reaching for her—*Stella!*

Stella tried to open the glass door, only to find that it had a lock she couldn't simply undo. She pulled her hairpin out to work on it when a fist crashed into the glass next to the lock, a second fist followed the first, shattering the door. Stella jumped back just as a heavy body burst through the rest of the glass door and then Sebastian was standing in the room.

Stella jumped into the arms of the waiting nightwalker, his eyes glowing like molten silver, his knuckles bleeding. He wrapped himself around her, his voice murmuring in her ears. "Thank god you're all right."

The locked door suddenly broke open and two of the shape shifters, still bearing a lot of fur, were standing in the doorway. One was clearly Harold and Stella thought it funny that he looked as much at home with his Uzi as he did with a tea tray.

He smiled at her. "Glad to see you're okay." Then he tilted his head and took in the rest of her outfit and grinned. "That's a different look for you."

Stella simply buried her head in Sebastian's shoulder.

Harold turned his attention back to the nightwalker in question. "We've got Vanessa in here and her companion, and one of the Watchers." He then noticed Donald against the wall, looking like he wanted to be invisible. "I see you've got someone here as well."

Harold wouldn't take well to Donald if he knew he'd been one of those who'd attacked him and Rebecca. Stella looked up at Sebastian. "This is Donald Morgan. You remember him from Napa."

The nightwalker looked suspiciously at the other man. "I remember him, but what's he doing here?"

"Acting as mole," Stella said. "He's the one who was sending me email, warning us about the attacks."

"Working with Vanessa, but against her at the same time? A dangerous game you were playing, young nightwalker."

Donald stood tall and pale. "I was working with her—she made me, after all. But I didn't like a lot of the things she did."

Harold spoke up. "We don't have a lot of time. We've put a hold on the elevator and have blocked the stairs but the rest of the Watchers will be up here soon. Since we've got what we came for—Stella—we should go."

"Good idea. We'll take Vanessa with us and interrogate her later."

Stella reached into her bag and got the handcuffs. "These might come in handy."

Harold took them from her with a grin. "Just what we need." He then disappeared into the other room. Stella heard a woman scream and men's voices rose, then the sounds disappeared in the direction of the patio. Through what was left of the window Stella saw Vanessa and Alex handcuffed together, being hustled toward the back of the helicopter under an armed shape shifter guard.

"We should go too," Sebastian said.

Stella grabbed her laptop case and her other bag, which she'd found under the bed. Sebastian took the bags while she collected the rest of her belongings.

Sebastian beckoned to Donald. "You come with us."

He glanced between Stella and Sebastian and shrugged his shoulders. "I suppose I better. I don't want to be here when the Watchers realize you've stolen their pet vampire." He followed them onto the patio.

Just as they got there, Vanessa broke free of her escort and, dragging Alex with her, ran toward them. Sebastian dropped the bags and lunged but the female nightwalker grabbed Stella and pulled her to one side with her free arm around her neck. Alex was dragged along, his eyes panicked, but he made no move to stop her. Instead he kept as far away as the handcuffs permitted. The nightwalker raised her knee and Stella felt her back bend under the pressure Vanessa put on it.

"I'll break her in half." The nightwalker pulled on Stella's neck and she couldn't help her whimper.

Sebastian stopped dead in his tracks and raised his hand, halting the shape shifters from charging. Everyone stood completely still and watched.

"What do you think this will accomplish, Vanessa? You can't possibly get away from us."

"What it will get me is a little satisfaction if I kill this woman you care about."

"What makes you think I care that much for her? When have I ever let a woman change my life?" He shook his head slowly.

Stella froze at the harshness of his words. Perhaps she was fooling herself at how much she meant to him.

But then in her mind she heard the gentle sound of his mental voice. *Be very still until I tell you to move.*

Vanessa sneered at him. "Of course you care. You came here tonight, didn't you, and put yourself on the line to rescue her? When was the last time you did something like that?"

Stella tried to make herself relax as Vanessa's knee pushed harder against the small of her spine, even though the pain was intense. Not much more and she really would end up with a broken back.

Sebastian's mask of nonchalance broke and she saw in his face the agony he felt seeing her in danger. It was as if the pain she felt were reflected in his eyes. He seemed to steel himself and she knew he was going to spring.

Something flashed in the corner of her eye and Vanessa gave a blood-curdling scream. The pressure around her neck eased and Stella broke free, dashing toward Sebastian, who caught her and pulled her away from the stricken nightwalker.

His arms tightened around her and she wished that he would never let her go.

A gurgling cry and Stella turned back to see a knife protruding from the female nightwalker's side, blood blackening the hilt. Donald stood nearby, one hand still thrust forward after completing his throw, and Stella realized it was his knife buried in the female nightwalker's side.

Alex cried out as well, but his was the sound of a man wounded in the soul, not the body. He clutched the woman to him. "No, Vanessa. Don't die."

She reached up to touch his face as if confused. "Alex?" She whispered through the pain, Stella realized she actually did care about the young man. Then her eyes closed and she lay lifeless in his arms.

Alex howled almost like a shape shifter. "We need to get her help!"

Donald shook his head slowly. "It was a silver blade. No help for her now."

Sebastian stared at him, accusation in his eyes. "You use a knife well. Her other companion was killed that way."

Donald met his stare and Stella read strength in the much-younger nightwalker. "I only kill when I have to…and the man you refer to would have taken your life."

"I'm not that easy a target."

"Perhaps not…but your lady is and he wasn't that particular."

Sebastian's eyes narrowed. "If you were in that field, then you must have been there when the shape shifters were hurt."

With a sudden shift of mood, Donald laughed, the sound strangely out of place. He nodded to Stella and Sebastian. "Listen, I'd love to hang around and discuss this further, but I have to be going now." Before Sebastian could move he took off, and faster than Stella could imagine possible Donald was at the low wall surrounding the patio and climbing over it, disappearing over the edge within a split second.

Stella and Sebastian both ran to where he'd disappeared and looked down. All they saw was a shadowy figure swinging from balcony to balcony down the side of the building.

"I guess he didn't want to come with us after all," Sebastian said grimly. He started to signal to the shape shifters to go after him but Stella took his arm.

"Even before he threw that knife, he was trying to save me. He was going to get me out of here and they caught him at it. I don't know what they were going to do to him but I took the handcuffs off him."

Some of the anger faded from Sebastian's face. "Then I owe him for that as well as the warnings he gave. There is still the matter of Harold and Rebecca..."

"I think he regretted that. He didn't mean to hurt her, at least."

Sebastian gave her a long searching look. "You really think he deserves the second chance you're giving him?"

She knew what he was asking her. Did she believe that Donald would make good on his promise not to go against the parafolk again? "Yes, I think he isn't our enemy anymore."

Sebastian waved back the shape shifter commandos who were on the edge of the balcony, poised to swing down in pursuit of the escaping nightwalker. He turned to Stella. "Very well, he can go...for now."

When they looked again the figure had reached the ground and streaked across the parking lot. There was the sound of a car starting and a small dark vehicle headed at full speed to the street beyond, disappearing from view almost immediately.

Sebastian pointed to Alex, still cradling Vanessa's limp body, and spoke to Harold and the others. "Bring them. At least we can keep her away from the Watchers."

The shape shifters released Alex from his former mistress and took both of them into the back of the chopper while Sebastian led Stella to the front of the vehicle. Moments later she sat in the copilot's seat next to him as they lifted off. Never comfortable in the air, she gripped the seat belt with white-knuckled fingers.

Sebastian looked over at her and chuckled over the high-pitched sound of the blades. After the strain of the previous hours it was good to hear him laugh.

He shook his head at her. "I'm definitely going to have to work on this fear of heights you have. I'm a registered pilot, little star. You can trust me in the air."

She couldn't resist responding. "I trust your flying, Sebastian. It's gravity I worry about."

She didn't think it was that funny, but Sebastian didn't stop laughing until they landed safely at the airport.

Chapter Nineteen

Stella stared at the computer screen and the empty window of the text editor that represented the first page of the third chapter of her latest novel. Empty because for the first time in her life she was actually blocked on a story. What should have been a simple tale of an ancient nightwalker living in contemporary times was not flowing from her fingers the way her stories always had before.

She had characters, setting, plot and conflict. She had notes and notes galore. There was a flowchart of potential scenes and a three-by-five card for each scene.

Sometimes she could even see the characters talking to each other.

Trouble was, it was all in her head and nothing she'd tried was allowing it to go onto the printed page.

Clearly there was something wrong. Her muse had never deserted her before so why would it now? Why was this story so hard to tell? Why wasn't she able to capture on the page her latest hero, a man both strong and tender and very, very sexy?

A man like Sebastian.

Maybe that was it. The hero she'd envisioned for her new book was a man like Sebastian and it was hard to put the words together to describe him when she was having trouble describing who he was in her real life.

Yes they were friends, and yes, oh yes, they were lovers. Even though the antidote had worked and he no longer needed her blood to keep healthy, he kept her close to him and they'd been nearly inseparable since he'd rescued her from the Watchers.

For the moment, they'd taken up residence in Jonathan's home. Sebastian had declared there would be no more hiding and no more safe houses for them. As soon as they'd arrived back at the parafolk stronghold he'd called the authorities in Napa, and with some persuasion gotten the authorities to back off on the search. Promising cooperation, he'd managed to provide to them the murder weapon in the case of Steven Coonsall, the dead man in his vineyard, a silver switchblade knife.

Which happened to be the same silver knife that had also killed a lady nightwalker whose death had not been reported. A silver knife that unfortunately bore no fingerprints to link it to a missing software engineer that nobody was looking for — something that would stay that way unless the young man made it necessary to go after him.

At this point the authorities were satisfied that the dead man had been a rogue parafolk and that his murderer, also a rogue, had been dealt with. Sebastian was still seen as in control and everyone was content with that.

The NorCal nightwalkers who'd been behind Vanessa had been informed that upon their prince's return they would have explanations to make. Some simply made a point of taking off to places unknown while others had come down to Los Angeles to make preemptive apologies. Most said they'd had no idea that Vanessa had planned to create her new world for nightwalkers by building it on the deaths of Sebastian and those who thought like him.

Stella could see the other nightwalkers' thoughts and so was often a silent observer at these meetings and would tell Sebastian who was and was not telling the truth. Those who were insincere were banished from California and the coup Vanessa had planned was dismantled bit by bit.

It was a slow process but Sebastian swore to Stella and his friends that he'd not return to his home in Napa until he was certain there would be no further threat to any of those he held dear.

In the meantime Sebastian had taken over the guest suite in Jonathan's home, and he'd been adamant about Stella sleeping in his bed every day. She stayed up with him all night and fell asleep at dawn in his arms but still woke in the afternoon a few hours before he roused.

She spent that time in his room and worked on her laptop, presumably writing her new book. However as soon as she knew the sun was going down, she crept back into bed so she was in his arms when he woke.

After that nature usually took its course. Stella had never had such great sex in her life.

It would have been a perfect life except for the writing. Trouble was, writing about a fictional version of Sebastian was almost impossible having been with the real one. Her imagination just couldn't keep up with the real thing.

She was close to giving up on this book, in spite of the emails from her editor and agent, which were just about daily now. When were they going to see something—anything—about the latest book?

Stella sighed. When she figured out what to write, and that was not happening at this point.

Abandoning her laptop, Stella stood and wandered over to the bed where Sebastian still lay in his daytime sleep.

What was wrong with her book? Was it that she was writing about a time period she wasn't comfortable with? Or was it something deeper...such as she didn't really want to expose Sebastian and the others by publishing a book that would lead to questions about them?

Or maybe it was something even deeper than that? She didn't want to write about Sebastian or his closest friends because if she did it would be like sharing them with the rest of the world. Before she'd created heroes and given them to other women, but somehow she couldn't create a fictional version of Sebastian to share.

She'd never felt so possessive of a man before but truthfully she didn't want other women knowing him the way she did.

Stella returned to the laptop. Perhaps what she needed was a complete change of direction. She'd write a new kind of story, something different. Not about vampires and not a Regency book. Possibly a bit offbeat, humorous and set in contemporary times...but with a twist.

Suddenly inspired, Stella dug off her hard-drive those old notes of hers about the kick-ass heroine she'd never gotten to write about but whose knowledge she'd taken advantage of all through her and Sebastian's recent adventure. Maybe if she gave it a paranormal twist she'd have something. Of course her heroine needed a name. Something kind of clever and unexpected.

Stella opened up a new screen and typed "Bubbles Brown".

Okay, good name. But what did a kick-ass heroine named Bubbles do? With a smile, Stella added "Private eye" to the title.

Good. But what was the paranormal twist? Stella thought for a moment, then her smile broadened into a grin. In her mind came the image of the female shape shifters who'd aided in her rescue, armed with their claws, fangs and Uzis, but still all woman.

Stella began typing and when she was done the page read, "Bubbles Brown—Werewolf, Private Eye."

Still grinning, she added "Chapter One" and then the first sentence.

"It's not easy being a female werewolf. For one thing, if the full moon and your period coincide, you get PMS with a vengeance. Sometimes a man took his life in his hands if he said anything to you on one of those nights, and that made it really tricky to keep a relationship going past the first month or so.

"And then there was the matter of manicures. Those never lasted beyond shifting and it got expensive to constantly replace nail polish.

"But these weren't the main issues Bubbles had on her mind as she eyed from the sidewalk the cheap-looking run-down bar in front of her. Sometimes being a werewolf meant you didn't have your pick of jobs and you had to take what you were given.

"Like this one. She headed inside and took in the interior. It was a gin joint like any other gin joint, but Bubbles wasn't in the market for gin. Wine was more her speed...a crisp Chardonnay with lots of oak her favorite. But alcohol of any kind wasn't why she was here this night. She was looking for trouble, and from the look of those giving her the once-over at the bar, she'd found it.

"Bubbles smiled to herself. On the other hand, maybe this job wasn't going to be so bad. In fact—*this could be fun!*"

And Stella, still grinning, hands pausing over the keyboard, nodded in agreement. *Yes, it could.*

And it was.

Four hours later, she was close to the end of chapter three when the lightproof shades began shifting across the windows, alerting her that dusk was here.

Stella saved her work and headed back to the bed, where Sebastian was shifting and stretching as he woke. Pulling off her sweatshirt and jeans, she slipped into the bed just in time to become wrapped in his arms.

He snuggled her close and kissed the back of her neck. "Good morning, Stella. How is my star this evening?"

"I'm well."

"And how is your work going?"

Suddenly she felt shy about telling him her revelation. "Going better."

"Better?"

"I'm up to chapter three already. It isn't the book I was going to write, but I really like it."

"A new book?" Reading her eagerness, Sebastian sat up and pushed the pillows against the headboard to support himself before pulling her again into his arms. "Tell me about it."

She did, and by the time she'd finished her description of the misadventures of a female werewolf private detective he was laughing heartily. "That's marvelous, Stella."

"I know a werewolf detective sounds pretty far-fetched."

"Oh you might be surprised," he said mysteriously. "But why did you decide on this and not the other book?"

"I couldn't seem to work on it...actually, I think maybe I was too close to the subject matter. And besides, I don't want other women fantasizing about you the way I do."

He leaned over and kissed her forehead. "So you don't want to share me with other women? I think I like that. Neither do I wish to share you with anyone. But I'm willing to compromise. You need to write, Stella—I understand how important that is to you."

"Not as important as you are."

That earned another kiss, this time on the lips. He kept the kiss up, pushing her further onto the bed until he lay above her, all six feet plus of him stretched out and covering her body.

With one hand he massaged her breasts then dipped his head to gently nibble on the tender tips. "I want you, Stella," he whispered.

"I want you too," she whispered back.

He reared up and over her, his hard cock probing gently at her entrance. Already wet, Stella guided him inside. It was often like this in their early evening couplings, his body fired up for her, and she from thinking about him during the afternoon.

After he'd sheathed himself within her he began to move slowly, taking his time now that he was actually within her. Tension and friction built between them until Stella reached her first climax, crying softly her pleasure.

He slowed now, taking his time and savoring what was between them. Stella reached out with her mind, infusing his silver with streaks of pink and purple. Their minds seemed to melt together and she read his hunger for more than her body. This was the sharing she'd come to enjoy almost as much as being in his mind and loving his body.

Drink from me, my love.

His fangs touched the side of her neck and sank within, sipping carefully from her, then more intently even as his body sped up again. She stopped him when he'd had enough, although she'd noticed recently that she rarely felt faint anymore after they'd made love.

Even so, he closed and erased the marks, then plunged into her over and over again, bringing both of them to climax. With their minds joined they couldn't help reaching that peak together and Stella's hands clutched his magnificent rear as he flexed one more time and emptied himself deep within her.

Afterwards, they lay together, replete as always, neither having much to say. *What on earth*, Stella thought, *could possibly be said after loving like that?* Words hardly seemed necessary.

Even so, Sebastian broke the silence. "Have you noticed I've not drunk from anyone but you in nearly a month now?"

Now that he mentioned it... "I guess that's true." Hope rose in Stella. So far they'd avoided the subject, but maybe it was time they discussed their future. "Does that mean..." her voice trailed off

"Does it mean you are my bloodmate? Yes, I think it does. If that's good with you?"

"That's wonderful, Sebastian," she said and she meant it. After all, Sharon had told her it was as close to marriage as a nightwalker could get.

"I'm glad you're pleased, but that's not all I have in mind."

With a mischievous look that seemed quite unlike him, he released her. Still naked, Sebastian slipped onto the floor and knelt on one knee beside the mattress. From under the bed he pulled out a small jewelry box and opened it. Stella's jaw dropped as she took in the rings inside, including a solitaire set with a beautiful ruby.

"I have read all of your books, Stella, and at some point, your hero always gets around to insisting on making his relationship with his lady a permanent one."

Stella's heart seemed to go into overdrive. "Are you asking me..."

He nodded solemnly, his silver-gray eyes alive with emotion and warmth. He cleared his throat. "Stella Robertson," he intoned in that deep, rich voice of his. "Will you do me the honor of becoming my wife?"

With a shriek, Stella jumped off the bed and into his arms, knocking the rings to the floor. Throwing her arms around him, she kissed his face and neck and anyplace else she could reach.

Laughing, Sebastian managed to contain her. "Does this mean yes?"

"Of course it does!"

She managed to control her excitement as he recovered the ring box and pulled out the solitaire, fitting it onto her finger. It was a perfect fit, of course.

Stella admired the beautiful stone. "It's perfect, Sebastian. I can't wait to show Sharon."

He tilted his head as if listening to something then grinned. "Ah yes...well, maybe you can compare rings on the plane. Jonathan and I hatched up a scheme to take one of my small jets to Las Vegas this evening...assuming you can get over this fear of flying you have with me."

"Vegas, tonight? You mean Sharon and Jonathan are getting married too?"

"If the squeal of joy I just overheard from the master bedroom is any indication, it would seem so."

"But I didn't think your people got married?"

"There is no reason we can't. Jonathan and I have decided to start a new tradition among nightwalkers." He grinned at her. "Legal marriage will help cement our relationship as far as the authorities are concerned and make us more normal to them."

He pulled her closer. "Besides, I still remember what marriage means to the world and I want that too. I can't wait to exchange vows with you and make a permanent statement of what you mean to me. Are you willing to do the same with me?"

Stella looked at him, her golden-haired vampire hero who wanted to be known as her husband. "A permanent statement of what we are to each other. Yes, I would love that...even if I have to get into a plane with you."

She said it and she meant every word.

Chapter Twenty
ಐ

Maybe she should give her agent a bonus. Stella pondered that thought as she reached for another book to sign for the extremely happy fan who'd finally made her way through the line of similar fans at Stella's now-annual late-night Halloween booksigning in San Francisco.

While the first signing had been a bust, the second had done well and now, two years later, Stella had a crowd of people waiting in the bookstore for her to autograph her latest Estelle Roberts novel. The bookstore owner was ecstatic about the turnout, saying people had begun lining up shortly after dark to buy books, in spite of the nine p.m. start for the signing.

Stella could have told her that much of the costumed crowd hadn't been able to come until after dark…not all of the visible fangs on the patrons were part of a costume. Since becoming Sebastian's bloodmate and wife, she'd found a whole new audience for her books, and was the most popular romance novelist in the parafolk world.

She was even writing screenplays in her free time for Fly By Night Films. Mostly shorter works that didn't require a lot of her time, but she had hopes of doing a longer one sometime soon. She even occasionally worked with Bernie Williams, a nightwalker with a long list of hit films to his name…or to his many pseudonyms, as he'd lived long enough to have to take different pen names every decade or so.

But it was still romance writing that she loved and this series, which had started with the book she'd written while first living with Sebastian, was her favorite to date. The first one, *Bubbles Brown, Werewolf Private Eye,* had become a bestseller nearly overnight as Stella discovered that she had other hidden talents than being a Regency author. Reviewers and readers alike loved the fact that she had Bubbles open locks with a hairpin rather than simply tear the door off its hinges.

She still planned another vampire Regency, and this time the hero would be a blond with a penchant for rich red wines—a man who, after all, belonged in one of her books. A hero of the first water—just changed enough so that no one would recognize him.

It was nearing midnight when Stella looked up at the last person in line, who'd been waiting nearly an hour for the privilege.

"Emily," the lady said happily. "Please make it to Emily."

Stella did so, handed the book to her and leaned back with a satisfied sigh. The woman she gave the book to beamed back—her nose adorned with a large fake mole and her false teeth comically crooked to go with her truly ridiculous witch costume. Obviously not a parafolk, but that didn't matter tonight.

On Halloween they were all parafolk in one way or another. The "witch" turned just in time to see Sebastian walk into the room and her eyes went wide. "Wow...is that your cover model?"

Stella had to laugh. "Not really. You might say he's my inspiration though."

Emily sighed at the tall blond man wearing a tuxedo and black cape. "Inspiring is right. He looks like one of your heroes, Ms. Roberts."

As the fan continued to gawk, Sebastian came over to the table. Stella looked at him and then at Emily. "Actually he's my true-life hero, Emily. This is my husband, Sebastian Moret."

He smiled at both of them and Emily seemed to swoon over his fangs. "Oh! He's even in costume."

Sebastian made his most courtly bow, giving Stella a little wink on the side. "But of course. It's Halloween, isn't it?" He turned his lethal smile on Stella, who felt a little swoon of her own.

"So, little star, are you ready to leave?"

"Just about." She cleared her space and claimed her bag from under the table.

Sebastian looked at Emily, preening over his attention. "If I may reclaim my lady?"

Flustered, she just nodded and Sebastian led Stella away. "There is merriment around and much to do tonight. Shall we go?"

They were halfway to the door when his mind spoke to her. *I heard what you said about being a hero, little star. I must admit — I am flattered to be yours.*

She paused at the door and kissed him hard on the mouth. "You told me yourself that it was you I was writing about all those years. I'm just glad now I have you in the flesh."

He laughed. *Flesh is good, particularly when it leads to love. And I do love you.*

I love you too, Sebastian.

He gave her his most wicked angel smile. *I also love your romance books, my star, do you know why?*

All right, she'd ask. *Why do you love my books, Sebastian?*

I love your books because they always finish with a happy ending.

The End

Enjoy an excerpt from:

NIGHT VISIONS

Copyright © ARIANA DUPRE, 2007.
All Rights Reserved, Ellora's Cave Publishing, Inc.

∞

There was nowhere to hide.

Angie Benton watched the young woman running through the forest. As she fought the brush and bramble, her torn clothes ripped even more.

She tripped over a tree root and fell to the ground. Quickly, she struggled to her feet while leaves caught in her hair and briars slashed her arms, drawing blood.

Angie could feel the woman's terror—like a knife slicing through her own heart.

Just then a man appeared. Angie, watching from a high perch in the trees, trembled. What now?

Jaw clenched, eyes narrowed, the man opened and closed his fists repeatedly as he tramped toward the frightened woman. His shirt was unbuttoned, revealing the sweat glistening on his heaving chest. He looked so angry, so hostile. She could even hear the fury in his strong, deliberate footsteps.

The woman heard him too and looked over her shoulder.

Angie gasped. The woman's face was her own!

Horrified, Angie watched the woman who could be her twin run into a clearing, then pause and look frantically around. She could feel her desperation and when the other woman sprinted across the meadow toward an old shack, Angie experienced a jolt of hope and a burst of energy as she mentally followed her twin.

Arriving breathless at the cabin, the woman jumped onto the porch, pushed through the broken door and ran into the first room on her left.

Angie spotted an exit at the back of the shack. She willed her twin to find it and escape that way. Instead, the woman ran wildly through the house in terror, searching for a place to hide.

Entering the kitchen at last, she didn't run out the back door as Angie willed. Instead, she crouched in the corner behind an antique hutch.

The old pine floors creaked as if under a heavy weight.

Angie screamed, "Run! Run!" But the twin didn't move.

The man's footsteps moved methodically through the dilapidated old shack, searching, slowly, room by room.

Still her twin waited motionless, until, at last, the footsteps left the house.

Tentatively, the young woman stood up and glanced around. Inching toward the back door, she looked through the screen and out the side windows, surveying the yard with wide, frightened eyes.

All clear.

Cautiously, she opened the door and slipped out. With her back to the yard, she quietly closed the door behind her, then spun around to make a run for it.

And crashed right into her pursuer.

A loud whistle pierced Angie's hearing. What on earth was happening?

Someone was pulling her from her perch. Someone had a grip on her biceps and searing stabs of pain were shooting through her arms.

She looked up and stared into the angriest blue eyes she had ever seen.

Eyes belonging to the man she'd just seen outside the cabin door.

Her heart pounded. *How had she become the woman she'd been watching?*

The man's sandy brown hair hung over his face in wet strands, its blond highlights still noticeable. Sweat beaded across his brow. He clenched his jaw against chiseled cheeks and he tightened his grip by digging his fingers deeper into the soft flesh of her arms.

Angie *jerked her body violently, but could not* break his hold. Wave after wave of terror crashed through her. She had to escape!

"Angie!" he growled.

She snapped her head back to look up at his angry face.

A flash of light in her peripheral vision caught her attention and she turned to see someone, shadowed by trees, leveling a gun at them.

Angie froze. As if in slow motion, the muzzle of the gun moved until it was pointing straight at her. She heard a booming blast, so loud it hurt her ears. *Oh God, I'm going to die*, she thought in terror.

The man with the sandy hair whirled her around, using his body to shield her from the oncoming bullet. Suddenly, his face contorted, his back arched and his grip on her arms loosened, then released, as he fell to the ground.

Angie watched him land in a crumpled heap at her feet. She'd barely had time to take this in before she felt something hard and cold jab into her back and an arm clench around her neck, forcing her to look skyward. She heard a deep, raspy, laugh behind her as a man dragged her backward, knocking her off her feet with a quick pull, his laughter intensifying.

Angie struggled frantically with the gunman. She was so desperate, so frightened, that several seconds passed before she noticed that the man who had come between her and the bullet was no longer there.

Where had he gone?

The pressure increased against her throat.

Angie twisted and turned, trying to break free, trying to find the man who had saved her before.

But it was useless. He'd disappeared and the more she struggled, the more her assailant tightened his hold.

Then the realization hit her. The sandy haired man was dragging her across the yard. Somehow, he'd captured her.

A gunshot rang out.

Fire burned through her chest. The man pushed her and she sank to the ground, feeling her life ebbing away.

Enjoy an excerpt from:

ALL NIGHT INN

Copyright © JANET MILLER, 2005.
All Rights Reserved, Ellora's Cave Publishing, Inc.

☙

"Ms. Colson." Jonathan came upon her so quietly she startled, dropping the rag. He watched silently as she recovered her composure. "You did well tonight. I have no objection to continuing your employment." He eyed the cloth on the counter then turned his intense blue stare back to her. "What are your feelings about it?"

Shaken, but not deterred. With a boldness she didn't feel, she stared back at him. "I still want the job."

Just for an instant a smile slipped across his lips. "Very well." He inclined his head, and pointed to the hallway leading to his office. "That way, please."

She preceded him inside. It wasn't a large room. Jonathan's desk took up the bulk of the space in the middle. In one corner was a brown leather couch, easily six feet long, with a colorful striped blanket spread across the back. A mini-fridge sat next to it, doubling as a lamp stand. For a moment Sharon speculated as to what kind of drinks her future boss kept cold. Little plastic bags from the local blood bank, perhaps?

Heart pounding, she eyed the couch and waited. Jonathan followed her gaze, hesitated, and apparently decided against the intimacy that would afford. He directed her toward the top of the desk with an elegant wave of his hand. "If you will sit there, Ms. Colson?"

She did as he instructed, facing him as he approached. For the first time since that brief caress in the bar, he touched her, placed his hands on her shoulders. She'd thought they'd be cold, clammy, but there was perceptible warmth to them. She felt it through the thin material of her blouse. Not warm enough to be human, but there.

For a moment he studied her face. "You're sure about this?"

Sharon closed her eyes and steeled herself for the sensation of his mouth on her throat, the prick of his teeth piercing the skin. She hated pain. She was the kind to insist on local anesthesia before allowing a splinter to be removed.

"Just do it," she whispered.

He did nothing. She opened her eyes and his blue stare bore into her. "You must look into my eyes and let me into your mind, Ms. Colson. I'll take the fear from you and make it easy."

He wanted to link minds with her? Panicked, Sharon shook her head. "No, not that. I won't let you do that."

He frowned. "You don't understand. I can block what you feel and make it pleasurable for you. Without a mind link there will be pain."

"I do understand. I expect the pain. I can deal with it."

He shook his head, displeasure infusing his expression. "I'm not in the habit of causing discomfort. I enjoy feeding..." One long finger traced the vein in her neck. "I'd rather you enjoyed it, too."

"It isn't important I enjoy it," she said, her voice desperate. How could she make him understand? Sharon took a deep and ragged breath. "There was a man I met who did a mind link to me once." She shuddered at the memory. It had been...awful. She'd felt like she'd been ripped apart and afterward...no, she couldn't think about the "afterward."

"It was months before I could think straight. I'm willing to let you feed off me, but I can't let you into my mind."

He let go of her and stepped back, disappointment in his face. "I'm very sorry, Ms. Colson. I would have enjoyed having you here...but the role of a companion requires my being able to touch your mind."

Moving to the door, he gestured to her. "Come with me to the bar, and I'll pay you for this evening."

"No!" Nervously, she licked her lips. "Please...can't you make an exception? I really need this job."

Frustration showed in his face. "Exception to what? To the mark, no, it's too dangerous for me to have unmarked humans here."

Desperation made her bold. "What about the link, then? Just this once? Maybe when I know you better, can trust you more...I promise I'll let you into my mind."

For a moment she thought he was going to give up and send her on her way. Then she caught the hungry look in his eyes and the way he studied her neck with a possessive stare. She could tell he wanted this, to taste her, to mark her as his own. He might not ever take her blood again, but he wanted it this time.

The way he licked his lips told her that he wanted it bad enough to forego his principles and bleed her without the mind link.

"As you wish, then." The vampire returned to her and took a different hold with his hands. One moved to the back of her head, the other to just below her shoulder blades. It was a more intimate embrace than the one he'd taken before—and more secure. His hand caressed her hair, pulling it back, baring her neck. It might have been the prelude to a kiss.

Piercing blue eyes stared into hers. "I will hold you to that promise," he whispered.

His arms tightened and he moved so fast that she didn't have a chance to say anything, couldn't have pulled away if she wanted to. Held in his vise-like grip, sharp pain stabbed through her as his fangs plunged into her neck, unerringly locating the artery. A burning sensation followed as strong lips drew the blood through the tiny holes.

Pain. It was worse than she'd imagined. Sharon wanted to cry out, but couldn't. He held her so close she was crushed into his chest. His throat rippled as he swallowed and she felt his heartbeat stutter then pick up pace, growing faster, almost matching the furious pounding of hers.

She hadn't expected him to take so much, just a few swallows, a taste. This was more like a banquet for him as he guzzled her life's blood. Fear grew inside her...fear of what she'd promised, of what she would become at his hands.

A vampire and companion linked minds—it was "required". How was she ever going to deal with that?

As her body chilled, his grew warmer. A rushing noise sounded in her ears and dizziness encompassed her. She grew weak and faint and still he took from her until she began to wonder if he intended to stop feeding at all, or if her life would end in his arms.

Was she going to die?

A gasp of fear and pain escaped her. Abruptly his mouth stopped moving and simply rested. He breathed heavily, the heat of his breath scorching her throat. The worst of the pain ended at the same time, but the relief from it put tears into her eyes.

His grip eased, and he allowed her to pull back, but only briefly. "A moment," he whispered. "I must stop the flow." He pressed down, covering the aching places where his teeth had pierced the skin.

She felt the touch of his tongue move across the holes, sealing them but not healing. He gently licked the rest of her neck, cleaning the remaining blood and soothing her skin. The throbbing abated under his tender ministrations.

The vampire drew back, a warm possessive glow in his eyes. An odd thought slid into her mind. *He was a neat eater.* Only the smallest amount of blood lingered at the corners of his mouth, and as she watched his flitting tongue removed even that evidence.

Deep amusement laced his voice when he spoke. "Congratulations, Ms. Colson. You have the job."

Why an electronic book?

We live in the Information Age—an exciting time in the history of human civilization, in which technology rules supreme and continues to progress in leaps and bounds every minute of every day. For a multitude of reasons, more and more avid literary fans are opting to purchase e-books instead of paper books. The question from those not yet initiated into the world of electronic reading is simply: *Why?*

1. ***Price.*** An electronic title at Ellora's Cave Publishing and Cerridwen Press runs anywhere from 40% to 75% less than the cover price of the exact same title in paperback format. Why? Basic mathematics and cost. It is less expensive to publish an e-book (no paper and printing, no warehousing and shipping) than it is to publish a paperback, so the savings are passed along to the consumer.
2. ***Space.*** Running out of room in your house for your books? That is one worry you will never have with electronic books. For a low one-time cost, you can purchase a handheld device specifically designed for e-reading. Many e-readers have large, convenient screens for viewing. Better yet, hundreds of titles can be stored within your new library—on a single microchip. There are a variety of e-readers from different manufacturers. You can also read e-books on your PC or laptop computer. (Please note that Ellora's Cave does not endorse any specific brands. You can check our websites at www.ellorascave.com

or www.cerridwenpress.com for information we make available to new consumers.)

3. ***Mobility.*** Because your new e-library consists of only a microchip within a small, easily transportable e-reader, your entire cache of books can be taken with you wherever you go.

4. ***Personal Viewing Preferences.*** Are the words you are currently reading too small? Too large? Too… ANNOYING? Paperback books cannot be modified according to personal preferences, but e-books can.

5. ***Instant Gratification.*** Is it the middle of the night and all the bookstores near you are closed? Are you tired of waiting days, sometimes weeks, for bookstores to ship the novels you bought? Ellora's Cave Publishing sells instantaneous downloads twenty-four hours a day, seven days a week, every day of the year. Our webstore is never closed. Our e-book delivery system is 100% automated, meaning your order is filled as soon as you pay for it.

Those are a few of the top reasons why electronic books are replacing paperbacks for many avid readers.

As always, Ellora's Cave and Cerridwen Press welcome your questions and comments. We invite you to email us at Comments@ellorascave.com or write to us directly at Ellora's Cave Publishing Inc., 1056 Home Avenue, Akron, OH 44310-3502.

Cerridwen Press
Monthly Newsletter

News
Author Appearances
Book Signings
New Releases
Contests
Author Profiles
Feature Articles

Available online at
www.CerridwenPress.com

MAKE EACH DAY MORE *EXCITING* WITH OUR

ELLORA'S CAVEMEN
CALENDAR

☥ WWW.ELLORASCAVE.COM ☥

Cerridwen Press

Cerridwen, the Celtic goddess of wisdom, was the muse who brought inspiration to storytellers and those in the creative arts.

Cerridwen Press encompasses the best and most innovative stories in all genres of today's fiction.

Visit our website and discover the newest titles by talented authors who still get inspired—much like the ancient storytellers did…

once upon a time.

www.cerridwenpress.com